JOHN MACNAB

JOHN MACNAB

BY

JOHN BUCHAN

MACDONALD PUBLISHERS
Loanhead, Midlothian

First published in this Edition 1980 by
Macdonald Publishers
Edgefield Road, Loanhead, Midlothian

ISBN 0 904265 34 x   hardback
      0 904265 39 0   paperback

*The publishers acknowledge the financial
assistance of the Scottish Arts Council
in the publication of this volume*

Printed in Scotland by
Macdonald Printers (Edinburgh) Limited
Edgefield Road, Loanhead, Midlothian

To
ROSALIND MAITLAND

Contents

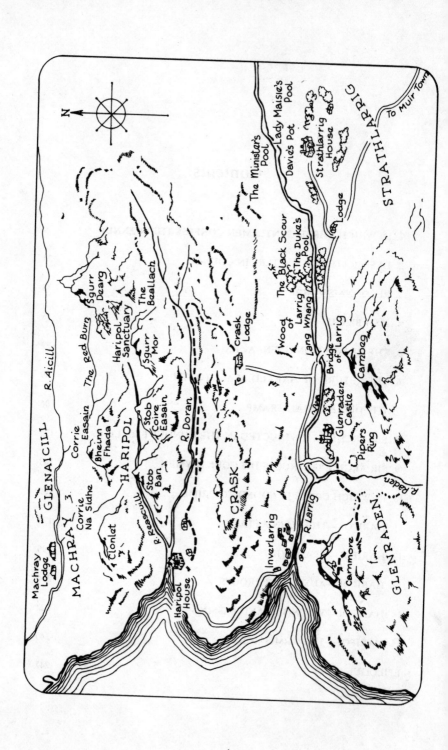

IN WHICH THREE GENTLEMEN CONFESS
THEIR ENNUI

THE great doctor stood on the hearth-rug looking down at his friend who sprawled before him in an easy-chair. It was a hot day in early July, and the windows were closed and the blinds half-down to keep out the glare and the dust. The standing figure had bent shoulders, a massive clean-shaven face, and a keen interrogatory air, and might have passed his sixtieth birthday. He looked like a distinguished lawyer, who would soon leave his practice for the Bench. But it was the man in the chair who was the lawyer, a man who had left forty behind him, but was still on the pleasant side of fifty.

"I tell you for the tenth time that there's nothing the matter with you."

"And I tell you for the tenth time that I'm miserably ill."

The doctor shrugged his shoulders. "Then it's a mind diseased, to which I don't propose to minister. What do you say is wrong?"

"Simply what my housekeeper calls a 'no-how' feeling."

"It's clearly nothing physical. Your heart and lungs are sound. Your digestion's as good as anybody's can be in London in Midsummer. Your nerves—well, I've tried all the stock tests, and they appear to be normal."

"Oh, my nerves are all right," said the other wearily.

"Your brain seems good enough, except for this dismal obsession that you are ill. I can find no earthly thing wrong, except that you're stale. I don't say run-down, for that you're not. You're stale in mind. You want a holiday."

"I don't. I may *need* one, but I don't *want* it. That's precisely

9

the trouble. I used to be a glutton for holidays, and spent my leisure moments during term planning what I was going to do. Now there seems to be nothing in the world I want to do—neither work nor play."

"Try fishing. You used to be keen."

"I've killed all the salmon I mean to kill. I never want to look the ugly brutes in the face again."

"Shooting?"

"Too easy and too dull."

"A yacht."

"Stop it, old fellow. Your catalogue of undesired delights only makes it worse. I tell you that there's nothing at this moment which has the slightest charm for me. I'm bored with my work, and I can't think of anything else of any kind for which I would cross the street. I don't even want to go into the country and sleep. It's been coming on for a long time—I daresay it's due somehow to the war—but when I was in office I did not feel it so badly, for I was in a service and not my own master. Now I've nothing to do except to earn an enormous income, which I haven't any need for. Work comes rolling in—I've got retainers for nearly every solvent concern in this land—and all that happens is that I want to strangle my clerk and a few eminent solicitors. I don't care a tinker's curse for success, and what is worse, I'm just as apathetic about the modest pleasures which used to enliven my life."

"You may be more tired than you think."

"I'm not tired at all." The speaker rose from his chair yawning, and walked to the windows to stare into the airless street. He did not look tired, for his movements were vigorous, and, though his face had the slight pallor of his profession, his eye was clear and steady. He turned round suddenly.

"I tell you what I've got. It's what the Middle Ages suffered from—I read a book about it the other day—and its called *taedium vitae*. It's a special kind of ennui. I can diagnose my ailment well enough, and Shakespeare has the words for it. I've come to a pitch where I find 'nothing left remarkable beneath the visiting moon.' "

10

"Then why do you come to me, if the trouble is not with your body?"

"Because you're *you*. I should come to you just the same if you were a vet., or a bone-setter, or a Christian Scientist. I want your advice, not as a fashionable consultant, but as an old friend and a wise man. It's a state of affairs that can't go on. What am I to do to get rid of this infernal disillusionment? I can't go through the rest of my life dragging my wing."

The doctor was smiling.

"If you ask my professional advice," he said, "I am bound to tell you that medical science has no suggestion to offer. If you consult me as a friend, I advise you to steal a horse in some part of the world where a horse-thief is usually hanged."

The other considered. "Pretty drastic prescription for a man who has been a Law Officer of the Crown."

"I speak figuratively. You've got to rediscover the comforts of your life by losing them for a little. You have good food and all the rest of it at your command—well, you've got to be in want for a bit to appreciate them. You're secure and respected and rather eminent—well, somehow or other get under the weather. If you could induce the newspapers to accuse you of something shady and have the devil of a job to clear yourself it might do the trick. The fact is, you've grown too competent. You need to be made to struggle for your life again—your life or your reputation. You have to find out the tonic of difficulty, and you can't find it in your profession. Therefore I say 'Steal a horse.'"

A faint interest appeared in the other's eyes.

"That sounds to me good sense. But, hang it all, it's utterly unpractical. I can't go looking for scrapes. I should feel like play-acting if in cold blood I got myself into difficulties, and I take it that the essence of your prescription is that I must feel desperately in earnest."

"I'm not prescribing. Heaven forbid that I should advise a friend to look for trouble. I'm merely stating how in the abstract I regard your case."

The patient rose to go. "Miserable comforters are ye all," he groaned. "Well, it appears you can do nothing for me except to suggest the advisability of crime. I suppose it's no good trying to make you take a fee?"

The doctor shook his head. "I wasn't altogether chaffing. Honestly, you would be the better of dropping for a month or two into another world—a harder one. A hand on a cattle-boat, for instance."

Sir Edward Leithen sighed deeply as he turned from the doorstep down the long hot street. He did not look behind him, or he would have seen another gentleman approach cautiously round the corner of a side-street, and, when the coast was clear, ring the doctor's bell. He was so completely fatigued with life that he neglected to be cautious at crossings, as was his habit, and was all but slain by a motor-omnibus. Everything seemed weary and over-familiar—the summer smell of town, the din of traffic, the panorama of faces, pretty women shopping, the occasional sight of a friend. Long ago, he reflected with disgust, there had been a time when he had enjoyed it all.

He found sanctuary at last in the shade and coolness of his club. He remembered that he was dining out, and bade the porter telephone that he could not come, giving no reason. He remembered, too, that there was a division in the House that night, an important division advertised by a three-line whip. He declined to go near the place. At any rate, he would have the dim consolation of behaving badly. His clerk was probably at the moment hunting feverishly for him, for he had missed a consultation in the great Argentine bank case which was in the paper next morning. That also could slide. He wanted, nay, he was determined, to make a mess of it.

Then he discovered that he was hungry, and that it was nearly the hour when a man may dine. "I've only one positive feeling left," he told himself, "the satisfaction of my brute needs. Nice position for a gentleman and a Christian!"

There was one other man in the dining-room, sitting at the little table in the window. At first sight he had the look of an undergraduate, a Rugby Blue, perhaps, who had just come down from the University, for he had the broad, slightly stooped shoulders of the football-player. He had a ruddy face, untidy sandy hair, and large reflective grey eyes. It was those eyes which declared his age, for round them were the many fine wrinkles which come only from the passage of time.

"Hullo, John," said Leithen. "May I sit at your table?"

The other, whose name was Palliser-Yeates, nodded.

"You may certainly eat in my company, but I've got nothing to say to you, Ned. I'm feeling as dried-up as a dead starfish."

They ate their meal in silence, and so preoccupied was Sir Edward Leithen with his own affairs that it did not seem to him strange that Mr Palliser-Yeates, who was commonly a person of robust spirits and plentiful conversation, should have the air of a deaf-mute. When they had reached the fish, two other diners took their seats and waved them a greeting. One of them was a youth with lean, high-coloured cheeks, who limped slightly; the other a tallish older man with a long dark face, a small dark moustache, and a neat pointed chin which gave him something of the air of a hidalgo. He looked weary and glum, but his companion seemed to be in the best of tempers, for his laugh rang out in that empty place with a startling boyishness. Mr Palliser-Yeates looked up angrily, with a shiver.

"Noisy brute, Archie Roylance!" he observed. "I suppose he's above himself since Ascot. His horse won some beastly race, didn't it? It's a good thing to be young and an ass."

There was that in his tone which roused Leithen from his apathy. He cast a sharp glance at the other's face.

"You're off-colour."

"No," said the other brusquely. "I'm perfectly fit. Only I'm getting old."

This was food for wonder, inasmuch as Mr Palliser-Yeates had a reputation for a more than youthful energy and, although forty-five years of age, was still accustomed to do startling things on the Chamonix *aiguilles*. He was head of an eminent banking firm and something of an authority on the aberrations of post-war finance.

A gleam of sympathy came into Leithen's eyes.

"How does it take you?" he asked.

"I've lost zest. Everything seems more or less dust and ashes. When you suddenly wake up and find that you've come to regard your respectable colleagues as so many fidgety old women and the job you've given your life to as an infernal squabble about trifles—why, you begin to wonder what's going to happen."

"I suppose a holiday ought to happen."

"The last thing I want. That's my complaint. I have no desire to do anything, work or play, and yet I'm not tired—only bored."

Leithen's sympathy had become interest.

"Have you seen a doctor?"

The other hesitated. "Yes," he said at length. "I saw old Acton Croke this afternoon. He was no earthly use. He advised me to go to Moscow and fix up a trade agreement. He thought that might make me content with my present lot."

"He told *me* to steal a horse."

Mr Palliser-Yeates stared in extreme surprise. "You! Do you feel the same way? Have you been to Croke?"

"Three hours ago. I thought he talked good sense. He said I must get into a rougher life so as to appreciate the blessings of the life that I'm fed up with. Probably he is right, but you can't take that sort of step in cold blood."

Mr Palliser-Yeates assented. The fact of having found an associate in misfortune seemed to enliven slightly, very slightly, the spirits of both. From the adjoining table came, like an echo from a happier world, the ringing voice and hearty laughter of youth. Leithen jerked his head towards them.

"I would give a good deal for Archie's gusto," he said. "My sound right leg, for example. Or, if I couldn't I'd like Charles Lamancha's insatiable ambition. If you want as much as he wants, you don't suffer from tedium."

Palliser-Yeates looked at the gentleman in question, the tall dark one of the two diners. "I'm not so sure. Perhaps he has got too much too easily. He has come on uncommon quick, you know, and, if you do that, there's apt to arrive a moment when you flag."

14

Lord Lamancha—the title had no connection with Don Quixote and Spain, but was the name of a shieling in a Border glen which had been the home six centuries ago of the ancient house of Merkland—was an object of interest to many of his countrymen. The Marquis of Liddesdale, his father, was a hale old man who might reasonably be expected to live for another ten years and so prevent his son's career being compromised by a premature removal to the House of Lords. He had a safe seat for a London division, was a member of the Cabinet, and had a high reputation for the matter-of-fact oratory which has replaced the pre-war grandiloquence. People trusted him, because, in spite of his hidalgo-ish appearance, he was believed to have that combination of candour and intelligence which England desires in her public men. Also he was popular, for his record in the war and the rumour of a youth spent in adventurous travel touched the imagination of the ordinary citizen. At the moment he was being talked of for a great Imperial post which was soon to become vacant, and there was gossip, in the alternative, of a Ministerial readjustment which would make him the pivot of a controversial Government. It was a remarkable position for a man to have won in his early forties, who had entered public life with every disadvantage of birth.

"I suppose he's happy," said Leithen. "But I've always held that there was a chance of Charles kicking over the traces. I doubt if his ambition is an organic part of him and not stuck on with pins. There's a fundamental daftness in all Merklands. I remember him at school."

The two men finished their meal and retired to the smoking-room, where they drank their coffee abstractedly. Each was thinking about the other, and wondering what light the other's case could shed on his own. The speculation gave each a faint glimmer of comfort.

Presently the voice of Sir Archibald Roylance was heard, and that ebullient young man flung himself down on a sofa beside Leithen, while Lord Lamancha selected a cigar. Sir Archie settled his game leg to his satisfaction, and filled an ancient pipe.

15

"Heavy weather," he announced. "I've been tryin' to cheer up old Charles and it's been like castin' a fly against a thirty-mile gale. I can't make out what's come over him. Here's a deservin' lad like me struggling at the foot of the ladder and not cast down, and there's Charles high up on the top rungs as glum as an owl and declarin' that the whole thing's foolishness. Shockin' spectacle for youth."

Lamancha, who had found an arm-chair beside Palliser-Yeates, looked at the others and smiled wryly.

"Is that true, Charles?" Leithen asked. "Are you also feeling hipped? Because John and I have just been confessing to each other that we're more fed up with everything in this gay world than we've ever been before in our useful lives."

Lamancha nodded. "I don't know what has come over me. I couldn't face the House to-night, so I telephoned to Archie to come and cheer me. I suppose I'm stale, but it's a new kind of staleness, for I'm perfectly fit in body, and I can't honestly say I feel weary in mind. It's simply that the light has gone out of the landscape. Nothing has any savour."

The three men had been at school together, they had been contemporaries at the University, and close friends ever since. They had no secrets from each other. Leithen, into whose face and voice had come a remote hint of interest, gave a sketch of his own mood, and the diagnosis of the eminent consultant. Archie Roylance stared blankly from one to the other, as if some new thing had broken in upon his simple philosophy of life.

"You fellows beat me," he cried. "Here you are, every one of you a swell of sorts, with everything to make you cheerful, and you're grousin' like a labour battalion! You should be jolly well ashamed of yourselves. It's fairly temptin' Providence. What you want is some hard exercise. Go and sweat ten hours a day on a steep hill, and you'll get rid of these notions."

"My dear Archie," said Leithen, "your prescription is too crude. I used to be fond enough of sport, but I wouldn't stir a foot to catch a sixty-pound salmon or kill a fourteen pointer. I don't want to. I see no fun in it. I'm *blasé*. It's too easy."

16

"Well, I'm dashed! You're the worst spoiled chap I ever heard of, and a nice example to democracy." Archie spoke as if his gods had been blasphemed.

"Democracy, anyhow, is a good example to us. I know now why workmen strike sometimes and can't give any reason. We're on strike—against our privileges."

Archie was not listening. "Too easy, you say?" he repeated. "I call that pretty fair conceit. I've seen you miss birds often enough, old fellow."

"Nevertheless, it seems to me too easy. Everything has become too easy, both work and play."

"You can screw up the difficulty, you know. Try shootin' with a twenty bore, or fishin' for salmon with a nine-foot rod and a dry-fly cast."

"I don't want to kill anything," said Palliser-Yeates. "I don't see the fun of it."

Archie was truly shocked. Then a light of reminiscence came into his eye. "You remind me of poor old Jim Tarras," he said thoughtfully.

There were no inquiries about Jim Tarras, so Archie volunteered further news.

"You remember Jim? He had a little place somewhere in Moray, and spent most of his time shootin' in East Africa. Poor chap, he went back there with Smuts in the war and perished of blackwater. Well, when his father died and he came home to settle down, he found it an uncommon dull job. So, to enliven it, he invented a new kind of sport. He knew all there was to be known about *shikar,* and from trampin' about the Highlands he had a pretty accurate knowledge of the country-side. So he used to write to the owner of a deer forest and present his compliments, and beg to inform him that between certain dates he proposed to kill one of his stags. When he had killed it he undertook to deliver it to the owner, for he wasn't a thief."

"I call that poaching on the grand scale," observed Palliser-Yeates.

"Wasn't it? Most of the fellows he wrote to accepted his challenge and told him to come and do his damnedest. Little

17

Avington, I remember, turned on every man and boy about the place for three nights to watch the forest. Jim usually worked at night, you see. One or two curmudgeons talked of the police and prosecutin' him, but public opinion was against them—too dashed unsportin'."

"Did he always get his stag?" Leithen asked.

"In-var-i-ably, and got it off the ground and delivered it to the owner, for that was the rule of the game. Sometimes he had a precious near squeak, and Avington, who was going off his head at the time, tried to pot him—shot a gillie in the leg too. But Jim always won out. I should think he was the best *shikari* God ever made."

"Is that true, Archie?" Lamancha's voice had a magisterial tone.

"True—as—true. I know all about it, for Wattie Lithgow, who was Jim's man, is with me now. He and his wife keep house for me at Crask. Jim never took but the one man with him, and that was Wattie, and he made him just about as cunning an old dodger as himself."

Leithen yawned. "What sort of a place is Crask?" he inquired.

"Tiny little place. No fishin' except some hill lochs and only rough shootin'. I take it for the birds. Most marvellous nestin' ground in Britain barrin' some of the Outer Islands. I don't know why it should be, but it is. Something to do with the Gulf Stream, maybe. Anyhow, I've got the greenshank breedin' regularly and the red-throated diver, and half a dozen rare duck. It's a marvellous stoppin' place in spring too, for birds goin' north."

"Are you much there?"

"Generally in April, and always from the middle of August till the middle of October. You see, it's about the only place I know where you can do exactly as you like. The house is stuck away up on a long slope of moor, and you see the road for a mile from the windows, so you've plenty of time to take to the hills if anybody comes to worry you. I roost there with old Sime, my butler, and the two Lithgows, and put up a pal now and then who likes the life. It's the jolliest bit of the year for me."

"Have you any neighbours?"

"Heaps, but they don't trouble me much. Crask's the earthenware pot among the brazen vessels—mighty hard to get to and nothing to see when you get there. So the brazen vessels keep to themselves."

Lamancha went to a shelf of books above a writing-table and returned with an atlas. "Who are your brazen vessels?" he asked.

"Well, my brassiest is old Claybody at Haripol—that's four miles off across the hill."

"Bit of a swine, isn't he?" said Leithen.

"Oh, no. He's rather a good old bird himself. Don't care so much for his family. Then there's Glenraden t'other side of the Larrig"—he indicated a point on the map which Lamancha was studying—"with a real old Highland grandee living in it—Alastair Raden—commanded the Scots Guards, I believe, in the year One. Family as old as the Flood and very poor, but just manage to hang on. He's the last Raden that will live there, but that doesn't matter so much as he has no son—only a brace of daughters. Then, of course, there's the show place, Strathlarrig—horrible great house as large as a factory, but wonderful fine salmon-fishin'. Some Americans have got it this year—Boston or Philadelphia, I don't remember which —very rich and said to be rather high-brow. There's a son, I believe."

Lamancha closed the atlas.

"Do you know any of these people, Archie?" he asked.

"Only the Claybodys—very slightly. I stayed with them in Suffolk for a covert shoot two years ago. The Radens have been to call on me, but I was out. The Bandicotts—that's the Americans—are new this year."

"Is the sport good?"

"The very best. Haripol is about the steepest and most sportin' forest in the Highlands, and Glenraden is nearly as good. There's no forest at Strathlarrig, but, as I've told you,

19

amazin' good salmon fishin'. For a west coast river, I should put the Larrig only second to the Laxford."

Lamancha consulted the atlas again and appeared to ponder. Then he lifted his head, and his long face, which had a certain heaviness and sullenness in repose, was now lit by a smile which made it handsomer and younger.

"Could you have me at Crask this autumn?" he asked. "My wife has to go to Aix for a cure and I have no plans after the House rises."

"I should jolly well think so," cried Archie. "There's heaps of room in the old house, and I promise you I'll make you comfortable. Look here, you fellows! Why shouldn't all three of you come? I can get in a couple of extra maids from Inverlarrig."

"Excellent idea," said Lamancha. "But you mustn't bother about the maids. I'll bring my own man, and we'll have a male establishment, except for Mrs Lithgow. . . . By the way, I suppose you can count on Mrs Lithgow?"

"How do you mean, 'count'?" asked Archie, rather puzzled. Then a difficulty struck him. "But wouldn't you be bored? I can't show you much in the way of sport, and you're not naturalists like me. It's a quiet life, you know."

"I shouldn't be bored," said Lamancha, "I should take steps to prevent it."

Leithen and Palliser-Yeates seemed to divine his intention, for they simultaneously exclaimed.—"It isn't fair to excite Archie, Charles," the latter said. "You know that you'll never do it."

Leithen and Palliser-Yeates seemed to divine his intention, for they simultaneously exclaimed.—"It isn't fair to excite Archie, Charles," the latter said. "You know that you'll never do it."

"I intend to have a try. Hang it, John, it's the specific we were talking about—devilish difficult, devilish unpleasant, and calculated to make a man long for a dull life. Of course you two fellows will join me."

"What on earth are you talkin' about?" said the mystified Archie. "Join what?"

20

"We're proposing to quarter ourselves on you, my lad, and take a leaf out of Jim Tarras's book."

Sir Archie first stared, then he laughed nervously, then he called upon his gods, then he laughed freely and long. "Do you really mean it? What an almighty rag! . . . But hold on a moment. It will be rather awkward for me to take a hand. You see I've just been adopted as prospective candidate for that part of the country."

"So much the better. If you're found out—which you won't be—you'll get the poaching vote solid, and a good deal more. Most men at heart are poachers."

Archie shook a doubting head. "I don't know about that. They're an awfully respectable lot up there, and all those dashed stalkers and keepers and gillies are a sort of trade-union. The scallywags are a hopeless minority. If I get sent to quod—"

"You won't get sent to quod. At the worst it will be a fine, and you can pay that. What's the extreme penalty for this kind of offence, Ned?"

"I don't know," Leithen answered. "I'm not an authority on Scots law. But Archie's perfectly right. We can't go making a public exhibition of ourselves like this. We're too old to be listening to the chimes at midnight."

"Now, look here." Lamancha had shaken off his glumness and was as tense and eager as a schoolboy. "Didn't your doctor advise you to steal a horse? Well, this is a long sight easier than horse-stealing. It's admitted that we three want a tonic. On second thoughts Archie had better stand out—he hasn't our ailment, and a healthy man doesn't need medicine. But we three need it, and this idea is an inspiration. Of course we take risks, but they're sound sporting risks. After all, I've a reputation of a kind, and I put as much into the pool as anyone."

His hearers regarded him with stony faces, but this in no way checked his ardour.

"It's a perfectly first-class chance. A lonely house where you can see visitors a mile off, and an unsociable dog like Archie for

21

a host. We write the letters and receive the answers at a London address. We arrive at Crask by stealth, and stay there unbeknown to the country-side, for Archie can count on his people and my man in a sepulchre. Also we've got Lithgow, who played the same game with Jim Tarras. We have a job which will want every bit of our nerve and ingenuity with a reasonable spice of danger—for, of course, if we fail we should cut queer figures. The thing is simply ordained by Heaven for our benefit. Of course you'll come."

"I'll do nothing of the kind," said Leithen.

"No more will I," said Palliser-Yeates.

"Then I'll go alone," said Lamancha cheerfully. "I'm out for a cure, if you're not. You've a month to make up your mind, and meanwhile a share in the syndicate remains open to you."

Sir Archie looked as if he wished he had never mentioned the fatal name of Jim Tarras, "I say, you know, Charles," he began hesitatingly, but was cut short.

"Are you going back on your invitation?" asked Lamancha sternly. "Very well, then, I've accepted it, and what's more I'm going to draft a specimen letter that will go to your Highland grandee, and Claybody and the American."

He rose with a bound and fetched a pencil and a sheet of notepaper from the nearest writing-table."Here goes—*Sir, I have the honour to inform you that I propose to kill a stag*—or a salmon as the case may be—*on your ground between midnight on——and midnight——*. We can leave the dates open for the present. *The animal, of course, remains your property and will be duly delivered to you. It is a condition that it must be removed wholly outside your bounds. In the event of the undersigned failing to achieve his purpose he will pay as forfeit one hundred pounds, and if successful fifty pounds to any charity you may appoint. I have the honour to be, your obedient humble servant.*"

"What do you say to that?" he asked. "Formal, a little official, but perfectly civil, and the writer proposes to pay his way like a gentleman. Bound to make a good impression."

"You've forgotten the signature," Leithen observed dryly.

22

"It must be signed with a *nom de guerre*." He thought for a moment. "I've got it. At once business-like and mysterious." At the bottom of the draft he scrawled the name "John Macnab."

2

DESPERATE CHARACTERS IN COUNCIL

CRASK—which is properly Craoisg and is so spelled by the Ordnance Survey—when the traveller approaches it from the Larrig Bridge has the air of a West Highland terrier, *couchant* and *regardant*. You are to picture a long tilt of moorland running east and west, not a smooth lawn of heather, but seamed with gullies and patched with bogs and thickets and crowned at the summit with a low line of rocks above which may be seen peeping the spikes of the distant Haripol hills. About three-quarters of the way up the slope stands the little house, whitewashed, slated, grey stone framing the narrow windows, with that attractive jumble of masonry which belongs to an adapted farm. It is approached by a road which scorns detours and runs straight from the glen highway, and it looks south over broken moorland to the shining links of the Larrig, and beyond them to the tributary vale of the Raden and the dark mountains of its source. Such is the view from the house itself, but from the garden behind there is an ampler vista, since to the left a glimpse may be had of the policies of Strathlarrig and even of a corner of that monstrous mansion, and to the right of the tidal waters of the river and the yellow sands on which in the stillest weather the Atlantic frets. Crask is at once a sanctuary and a watchtower; it commands a wide countryside and yet preserves its secrecy, for, though officially approached by a road like a ruler, there are a dozen sheltered ways of reaching it by the dips and crannies of the hill-side.

So thought a man who about five o'clock on the afternoon of the 24th of August was inconspicuously drawing towards it by way of a peat road which ran from the east through a wood

24

of birches. Sir Edward Leithen's air was not more cheerful that when we met him a month ago, except that there was now a certain vigour in it which came from ill-temper. He had been for a long walk in the rain, and the scent of wet bracken and birches and bog myrtle, the peaty fragrance of the hills salted with the tang of the sea, had failed to comfort, though, not so long ago, it had had the power to intoxicate. Scrambling in the dell of a burn, he had observed both varieties of the filmy fern and what he knew to be a very rare cerast, and, though an ardent botanist, he had observed them unmoved. Soon the rain had passed, the west wind blew aside the cloud-wrack, and the Haripol tops had come out black against a turquoise sky, with Sgurr Dearg, awful and remote, towering above all. Though a keen mountaineer, the spectacle had neither exhilarated nor tantalised him. He was in a bad temper, and he knew that at Crask he should find three other men in the same case, for even the debonair Sir Archie was in the dumps with a toothache.

He told himself that he had come on a fool's errand, and the extra absurdity was that he could not quite see how he had been induced to come. He had consistently refused: so had Palliser-Yeates; Archie as a prospective host had been halting and nervous; there was even a time when Lamancha, the source of all the mischief, had seemed to waver. Nevertheless, some occult force — false shame probably — had shepherded them all here, unwilling, unconvinced, cold-footed, destined to a preposterous adventure for which not one of them had the slightest zest. . . . Yet they had taken immense pains to arrange the thing, just as if they were all exulting in the prospect. His own clerk was to attend to the forwarding of their letters including any which might be addressed to "John Macnab." The newspapers had contained paragraphs announcing that the Countess of Lamancha had gone to Aix for a month, where she would presently be joined by her husband, who intended to spend a week drinking the waters before proceeding to his grouse-moor of Leriot on the Borders. *The Times,* three days ago, had recorded Sir Edward Leithen and Mr John Palliser-Yeates as among those who had left Euston for Edinburgh, and more than one social paragrapher had mentioned that the ex-Attorney-General would be spending his holiday fishing on the Tay, while the eminent banker was to be the guest of the Chancellor of the Exchequer at an informal vacation conference on the nation's precarious finances. Lamancha had been fetched under cover of night by Archie from a station so remote that no one but a lunatic would think of using it. Palliser-Yeates had tramped for two days across the hills from the south, and Leithen himself, having been instructed to bring a Ford car, had had a miserable drive of a hundred and fifty miles in the rain, during which he had repeatedly lost his way. He had carried out his injunctions as to secrecy by arriving at two in the morning by means of this very peat road. The troops had achieved their silent concentration, and the silly business must now begin. Leithen groaned, and anathematised the memory of Jim Tarras.

As he approached the house he saw, to his amazement, a large closed car making its way down the slope. Putting his glass on it, he watched it reach the glen road and then turn east, passing the gates of Strathlarrig, till he lost it behind a shoulder of hill. Hurrying across the stable-yard, he entered the house by the back-door, disturbing Lithgow the keeper in the midst of a whispered confabulation with Lamancha's man, whose name was Shapp. Passing through the gun-room he found, in the big smoking-room which looked over the valley, Lamancha and Palliser-Yeates with the crouch of conspirators flattening their noses on the windowpanes.

The sight of him diverted the attention of the two from the landscape.

"This is an infernal plant," Palliser-Yeates exclaimed. "Archie swore to us that no one ever came here, and the second day a confounded great car arrives. Charles and I had just time to nip in here and lock the door, while Archie parleyed with them. He's been uncommon quick about it. The brutes didn't stay for more than five minutes."

"Who were they?" Leithen asked.

"Only got a side glance at them. They seemed to be a stout

woman and a girl—oh, and a yelping little dog. I expect Archie kicked him, for he was giving tongue from the drawing-room."

The door opened to admit their host, who bore in one hand a large whisky-and-soda. He dropped wearily into a chair, where he sipped the beverage. An observer might have noted that what could be seen of his wholesome face was much inflamed, and that a bandage round chin and cheeks which ended in a top-knot above his scalp gave him the appearance of Ricquet with the Tuft in the fairytale.

"That's all right," he said, in the tone of a man who has done a good piece of work. "I've choked off visitors at Crask for a bit, for the old lady will put it all round the country-side."

"Put what?" said Leithen, and "Who is the old lady?" asked Lamancha, and "Did you kick the dog?" demanded Palliser-Yeates.

Archie looked drearily at his friends. "It was Lady Claybody and a daughter—I think the second one—and their horrid little dog. They won't come back in a hurry—nobody will come back—I'm marked down as a pariah. Hang it, I may as well chuck my candidature. I've scuppered my prospects for the sake of you three asses."

"What has the blessed martyr been and done?" asked Palliser-Yeates.

"I've put a barrage round this place, that's all. I was very civil to the Claybodys, though I felt a pretty fair guy with my head in a sling. I bustled about, talking nonsense and offerin' tea, and then, as luck would have it, I trod on the hound. That's the worst of my game leg. The brute nearly had me over, and it started howlin'—you must have heard it. That dog's a bit weak in the head, for it can't help barkin' just out of pure cussedness—Lady Claybody says it's high-strung because of its fine breedin'. It got something to bark for this time, and the old woman had it in her arms fondlin' it and lookin' very old-fashioned at me. It seems the beast's name is Roguie and she called it her darlin' Wee Roguie, for she's pickin' up a bit of Scots since she came to live in these parts. . . . Lucky Mackenzie wasn't at home. He'd have eaten it. . . . Well,

27

after that things settled down, and I was just goin' to order tea, when it occurred to the daughter to ask what was wrong with my face. Then I had an inspiration."

Archie paused and smiled sourly.

"I said I didn't know, but I feared I might be sickenin' for small-pox. I hinted that my face was a horrid sight under the bandage."

"Good for you, Archie," said Lamancha. "What happened then?"

"They bolted—fairly ran for it. They did record time into their car—scarcely stopped to say goodbye. I suppose you realise what I've done, you fellows. The natives here are scared to death of infectious diseases, and if we hadn't our own people we wouldn't have a servant left in the house. The story will be all over the country-side in two days, and my only fear is that it may bring some medical officer of health nosin' round. . . . Anyhow, it will choke off visitors."

"Archie, you're a brick," was Lamancha's tribute.

"I'm very much afraid I'm a fool, but thank Heaven I'm not the only one. Sime," he shouted in a voice of thunder, "what's happened to tea?"

The shout brought the one-armed butler and Shapp with the apparatus of the meal, and an immense heap of letters all addressed to Sir Archibald Roylance.

"Hullo! the mail has arrived," cried the master of the house. "Now let's see what's the news of John Macnab?"

He hunted furiously among the correspondence, tearing open envelopes and distributing letters to the others with the rapidity of a conjurer. One little sealed packet he reserved to the last, and drew from it three missives bearing the same superscription.

These he opened, glanced at, and handed to Lamancha. "Read 'em out, Charles," he said. "It's the answers at last."

Lamancha read slowly the first document, of which this is the text:

28

GLENRADEN CASTLE,
STRATHLARRIG,
Aug. — 19—.

SIR,

I have received your insolent letter. I do not know what kind of rascal you may be, except that you have the morals of a bandit and the assurance of a halfpenny journalist. But since you seem in your perverted way to be a sportsman, I am not the man to refuse your challenge. My reply is, sir, damn your eyes and have a try. I defy you to kill a stag in my forest between midnight on the 28th of August and midnight of the 30th. I will give instructions to my men to guard my marches, and if you should be roughly handled by them you have only to blame yourself.

Yours faithfully,

ALASTAIR RADEN.

John Macnab, Esq.

"That's a good fellow," said Archie with conviction. "Just the sort of letter I'd write myself. He takes things in the proper spirit. But it's a blue look-out for your chances, my lads. What old Raden doesn't know about deer isn't knowledge."

Lamancha read the second reply:

STRATHLARRIG HOUSE,
STRATHLARRIG,
Aug. —, 19—.

MY DEAR SIR,

Your letter was somewhat of a surprise, but as I am not yet familiar with the customs of this country, I forbear to enlarge on this point, and since you have marked it 'Confidential' I am unable to take advice. You state that you intend to kill a salmon in the Strathlarrig water between midnight on September 1 and midnight on September 3, this salmon, if killed, to remain my property. I have consulted such books as might give me guidance, and I am bound to

29

state that in my view the laws of Scotland are hostile to your suggested enterprise. Nevertheless, I do not take my stand on the law, for I presume that your proposition is conceived in a sporting spirit, and that you dare me to stop you. Well, sir, I will see you on that hand. The fishing is not that good at present that I am inclined to quarrel about one salmon. I give you leave to use every method that may occur to you to capture that fish, and I promise to use every method that may occur to me to prevent you. In your letter you undertake to use only 'legitimate means.' I would have pleasure in meeting you in the same spirit, but I reckon that all means are counted legitimate in the capture of poachers.

Cordially,

Junius Theodore Bandicott.

Mr J. Macnab.

"That's the young 'un," Archie observed. "The old man was christened 'Acheson,' and don't take any interest in fishin'. He spends his time in lookin' for Norse remains."

"He seems a decent sort of fellow," said Palliser Yeates, "but I don't quite like the last sentence. He'll probably try shooting, same as his countrymen once did on the Beauly. Whoever gets this job will have some excitement for his money."

Lamancha read out the last letter:

227 North Melville Street,
Edinburgh,
Aug.—, 19—.

Sir,

Re Haripol Forest

Our client, the Right Honourable Lord Claybody, has read to us on the telephone your letter of Aug. — and has desired us to reply to it. We are instructed to say that our client is at a loss to understand how to take your communication, whether as a piece of impertinence or as a serious threat. If it is the latter, and you persist in your intention, we are instructed to apply to the Court for a summary interdict to prevent your entering upon his lands. We would also point out that under the Criminal Law of Scotland, any person whatsoever who commits a trespass in the daytime by entering upon any land without leave of the proprietor, in pursuit of, *inter alia,* deer, is liable to a fine of £2, while, if such person have his face blackened, or if five or more persons acting in concert commit the trespass, the penalty is £5 (2 & 3 William IV, c. 68).

> We are, sir,
> Your obedient servants,
> PROSSER, McKELPIE, AND MACLYMONT.

John Macnab, Esq.

Lamancha laughed. "Is that good law, Ned?"

Leithen read the letter again. "I suppose so. Deer being *ferae naturae,* there is no private property in them or common law crime in killing them, and the only remedy is to prevent trespass in pursuit of them or to punish the trespasser."

"It seems to me that you get off pretty lightly," said Archie. "Two quid is not much in the way of a fine, for I don't suppose you want to black your faces or march five deep into Haripol. . . . But what a rotten sportsman old Claybody is!"

Palliser-Yeates heaved a sigh of apparent relief. "I am bound to say the replies are better than I expected. It will be a devil of a business, though, to circumvent that old Highland chief, and that young American sounds formidable. Only, if we're caught out there, we're dealing with sportsmen and can appeal to their higher nature, you know. Claybody is probably the easiest proposition so far as getting a stag is concerned, but if we're nobbled by him we needn't look for mercy. Still, it's only a couple of pounds."

"You're an ass, John," said Leithen. "It's only a couple of pounds for John Macnab. But if these infernal Edinburgh lawyers get on the job, it will be a case of producing the person of John Macnab, and then we're all in the cart. Don't you

31

realise that in this fool's game we simply cannot afford to lose—none of us?"

"That," said Lamancha, "is beyond doubt the truth, and it's just there that the fun comes in."

The reception of the three letters had brightened the atmosphere. Each man had now something to think about, and, till it was time to dress for dinner, each was busy with sheets of the Ordnance maps. The rain had begun again, the curtains were drawn, and round a good fire of peats they read and smoked and dozed. Then they had hot baths, and it was a comparatively cheerful and very hungry party that assembled in the dining-room. Archie proposed champagne, but the offer was unanimously declined. "We ought to be in training," Lamancha warned him. "Keep the Widow for the occasions when we need comforting. They'll come all right."

Palliser-Yeates was enthusiastic about the food. "I must say, you do us very well," he told his host. "These haddocks are the best things I've ever eaten. How do you manage to get fresh sea-fish here?"

Archie appealed to Sime. "They come from Inverlarrig, Sir Erchibald," said the butler. "There's a wee laddie comes up here sellin' haddies verra near every day."

"Bless my soul, Sime. I thought no one came up here. You know my orders."

"This is just a tinker laddie, Sir Erchibald. He sleeps in a cairt down about Larrigmore. He just comes wi' his powny and awa' back, and doesna bide twae minutes. Mistress Lithgow was anxious for haddies, for she said gentlemen got awfu' tired of saumon and trout."

"All right, Sime. I'll speak to Mrs Lithgow. She'd better tell him we don't want any more. By the way, we ought to see Lithgow after dinner. Tell him to come to the smoking-room."

When Sime had put the port on the table and withdrawn, Leithen lifted up his voice.

"Look here, before we get too deep into this thing, let's make sure that we know where we are. We're all three turned up here—why, I don't know. But there's still time to go back.

32

We realise now what we're in for. Are you clear in your minds that you want to go on?"

"I am," said Lamancha doggedly. "I'm out for a cure. Hang it, I feel a better man already."

"I suppose your profession makes you take risks," said Leithen dryly, "Mine doesn't. What about you, John?"

Palliser-Yeates shifted uneasily in his chair. "I don't want to go on. I feel no kind of keenness, and my feet are rather cold. And yet—you know—I should feel rather ashamed to turn back."

Archie uplifted his turbaned head. "That's how I feel, though I'm not on myself in this piece. We've given hostages, and the credit of John Macnab is at stake. We've dared old Raden and young Bandicott, and we can't decently cry off. Besides, I'm advertised as a smallpox patient, and it would be a pity to make a goat of myself for nothing. Mind you, I stand to lose as much as anybody, if we bungle things."

Leithen had the air of bowing to the inevitable. "Very well, that's settled. But I wish to Heaven I saw myself safely out of it. My only inducement to go on is to score off that bounder Claybody. He and his attorney's letter put my hackles up."

In the smoking-room Lamancha busied himself with preparing three slips of paper and writing on them three names.

"We must hold a council of war," he said. "First of all, we have taken measures to keep our presence here secret. My man Shapp is all right. What about your people, Archie?"

"Sime and Carfrae have been warned, and you may count on them. They're the class of lads that ask no questions. So are the Lithgows. We've no neighbours, and they're anyway not the gossiping kind, and I've put them on their Bible oath. I fancy they think the reason is politics. They're a trifle scared of you, Charles, and your reputation, for they're not accustomed to hidin' Cabinet Ministers in the scullery. Lithgow's a fine crusted old Tory."

"Good. Well, we'd better draw for beats, and get Lithgow in."

33

The figure that presently appeared before them was a small man, about fifty years of age, with a great breadth of shoulder and a massive face decorated with a wispish tawny beard. His mouth had the gravity and primness of an elder of the Kirk, but his shrewd blue eyes were not grave. The son of a Tweeddale shepherd who had emigrated years before to a cheviot farm in Sutherland, he was in every line and feature the Lowlander, and his speech had still the broad intonation of the Borders. But all his life had been spent in the Highlands on this and that deer forest, and as a young stalker he had been picked out by Jim Tarras for his superior hill craft. To Archie his chief recommendation was that he was a passionate naturalist, who was as eager to stalk a rare bird with a field-glass as to lead a rifle up to deer. Other traits will appear in the course of this narrative; but it may be noted here that he was a voracious reader and in the long winter nights had amassed a store of varied knowledge, which was patently improving his master's mind. Archie was accustomed to quote him for most of his views on matters other than ornithology and war.

"Do you mind going over to that corner and shuffling these slips? Now, John, you draw first."

Mr Palliser-Yeates extracted a slip from Lithgow's massive hand.

"Glenraden," he cried. "Whew! I'm for it this time."

Leithen drew next. His slip read Strathlarrig.

"Thank God, I've got old Claybody," said Lamancha. "Unless you want him very badly, Ned?"

Leithen shook his head. "I'm content. It would be a bad start to change the draw."

"Sit down, Wattie," said Archie. "Here's a dram for you. We've summoned you to a consultation. I daresay you've been wonderin' what all this fuss about secrecy has meant. I'm going to tell you. You were with Jim Tarras, and you've often told me about his poachin'. Well, these three gentlemen want to have a try at the same game. They're tired of ordinary sport, and want something more excitin'. It wouldn't do, of course, for them to appear under their real names, so they've invented a *nom de guerre*—that's a bogus name, you know. They call themselves collectively, as you might say, John Macnab. John Macnab writes from London to three proprietors, same as Jim Tarras used to do, and proposes to take a deer or a salmon on their property within certain dates. There's a copy of the letter, and here are the replies that arrived tonight. Just you read 'em."

Lithgow, without moving a muscle of his face, took the documents. He nodded approvingly over the original letter. He smiled broadly at Colonel Raden's epistle, puzzled a little at Mr Bandicott's, and wrinkled his brows over that of the Edinburgh solicitors. Then he stared into the fire, and emitted short grunts which might have equally well been chuckles or groans.

"Well, what do you think of the chances?" asked Archie at length.

"Would the gentlemen be good shots?" asked Lithgow.

"Mr Palliser-Yeates, who has drawn Glenraden, is a very good shot," Archie replied, "and he has stalked on nearly every forest in Scotland. Lord Lamancha— Charles, you're pretty good, aren't you?"

"Fair," was the answer. "Good on my day."

"And Sir Edward Leithen is a considerable artist on the river. Now, Wattie, you understand that they want to win—want to get the stags and the salmon—but it's absolute sheer naked necessity that, whether they fail or succeed, they mustn't be caught. John Macnab must remain John Macnab, an unknown blighter from London. You know who Lord Lamancha is, but perhaps you don't know that Sir Edward Leithen is a great lawyer, and Mr Palliser-Yeates is one of the biggest bankers in the country."

"I ken all about the gentlemen," said Lithgow gravely. "I was readin' Mr Yeates's letter in *The Times* about the debt we was owin' America, and I mind fine Sir Edward's speeches in Parliament about the Irish Constitution. I didna altogether agree with him."

"Good for you, Wattie. You see, then, how desperately important it is that the thing shouldn't get out. Mr Tarras didn't much care if he was caught, but if John Macnab is uncovered there will be a high and holy row. Now you grasp the problem, and you've got to pull up your socks and think it out. I don't want your views to-night, but I should like to have your notion of the chances in a general way. What's the bettin'? Twenty to one against?"

"Mair like a thousand," said Lithgow grimly. "It will be verra, verra deeficult. It will want a deal o' thinkin'." Then he added, "Mr Tarras was an awfu' grand shot. He would kill a runnin' beast at fower hundred yards—aye, he could make certain of it."

"Good Lord, I'm not in that class," Palliser-Yeates exclaimed.

"Aye, and he was more than a grand shot. He could creep up to a sleepin' beast in the dark and pit a knife in its throat. The sauvages in Africa had learned him that. There was plenty o' times when him and me were out that it wasna possible to use the rifle."

"We can't compete there," said Lamancha dolefully.

"But I wad not say it was impossible," Lithgow added more briskly. "It will want a deal o' thinkin'. It might be done on Haripol—I wadna say but it might be done, but yon auld man at Glenraden will be ill to get the better of. And the Strathlarrig water is an easy water to watch. Ye'll be for only takin' shootable beasts, like Mr Tarras, and ye'll not be wantin' to cleek a fish? It might be not so hard to get a wee staggie, or to sniggle a salmon in one of the deep pots."

"No, we must play the game by the rules. We're not poachers."

"Then it will be verra, verra deeficult."

"You understand," put in Lamancha, "that, though we count on your help, you yourself mustn't be suspected. It's as important for you as for us to avoid suspicion, for if they got you it would implicate your master, and that mustn't happen on any account."

"I ken that. It will be verra, verra deeficult. I said the odds were a thousand to one, but I think ten thousand wad be liker the thing."

36

"Well, go and sleep on it, and we'll see you in the morning. An tell your wife I don't want any boys comin' up to the house with fish. She must send elsewhere and buy 'em. Good-night, Wattie."

When Lithgow had withdrawn the four men sat silent and meditative in their chairs. One would rise now and then and knock out his pipe, but scarcely a word was spoken. It is to be presumed that the thoughts of each were on the task in hand, but Leithen's must have wandered. "By the way, Archie," he said, "I saw a very pretty girl on the road this afternoon, riding a yellow pony. Who could she be?"

"Lord knows!" said Archie. "Probably one of the Raden girls. I haven't seen 'em yet."

When the clock struck eleven Sir Archie arose and ordered his guests to bed.

"I think my toothache is gone," he said, switching off his turban and revealing a ruffled head and scarlet cheek. Then he muttered: "A thousand to one! Ten thousand to one! It can't be done, you know. We've got to find some way of shortenin' the odds!"

3

RECONNAISSANCE

Rosy-Fingered Dawn, when, attended by mild airs and a sky of Italian blue, she looked in at Crask next morning, found two members of the household already astir. Mr Palliser-Yeates, coerced by Wattie Lithgow, was starting with bitter self-condemnation to prospect what his guide called "the yont side o' Glenraden." A quarter of an hour later Lamancha, armed with a map and a telescope, departed alone for the crest of hill behind which lay the Haripol forest. After that peace fell on the place, and it was not till the hour of ten that Sir Edward Leithen descended for breakfast.

The glory of the morning had against his convictions made him cheerful. The place smelt so good within and without, Mrs Lithgow's scones were so succulent, the bacon so crisp, and Archie, healed of the toothache, was so preposterous and mirthful a figure that Leithen found a faint zest again in the contemplation of the future. When Archie advised him to get busy about the Larrig he did not complain, but accompanied his host to the gun-room, where he studied attentively on a large-scale map the three miles of the stream in the tenancy of Mr Bandicott.

It seemed to him that he had better equip himself for the part by some simple disguise, so, declining Archie's suggestion of a kilt, he returned to his bedroom to refit. Obviously the best line was the tourist, so he donned a stiff white shirt and a stiff dress collar with a tartan bow-tie contributed from Sime's wardrobe. Light brown boots in which he had travelled from London took the place of his nailed shoes, and his thick knickerbocker stockings bulged out above them. Sime's watch-chain, from which depended a football club medal, a vulgar green Homburg hat of Archie's, and a camera slung on his shoulders completed the equipment. His host surveyed him with approval.

"The Blackpool season is beginning," he observed. "You're the born tripper, my lad. Don't forget the picture post cards." A bicycle was found, and the late Attorney-General zigzagged warily down the steep road to the Larrig bridge.

He entered the highway without seeing a human soul, and according to plan turned down the glen towards Inverlarrig. There at the tiny post-office he bought the regulation picture post cards, and conversed in what he imagined to be the speech of Cockaigne with the aged post-mistress. He was eloquent on the beauties of the weather and the landscape and not reticent as to his personal affairs. He was, he said, a seeker for beauty-spots, and had heard that the best were to be found in the demesne of Strathlarrig. "It's private grund," he was told, "but there's Americans bidin' there and they're kind folk and awfu' free with their siller. If ye ask at the lodge, they'll maybe let ye in to photograph." The sight of an array of ginger-beer bottles inspired him to further camouflage, so he purchased two which he stuck in his side-pockets.

East of the Bridge of Larrig he came to the chasm in the river above which he knew began the Strathlarrig water. The first part was a canal-like stretch among bogs, which promised ill for fishing, but beyond a spit of rock the Larrig curled in towards the road edge, and ran in noble pools and swift streams under the shadow of great pines. This, Leithen knew from the map, was the Wood of Larrigmore, a remnant of the ancient Caledonian Forest. By the water's edge the covert was dark, but towards the roadside the trees thinned out, and the ground was delicately carpeted with heather and thymy turf. There grazed an aged white pony, and a few yards off, on the shaft of a dilapidated fish-cart, sat a small boy.

Leithen, leaning his bicycle against a tree, prospected the murky pools with the air rather of an angler than a photographer, and in the process found his stiff shirt and collar a vexation. Also the ginger-beer bottles bobbed unpleasantly at his side. So, catching sight of the boy, he beckoned him near. "Do you like ginger-beer?" he asked, and in reply to a vigorous nod bestowed the pair on him. The child returned like a dog to the shelter of the cart, whence might have been presently heard the sound of gluttonous enjoyment. Leithen, having satisfied himself that no mortal could take a fish in that thicket, continued up-stream till he struck the wall of the Strathlarrig domain and a vast castellated lodge.

The lodge-keeper made no objection when he sought admittance, and he turned from the gravel drive towards the river, which now flowed through a rough natural park. For a fisherman it was the water of his dreams. The pools were long and shelving, with a strong stream at the head and, below, precisely the right kind of boulders and outjutting banks to shelter fish. There were three of these pools—the "Duke's," the "Black Scour," and "Davie's Pot," were the names Archie had told him—and beyond, almost under the windows of the house, "Lady Maisie's," conspicuous for its dwarf birches and the considerable waterfall above it. Here he made believe to take a photograph, though he had no idea how a camera worked, and reflected dismally upon the magnitude of his task. The whole place was as bright and open as the Horse Guards Parade. The house commanded all four pools, which he knew to be the best, and even at midnight, with the owner unsuspecting, poaching would be nearly impossible. What would it be when the owner was warned, and legitimate methods of fishing were part of the contract?

After a glance at the house, which seemed to be deep in noontide slumber, he made his inconspicuous way past the end of a formal garden to a reach where the Larrig flowed wide and shallow over pebbles. Then came a belt of firs, and then a long tract of broken water which was obviously not a place to hold salmon. He realised, from his memory of the map, that he must be near the end of the Strathlarrig beat, for the topmost mile was a series of unfishable linns. But presently he came to a noble pool. It lay in a meadow where the hay had just been cut and was liker a bit of Tweed or Eden than a Highland stream. Its shores were low and on the near side edged with fine gravel, the far bank was a green rise unspoiled by scrub, the current entered it with a proud swirl, washed the high bank, and spread itself out in a beautifully broken tail, so that every yard of it spelled fish. Leithen stared at it with appreciative eyes. The back of a moving monster showed in mid-stream, and automatically he raised his arm in an imaginary cast.

The next second he observed a man walking across the meadow towards him, and remembered his character. Directing his camera hastily at the butt-end of a black-faced sheep on the opposite shore, he appeared to be taking a careful photograph, after which he restored the apparatus to its case and turned to reconnoitre the stranger. This proved to be a middle-aged man in ancient tweed knickerbockers of an outrageous pattern known locally as the "Strathlarrig tartan." He was obviously a river-keeper, and was advancing with a resolute and minatory air.

Leithen took off his hat with a flourish.

"Have I the honour, sir, to address the owner of this lovely spot?" he asked in what he hoped was the true accent of a tripper.

The keeper stopped short and regarded him sternly.

"What are ye daein' here?" he demanded.

"Picking up a few pictures, sir. I inquired at your lodge, and was told that I might presume upon your indulgence. Pardon me, if I 'ave presumed too far. If I 'ad known that the proprietor was at 'and I would have sought 'im out and addressed my 'umble request to 'imself."

"Ye're makin' a mistake. I'm no the laird. The laird's awa' about India. But Mr Bandicott—that's him that's the tenant—has given strict orders that naebody's to gang near the watter. I wonder Mactavish at the lodge hadna mair sense."

"I fear the blame is mine," said the agreeable tourist. "I only asked leave to enter the grounds, but the beauty of the scenery attracted me to the river. Never 'ave I seen a more exquisite spot." He waved his arm towards the pool.

41

"It's no that bad. But ye maun awa' out o' this. Ye'd better gang by the back road, for fear they see ye frae the hoose."

Leithen followed him obediently, after presenting him with a cigarette, which he managed to extract without taking his case from his pocket. It should have been a fag, he reflected, and not one of Archie's special Egyptians. As they walked he conversed volubly.

"What's the name of the river?" he asked. "Is it the Strathlarrig?"

"No, it's the Larrig, and that bit you like sae weel is the Minister's Pool. There's no a pool like it in Scotland."

"I believe you. There is not," was the enthusiastic reply.

"I mean for fish. Ye'll no ken muckle aboot fishin'."

"I've done a bit of anglin' at 'ome. What do you catch here? Jack and perch?"

"Jack and perch!" cried the keeper scornfully. "Saumon, man. Saumon up to thirty pounds' wecht."

"Oh, of course, salmon. That must be a glorious sport. But a friend of mine, who has seen it done, told me it wasn't 'ard. He said that even I could catch a salmon."

"Mair like a saumon wad catch you. Now, you haud down the back road, and ye'll come out aside the lodge gate. And dinna you come here again. The orders is strict, and if auld Angus was to get a grip o' ye, I wadna say what wad happen. Guid day to ye, and dinna stop till ye're out o' the gates."

Leithen did as he was bid, circumnavigated the house, struck a farm track, and in time reached the high road. It was a very doleful tourist who trod the wayside heather past the Wood of Larrigmore. Never had he seen a finer stretch of water or one so impregnably defended. No bluff or ingenuity would avail an illicit angler on that open greensward, with every keeper mobilised and on guard. He thought less now of the idiocy of the whole proceeding than of the folly of plunging in the dark upon just that piece of river. There were many streams where Jim Tarras's feat might be achieved, but he had chosen the one stretch in all Scotland where it was starkly impossible.

The recipient of the ginger-beer was still sitting by the shafts of his cart. He seemed to be lunching, for he was carving attentively a hunk of cheese and a loaf-end with a gully-knife. As he looked up from his task Leithen saw a child of perhaps twelve summers, with a singularly alert and impudent eye, a much-freckled face, and a thatch of tow-coloured hair bleached almost white by the sun. His feet were bare, his trousers were those of a grown man, tucked up at the knees and hitched up almost under his armpits, and for a shirt he appeared to have a much-torn jersey. Weather had tanned his whole appearance into the blend of greys and browns which one sees on a hill-side boulder. The boy nodded gravely to Leithen, and continued to munch.

Below the wood lay the half-mile where the Larrig wound sluggishly through a bog before precipitating itself into the chasm above the Bridge of Larrig. Leithen left his bicycle by the roadside and crossed the waste of hags and tussocks to the water's edge. It looked a thankless place for the angler. The clear streams of the Larrig seemed to have taken on the colour of their banks, and to drowse dark and deep and sullen in one gigantic peat-hole. In spite of the rain of yesterday there was little current. The place looked oily, stagnant, and unfishable—a tract through which salmon after mounting the fall would hurry to the bright pools above.

Leithen sat down in a clump of heather and lit his pipe. Something might be done with a worm after a spate, he considered, but any other lure was out of the question. The place had its merits for every purpose but taking salmon. It was a part of the Strathlarrig water outside the park pale, and it was so hopeless that it was not likely to be carefully patrolled. The high road, it was true, ran near, but it was little frequented. If only. . . . He suddenly sat up, and gazed intently at a ripple on the dead surface. Surely that was a fish on the move. . . . He kept his eyes on the river, until he saw something else which made him rub them, and fall into deep reflection. . . .

He was roused by a voice at his shoulder.

"What for will they no let me come up to Crask ony mair?" the voice demanded in a sort of tinker's whine.

43

Leithen turned and found the boy of the ginger-beer.

"Hullo! You oughtn't to do that, my son. You'll give people heart disease. What was it you asked?"

"What . . . for . . . will . . . they . . . no . . . let . . . me come . . . up to Crask . . . ony mair?"

"I'm sure I don't know. What's Crask?"

"Ye ken it fine. It's the big hoose up the hill. I seen you come doon frae it yoursel' this mornin'."

Leithen was tempted to deny this allegation and assert his title of tourist, but something in the extreme intelligence of the boy's face suggested that such a course might be dangerous. Instead he said, "Tell me your name, and what's your business at Crask?"

"My name's Benjamin Bogle, but I get Fish Benjie frae most folks. I've sell't haddies and flukes to Crask these twa months. But this mornin' I was tell't no to come back, and when I speired what way, the auld wife shut the door on me."

A recollection of Sir Archie's order the night before returned to Leithen's mind, and with it a great sense of insecurity. The argus-eyed child, hot with a grievance, had seen him descend from Crask, and was therefore in a position to give away the whole show. What chance was there for secrecy with this malevolent scout hanging around?

"Where do you live, Benjie?"

"I bide in my cairt. My father's in jyle, and my mither's lyin' badly in Muirtown. I sell fish to a' the gentry."

"And you want to know why you can't sell them at Crask?"

"Aye, I wad like to ken that. The auld wife used to be a kind body and gie me jeely pieces. What's turned her into a draygon?"

Leithen was accustomed, in the duties of his profession, to quick decisions on tactics, and now he took one which was destined to be momentous.

"Benjie," he said solemnly, "there's a lot of things in the world that I don't understand, and it stands to reason that there must be more that you don't. I'm in a position in which I badly want somebody to help me. I like the look of you. You

44

look a trusty fellow and a keen one. Is all your time taken up selling haddies?"

" 'Deed no. Just twa hours in the mornin', and twa hours at nicht when I gang doun to the cobles at Inverlarrig. I've a heap o' time on my hands."

"Good. I think I can promise that you may resume your trade at Crask. But first I want you to do a job for me. There's a bicycle lying by the roadside. Bring it up to Crask this evening between six and seven. Have you a watch?"

"No, but I can tell the time braw and fine."

"Go to the stables and wait for me there. I want to have a talk with you." Leithen produced half a crown, on which the grubby paw of Fish Benjie instantly closed.

"And look here, Benjie. You haven't seen me here, or anybody like me. Above all, you didn't see me come down from Crask this morning. If anybody asks you questions, you only saw a man on a bicycle on the road to Inverlarrig."

The boy nodded, and his solemn face flickered for a second with a subtle smile.

"Well, that's a bargain." Leithen got up from his couch and turned down the river, making for the Bridge of Larrig, where the highway crossed. He looked back once, and saw Fish Benjie wheeling his bicycle into the undergrowth of the wood. He was in two minds as to whether he had done wisely in placing himself in the hands of a small ragamuffin, who for all he knew might be hand-in-glove with the Strathlarrig keepers. But the recollection of Benjie's face reassured him. He did not look like a boy who would be the pet of any constituted authority; he had the air rather of the nomad against whom the orderly world waged war. There had been an impish honesty in his face, and Leithen, who had a weakness for disreputable urchins, felt that he had taken the right course. Besides, the young sleuth-hound had got on his trail, and there had been nothing for it but to make him an ally.

He crossed the bridge, avoided the Crask road, and struck up hill by a track which followed the ravine of a burn. As he walked his mind went back to a stretch on a Canadian river, a

45

stretch of still unruffled water warmed all day by a July sun. It had been as full as it could hold of salmon, but no artifice of his could stir them. There in the later afternoon had come an aged man from Boston, who fished with a light trout rod and cast a deft line, and placed a curious little dry fly several feet above a fish's snout. Then, by certain strange manoeuvres, he had drawn the fly under water. Leithen had looked on and marvelled, while before sunset that ancient man hooked and landed seven good fish. . . . Somehow that bit of shining sunflecked Canadian river reminded him of the unpromising stretch of the Larrig he had just been reconnoitring.

At a turn of the road he came upon his host, tramping homeward in the company of a most unprepossessing hound. I pause for an instant to introduce Mackenzie. He was a mongrel collie of the old Highland stock, known as "beardies," and his touzled head, not unlike an extra-shaggy Dandie Dinmont's, was set upon a body of immense length, girth and muscle. His manners were atrocious to all except his master, and local report accused him of every canine vice except worrying sheep. He had been christened "The Bluidy Mackenzie" after a noted persecutor of the godly, by someone whose knowledge of history was greater than Sir Archie's, for the latter never understood the allusion. The name, however, remained his official one; commonly he was addressed as Mackenzie, but in moments of expansion he was referred to by his master as Old Bloody.

The said master seemed to be in a strange mood. He was dripping wet, having apparently fallen into the river, but his spirits soared, and he kept on smiling in a light-hearted way. He scarcely listened to Leithen, when he told him of his compact with Fish Benjie. "I daresay it will be all right," he observed idiotically. "Is your idea to pass off one of his haddies as a young salmon on the guileless Bandicott?" For an explanation of Sir Archie's conduct the chronicler must retrace his steps.

After Leithen's departure it had seemed good to him to take the air, so, summoning Mackenzie from a dark lair in the yard,

46

he made his way to the river—the beat below the bridge and beyond the high road, which was on Crask ground. There it was a broad brawling water, boulder-strewn and shallow, which an active man could cross dry-shod by natural stepping-stones. Sir Archie sat for a time on the near shore, listening to the sandpipers—birds which were his special favourites—and watching the whinchats on the hill-side and the flashing white breasts of the water-ousels. Mackenzie lay beside him, an uneasy sphinx, tormented by a distant subtle odour of badger.

Presently Sir Archie arose and stepped out on the half-submerged boulder. He was getting very proud of the way he had learned to manage his game leg, and it occurred to him that here was a chance of testing his balance. If he could hop across on the stones to the other side he might regard himself as an able-bodied man. Balancing himself with his stick as a rope-dancer uses his pole, he in due course reached the middle of the current. After that it was more difficult, for the stones were smaller and the stream more rapid, but with an occasional splash and flounder he landed safely, to be saluted with a shower of spray from Mackenzie, who had taken the deep-water route.

"Not so bad that, for a crock," he told himself, as he lay full length in the sun watching the faint line of the Haripol hills overtopping the ridge of Crask.

Half an hour was spent in idleness till the dawning of hunger warned him to return. The crossing as seen from this side looked more formidable, for the first stones could only be reached by jumping a fairly broad stretch of current. Yet the jump was achieved, and with renewed confidence Sir Archie essayed the more solid boulders. All would have gone well had not he taken his eyes from the stones and observed on the bank beyond a girl's figure. She had been walking by the stream and had stopped to stare at the portent of his performance. Now Sir Archie was aware that his style of jumping was not graceful and he was discomposed by his sudden gallery. Nevertheless, the thing was so easy that he could scarcely have failed had it not been for the faithful Mackenzie. That animal had resolved to

47

follow his master's footsteps, and was jumping steadily behind him. But three boulders from the shore they jumped simultaneously, and there was not standing-room for both. Sir Archie, already nervous, slipped, recovered himself, slipped again, and then, accompanied by Mackenzie, subsided noisily into three feet of water.

He waded ashore to find himself faced by a girl in whose face concern struggled with amusement. He lifted a dripping hand and grinned.

"Silly exhibition, wasn't it? All the fault of Mackenzie! Idiotic brute of a dog, not to remember my game leg!"

"You're horribly wet," the girl said, "but it was sporting of you to try that crossing. What about dry clothes?"

"Oh, no trouble about that. I've only to get up to Crask."

"You're Sir Archibald Roylance, aren't you? I'm Janet Raden. I've been with papa to call on you, but you're never at home."

Sir Archie, having now got the water out of his eyes and hair, was able to regard his interlocutor. He saw a slight girl with what seemed to him astonishingly bright hair and very blue and candid eyes. She appeared to be anxious about his dry clothes, for she led the way up the bank at a great pace, while he limped behind her. Suddenly she noticed the limp.

"Oh, please forgive me, I forgot about your leg. You had another smash, hadn't you, besides the one in the war—steeplechasing, wasn't it?"

"Yes, but it didn't signify. I'm all right again and get about anywhere, but I'm a bit slower on the wing, you know."

"You're keen about horses?"

"Love 'em."

"So do I. Agatha—that's my sister—doesn't care a bit about them. She would like to live all the year at Glenraden, but—I'm ashamed to say it—I would rather have a foggy November in Warwickshire than August in Scotland. I simply dream of hunting."

The ardent eyes and the young grace of the girl seemed marvellous things to Sir Archie. "I expect you go uncommon well," he murmured.

48

"No, only moderate. I only get scratch mounts. You see I stay with my Aunt Barbara, and she's too old to hunt, and has nothing in her stables but camels. But this year . . ." She broke off as she caught sight of the pools forming round Sir Archie's boots. "I mustn't keep you here talking. You be off home at once."

"Don't worry about me. I'm wet for days on end when I'm watchin' birds in the spring. You were sayin' about this year?"

Her answer was a surprising question. "Do you know anybody called John Macnab?"

Sir Archibald Roylance was a resourceful mountebank and did not hesitate.

"Yes. The distiller, you mean? Dhuniewassel Whisky? I've seen his advertisements—'They drink Dhuniewassel, In cottage and castle—' That chap?"

"No, no, somebody quite different. Listen, please, if you're not too wet, for I want you to help me. Papa has had the most extraordinary letter from somebody called John Macnab, saying he means to kill a stag in our forest between certain dates, and daring us to prevent him. He is going to hand over the beast to us if he gets it and pay fifty pounds, but if he fails he is to pay a hundred pounds. Did you ever hear of such a thing?"

"Some infernal swindler," said Archie darkly.

"No. He can't be. You see the fifty pounds arrived this morning."

"God bless my soul!"

"Yes. In Bank of England notes, posted from London. Papa at first wanted to tell him to go to—well, where Papa tells people he doesn't like to go. But I thought the offer so sporting that I persuaded him to take up the challenge. Indeed, I wrote the reply myself. Mr Macnab said that the money was to go to a charity, so Agatha is having the fifty pounds for her native weaving and dyeing—she's frightfully keen about that. But if we win the other fifty pounds papa says the best charity he can think of is to prevent me breaking my neck on hirelings, and I'm to have it to buy a hunter. So I'm very anxious to find out about Mr John Macnab."

"Probably some rich Colonial who hasn't learned manners."

"I don't think so. His manners are very good, to judge by his letter. I think he is a gentleman, but perhaps a little mad. We simply *must* beat him, for I've got to have that fifty pounds. And—and I want you to help me."

"Oh, well, you know—I mean to say—I'm not much of a fellow. . . ."

"You're very clever, and you've done all kinds of things. I feel that if you advised us we should win easily, for I'm sure you had far harder jobs in the war."

To have a pretty young woman lauding his abilities and appealing with melting eyes for his aid was a new experience in Sir Archie's life. It was so delectable an experience that he almost forgot its awful complications. When he remembered them he flushed and stammered.

"Really, I'd love to, but I wouldn't be any earthly good. I'm an old crock, you see. But you needn't worry—your Glenraden gillies will make short work of this bandit. . . . By Jove, I hope you get your hunter, Miss Raden. You've got to have it somehow. Tell you what, if I've any bright idea I'll let you know."

"Thank you so much. And may I consult you if I'm in difficulties?"

"Yes, of course. I mean to say, No. Hang it, I don't know, for I don't like interferin' with your father's challenge."

"That means you will. Now, you mustn't wait another moment. Good-bye. Will you come over to lunch at Glenraden?"

Then she broke off and stared at him. "I forgot. Haven't you smallpox?"

"What! Smallpox? Oh, I see! Has old Mother Claybody been putting that about?"

"She came to tea yesterday twittering with terror, and warned us all not to go within a mile of Crask."

Sir Archie laughed somewhat hollowly. "I had a bad toothache and my head tied up, and I daresay I said something

50

silly, but I never thought she would take it for gospel. You see for yourself that I've nothing the matter with me."

"You'll have pneumonia the matter with you, unless you hurry home. Good-bye. We'll expect you to lunch the day after to-morrow." And with a wave of her hand she was gone.

The extraordinary fact was that Sir Archie was not depressed by the new tangle which encumbered him. On the contrary, he was in the best of spirits. He hobbled gaily up the by-road to Crask, listened to Leithen, when he met him, with less than half an ear, and was happy with his own thoughts. I am at a loss to know how to describe the first shattering impact of youth and beauty on a susceptible mind. The old plan was to borrow the language of the world's poetry, the new seems to be to have recourse to the difficult jargon of psychologists and physicians; but neither, I fear, would suit Sir Archie's case. He did not think of nymphs and goddesses or of linnets in spring; still less did he plunge into the depths of a subconscious self which he was not aware of possessing. The unromantic epithet which rose to his lips was "jolly." This was for certain the jolliest girl he had ever met—regular young sportswoman and amazingly good-lookin', and he was dashed if she wouldn't get her hunter. For a delirious ten minutes, which carried him to the edge of the Crask lawn, he pictured his resourcefulness placed at her service, her triumphant success, and her bright-eyed gratitude.

Then he suddenly remembered that alliance with Miss Janet Raden was treachery to his three guests. The aid she had asked for could only be given at the expense of John Macnab. He was in the miserable position of having a leg in both camps, of having unhappily received the confidences of both sides, and whatever he did he must make a mess of it. He could not desert his friends, so he must fail the lady; wherefore there could be no luncheon for him, the day after to-morrow, since another five minutes' talk with her would entangle him beyond hope. There was nothing for it but to have a return of smallpox. He groaned aloud.

"A twinge of that beastly toothache," he explained in reply to his companion's inquiry.

When the party met in the smoking-room that night after dinner two very weary men occupied the deepest arm-chairs. Lamancha was struggling with sleep; Palliser-Yeates was limp with fatigue, far too weary to be sleepy. "I've had the devil of a day," said the latter. "Wattie took me at a racing gallop about thirty miles over bogs and crags. Lord! I'm stiff and footsore. I believe I crawled more than ten miles, and I've no skin left on my knees. But we spied the deuce of a lot of ground, and I see my way to the rudiments of a plan. You start off, Charles, while I collect my thoughts."

But Lamancha was supine.

"I'm too drunk with sleep to talk," he said. "I prospected all the south side of Haripol—all this side of the Reascuill, you know. I got a good spy from Sgurr Mor, and I tried to get up Sgurr Dearg, but stuck on the rocks. That's a fearsome mountain, if you like. Didn't see a blessed soul all day—no rifles out—but I heard a shot from the Machray ground. I got my glasses on to several fine beasts. It struck me that the best chance would be in the corrie between Sgurr Mor and Sgurr Dearg—there's a nice low pass at the head to get a stag through and the place is rather tucked away from the rest of the forest. That's as far as I've got at present. I want to sleep."

Palliser-Yeates was in a very different mood. With an ordnance map spread out on his knees he expounded the result of his researches, waving his pipe excitedly.

"It's a stiff problem, but there's just the ghost of a hope. Wattie admitted that on the way home. Look here, you fellows—Glenraden is divided, like Gaul, into three parts. There's the Home beat—all the low ground of the Raden glen and the little hills behind the house. Then there's the Carnbeg beat to the east, which is the best I fancy—very easy going, not very high and with peat roads and tracks where you could shift a beast. Last there's Carnmore, miles from anywhere, with all the highest tops and as steep as Torridon. It would be the devil of a business, if I got a stag there, to move it. Wattie and I went round the whole marches, mostly on our bellies. No, we weren't seen—Wattie took care of that. What a noble *shikari* the old chap is!"

"Well, what's your conclusion?" Leithen asked.

Palliser-Yeates shook his head. "That's just where I'm stumped. Try to put yourself in old Raden's place. He has only one stalker and two gillies for the whole forest, for he's very short-handed, and as a matter of fact he stalks his beasts himself. He'll consider where John Macnab is likeliest to have his try, and he'll naturally decide on the Carnmore beat, for that's by far the most secluded. You may take it from me that he has only enough men to watch one beat properly. But he'll reflect that John Macnab has got to get his stag away, and he'll wonder how he'll manage it on Carnmore, for there's only one bad track up from Inverlarrig. Therefore he'll conclude that John Macnab may be more likely to try Carnbeg, though it's a bit more public. You see, his decision isn't any easier than mine. On the whole, I'm inclined to think he'll plump for Carnmore, for he must think John Macnab a fairly desperate fellow who will aim first at killing his stag in peace, and will trust to Providence for the rest. So at the moment I favour Carnbeg."

Leithen wrinkled his brow. "There are three of us," he said. "That gives us a chance of a little finesse. What about letting Charles or me make a demonstration against Carnmore, while you wait at Carnbeg?"

"Good idea! I thought of that too."

"You'd better assume Colonel Raden to be in very full possession of his wits," Leithen continued. "The simple bluff won't do—he'll see through it. He'll think that John Macnab is the same wary kind of old bird as himself. I found out in the war that it didn't do to underrate your opponent's brains. He's pretty certain to expect a feint and not to be taken in. I'm for something a little subtler."

"Meaning?"

"Meaning that you feint in one place, so that your opponent believes it to be a feint and pays no attention—and then you sail in and get to work in that very place."

Palliser-Yeates whistled. "That wants thinking over. . . . How about yourself?"

"I've studied the river, and you never in your life saw such a hopeless proposition. All the good pools are as open as the Serpentine. Wattie stated the odds correctly."

"Nothing doing there?"

"Nothing doing, unless I take steps to shorten the odds. So I've taken in a partner."

The others stared, and even Lamancha woke up.

"Yes. I interviewed him in the stable before dinner. It's the little ragamuffin who sells fish—Fish Benjie is the name he goes by. Archie, I hope you don't mind, but I told him to resume his morning visits. They're my best chance for consultations."

"You're taking a pretty big risk, Ned," said his host. "D'you mean to say you've let that boy into the whole secret?"

"I've told him everything. It was the only way, for he had begun to suspect. I admit it's a gamble, but I believe I can trust the child. I think I know a sportsman when I see him."

Archie still shook his head. "There's something else I may as well tell you. I met one of the Raden girls to-day—the younger—she was on the bank when I fell into the Larrig. She asked me point-blank if I knew anybody called John Macnab?"

Lamancha was wide awake. "What did you say?" he asked sharply.

"Oh, lied of course. Said I supposed she meant the distiller. Then she told me the whole story—said she had written the letter her father signed. She's mad keen to win the extra fifty quid, for it means a hunter for her this winter down in Warwickshire. Yes, and she asked me to help. I talked a lot of rot about my game leg and that sort of thing, but I sort of promised to go and lunch at Glenraden the day after to-morrow."

"That's impossible," said Lamancha.

"I know it is, but there's only one way out of it. I've got to have smallpox again."

"You've got to go to bed and stay there for a month," said Palliser-Yeates severely. "Now, look here, Archie. We simply can't have you getting mixed up with the enemy, especially the enemy women. You're much too susceptible and far too great an ass."

"Of course not," said Archie, with a touch of protest in his voice. "I see that well enough, but it's a black look-out for me. I wish to Heaven you fellows had chosen to take your cure somewhere else. I'm simply wreckin' all my political career. I had a letter from my agent to-night, and I should be touring the constituency instead of playin' the goat here. All I've got to say is that you've a dashed lot more than old Raden against you. You've got that girl, crazy about her hunter, and anyone can see that she's as clever as a monkey."

But the laird of Crask was not thinking of Miss Janet Raden's wits as he went meditatively to bed. He was wondering why her eyes were so blue, and as he ascended the stairs he thought he had discovered the reason. Her hair was spun-gold, but she had dark eye-lashes.

4

FISH BENJIE

On the roads of the north of Scotland, any time after the last
snow-wreaths have melted behind the dykes, you will meet a
peculiar kind of tinker. They are not the copper-nosed
scarecrows of the lowlands, sullen and cringing, attended by
sad infants in ramshackle perambulators. Nor are they in any
sense gipsies, for they have not the Romany speech or
colouring. They travel the roads with an establishment, usually
a covered cart and one or more lean horses, and you may find
their encampments any day by any burnside. Of a rainy night
you can see their queer little tents, shaped like a segment of
sausage, with a fire hissing at the door, and the horses cropping
the roadside grass; of a fine morning the women will be
washing their duds on the loch shore and their young fighting
like ferrets among the shingle. You will meet with them in the
back streets of the little towns, and at the back doors of
wayside inns, but mostly in sheltered hollows of the moor or
green nooks among the birches, for they are artists in choosing
camping-grounds. They are children of Esau who combine a
dozen crafts—tinkering, fish-hawking, besom-making, and
the like—with their natural trades of horse-coping and
poaching. At once brazen and obsequious, they beg rather as
an art than a necessity; they will whine to a keeper with pockets
full of pheasants' eggs, and seek permission to camp from a
laird with a melting tale of hardships, while one of his salmon
lies hidden in the bracken on their cart floor. The men are an
upstanding race, keen-eyed, resourceful, with humour in their
cunning; the women, till life bears too hardly on them, are
handsome and soft-spoken; and the children are burned and
weathered like imps of the desert. Their speech is neither

lowland nor highland, but a sing-song Scots of their own, and if they show the Celt in their secret ways there is a hint of Norse blood in the tawny hair and blue eyes so common among them.

Ebenezer Bogle was born into this life, and for fifty-five years travelled the roads from the Reay country to the Mearns and from John o' Groats to the sea-lochs of Appin. Sickness overtook him one October when camped in the Black Isle, and, feeling the hand of death on him, he sent for two people. One was the nearest Free Kirk minister—for Ebenezer was theologically of the old school; the other was a banker from Muirtown. What he said to the minister I do not know; but what the banker said to him may be gathered from the fact that he informed his wife before he died that in the Muirtown bank there lay to his credit a sum of nearly three thousand pounds. Ebenezer had been a sober and careful man, and a genius at horse-coping. He had bought the little rough shelties of the North and the Isles, and sold them at lowland fairs, he had dabbled in black cattle, he had done big trade in sheep-skins when a snowstorm decimated the Sutherland flocks, and he had engaged, perhaps, in less reputable ventures, which might be forbidden by the law of the land, but were not contrary, so he believed, to the Bible. Year by year his bank balance had mounted, for he spent little, and now he had a fortune to bequeath. He made no will; all went to his wife, with the understanding that it would be kept intact for his son; and in this confidence Ebenezer closed his eyes.

The wife did not change her habit of life. The son Benjamin accompanied her as before in the long rounds between May and October, and in the winter abode in the fishing quarter of Muirtown, and intermittently attended school. Presently his mother took a second husband, a Catholic Macdonald from the West, for the road is a lonely occupation for a solitary woman. Her new man was a cheerful being—very little like the provident Ebenezer— much addicted to the bottle and a lover of all things but legitimate trade. But he respected the dead man's wishes and made no attempt to touch the hoard in the Muirtown bank; he was kind, too, to the boy, and taught him

57

many things that are not provided for in the educational system of Scotland. From him Benjie learned how to take a nesting grouse, how to snare a dozen things, from hares to roebuck, how to sniggle salmon in the clear pools, and how to poach a hind when the deer came down in hard weather to the meadows. He learned how to tell the hour by the sun, and to find his way by the stars, and what weather was foretold by the starlings packing at nightfall, or the crows sitting with their beaks to the wind, or a badger coming home after daylight. The boy knew how to make cunning whistles from ash and rowan with which to imitate a snipe's bleat or the call of an otter, and he knew how at all times and in all weathers to fend for himself and find food and shelter. A tough little nomad he became under this tutelage, knowing no boys' games, with scarcely an acquaintance of his age, but able to deal on equal terms with every fisherman, gillie, and tinker north of the Highland line.

It chanced that in the spring of this year Mrs Bogle had fallen ill for the first time in her life. It was influenza, and, being neglected, was followed by pneumonia, so that when May came she was in no condition to take the road. By ill luck her husband had been involved in a drunken row, when he had assaulted two of his companions with such violence and success that he was sent for six months to prison. In these circumstances there was nothing for it but that Benjie should set out alone with the cart, and it is a proof of the stoutheartedness of the family tradition that his mother never questioned the propriety of this arrangement. He departed with her blessing, and weekly despatched to her a much-blotted scrawl describing his doings. There was something of his father's hard fibre in the child, for he was a keen bargainer and as wary as a fox against cajolery. He met friends of his family who let him camp beside them, and with their young he did battle, when they dared to threaten his dignity. Benjie fought in no orthodox way, but like a weasel, using every weapon of tooth and claw, but in his sobbing furies he was unconquerable, and was soon left in peace. Presently he found that he preferred to camp alone, so with his old cart and horse he made his way up and down the long glens of the West to the Larrig. There, he remembered, the fish trade had been profitable in past years, so he sat himself down by the roadside, to act as middleman between the fishing-cobles of Inverlarrig and the kitchens of the shooting lodges. It would be untrue to say that this was his only means of livelihood, and I fear that the contents of Benjie's pot, as it bubbled of an evening in the Wood of Larrigmore, would not have borne inspection by any keeper who chanced to pass. The weekly scrawls went regularly to his now convalescent mother, and once a parcel arrived for him at the Inverlarrig post-office containing a gigantic new shirt, which he used as a blanket. For the rest, he lived as Robinson Crusoe lived, on the country-side around him, asking no news of the outer world.

On the morning of the 27th of August he might have been seen, a little after seven o'clock, driving his cart up the fine beech avenue which led to Glenraden Castle. It was part of his morning round, but hitherto he had left his cart at the lodge-gate, and carried his fish on foot to the house; wherefore he had some slight argument with the lodge-keeper before he was permitted to enter. He drove circumspectly to the back regions, left his fish at the kitchen door, and then proceeded to the cottage of the stalker, one Macpherson, which stood by itself in a clump of firs. There he waited for some time till Mrs Macpherson came to feed her hens. A string of haddocks changed hands, and Benjie was bidden indoors, where he was given a cup of tea, while old Macpherson smoked his early pipe and asked questions. Half an hour later Benjie left, with every sign of amity, and drove very slowly down the woodland road towards the haugh where the Raden, sweeping from the narrows of the glen, spreads into broad pools and shining shallows. There he left the cart and squatted inconspicuously in the heather in a place which commanded a prospect of the home woods. From his observations he was aware that one of the young ladies regularly took her morning walk in this quarter.

Meantime in the pleasant upstairs dining-room of the Castle breakfast had begun. Colonel Alastair Raden, having read prayers to a row of servants from a chair in the window—there was a family tradition that he once broke off in a petiton to call excitedly his Maker's attention to a capercailzie on the lawn—and having finished his porridge, which he ate standing, with bulletins interjected about the weather, was doing good work on bacon and eggs. Breakfast, he used to declare, should consist of no kickshaws like kidneys and omelettes; only bacon and eggs, and plenty of 'em. The master of the house was a lean old gentleman dressed in an ancient loud-patterned tweed jacket and a very faded kilt. Still erect as a post, he had a barrack-square voice, a high-boned, aquiline face, and a kindly but irritable blue eye. His daughters were devoting what time was left to them from attending to the breakfasts of three terriers to an animated discussion of a letter which lay before them. The morning meal at Glenraden was rarely interrupted by correspondence, for the post did not arrive till the evening, but this missive had been delivered by hand.

"He can't come," the younger cried. "He says he's seedy again. It may really be smallpox this time."

"Who can't come, and who has smallpox?" her father demanded.

"Sir Archibald Roylance. I told you I met him and asked him to lunch here to-day. We really ought to get to know our nearest neighbour, and he seems a very pleasant young man."

"I think he is hiding a dark secret," said the elder Miss Raden. "Nobody who calls there ever finds him in—except Lady Claybody, and then he told her he had smallpox. Old Mr Bandicott said he went up the long hill to Crask yesterday, and found nobody at home, though he was perfectly certain he saw one figure slinking into the wood and another moving away from a window. I wonder if Sir Archibald is really all right. We don't know anything about him, do we?"

"Of course he's all right—bound to be—dashed gallant, sporting fellow. Sorry he's not coming to luncheon—I want to meet him. He's probably afraid of Nettie, and I don't blame him, for she's a brazen hussy, and he does well to be shy of old Bandicott. I'm scared to death by the old fellow myself."

"You know you've promised to let him dig in the Piper's Ring, papa."

"I know I have, and I would have promised to let him dig up my lawn to keep him quiet. Never met a man with such a flow of incomprehensible talk. He had the audacity to tell me that I was no more Celtic than he was, but sprung from some blackguard Norse raiders a thousand years back. Judging by the sketch he gave me of their habits, I'd sooner the Radens were descended from Polish Jews."

"I thought him a darling," said his elder daughter, "and with such a beautiful face."

"He may be a darling for all I know, but his head is stuffed with maggots. If you admired him so much, why didn't you take him off my hands? I liked the look of the young fellow and wanted to have a word with him. More by token"—the Colonel was hunting about for the marmalade—"what were you two plotting with him in the corner after dinner?"

"We were talking about John Macnab."

The Colonel's face became wrathful.

"Then I call it dashed unfilial conduct of you not to have brought me in. There was I, deafened with the old man's chatter—all about a fellow called Harald Blacktooth or Bottlenose or some such name, that he swears is buried in my grounds and means to dig up—when I might have been having a really fruitful conversation. What was young Bandicott's notion of John Macnab?"

"Mr Junius thinks he is a lunatic," said the elder Miss Raden. She was in every way her sister's opposite, dark of hair and eye where Janet was fair, tall where Janet was little, slow and quiet of voice where Janet was quick and gusty.

"I entirely differ from him. I think John Macnab is perfectly sane, and probably a good fellow, though a dashed insolent one. What's Bandicott doing about his river?"

"Patrolling it day and night between the 1st and 3rd of September. He says he's taking no chances, though he'd bet

Wall Street to a nickel that the poor poop hasn't the frozenest outside."

"Nettie, he said nothing of the kind!" Miss Agatha was indignant. "He talks beautiful English, with no trace of an accent—all Bostonians do, he told me."

"Anyhow, he asked what steps we were taking and advised us to get busy. We come before him, you know. . . . Heavens, papa, it begins to-morrow night! Oh, and I did so want to consult Sir Archibald. I'm sure he could help."

Colonel Raden, having made a satisfactory breakfast, was lighting a pipe.

"You need not worry, my dear. I'm an old campaigner and have planned out the thing thoroughly. I've been in frequent consultation with Macpherson, and yesterday we had Alan and James Fraser in, and they entirely agreed."

He produced from his pocket a sheet of foolscap on which had been roughly drawn a map of the estate.

"Now, listen to me. We must assume this fellow Macnab to be in possession of his senses, and to have more or less reconnoitred the ground—though I don't know how the devil he can have managed it, for the gillies have kept their eyes open, and nobody's been seen near the place. Well, here are the three beats. Unless young Bandicott is right and the man's a lunatic, he won't try the Home beat, for the simple reason that a shot there would be heard by twenty people and he could not move a beast twenty yards without being caught. There remains Carnmore and Carnbeg. Macpherson was clear that he would try Carnmore, as being farthest away from the house. But I, with my old campaigning experience"—here Colonel Raden looked remarkably cunning—"pointed out at once that such reasoning was rudimentary. I said 'He'll bluff us, and just because he thinks that *we* think he'll try Carnmore, he'll try Carnbeg. Therefore, since we can only afford to watch one beat thoroughly, we'll watch Carnbeg.' What do you think of that, my dears?"

"I think you're very clever, papa," said Agatha. "I'm sure you're right."

62

"And you, Nettie?"

Janet was knitting her brows and looking thoughtful.

"I'm . . . not . . . so . . . sure. You see we must assume that John Macnab is very ingenious. He probably made his fortune in the colonies by every kind of dodge. He's sure to be very clever."

"Well but, my dear," said her father, "it's just that cleverness that I propose to match."

"But do you think you have quite matched it? You have tried to imagine what John Macnab would be thinking, and he will have done just the same by you. Why shouldn't he have guessed the conclusion you have reached and be deciding to go one better?"

"How do you mean, Nettie?" asked her puzzled parent. He was inclined to be annoyed, but experience had taught him that his younger daughter's wits were not to be lightly disregarded.

Nettie took the estate map from his hand and found a stump of pencil in the pocket of her jumper.

"Please look at this, papa. Here is A and B. B offers a better chance, so Macpherson says John Macnab will take B. You say, acutely, that John Macnab is not a fool, and will try to bluff us by taking A. I say that John Macnab will have anticipated your acumen."

"Yes, yes," said her father impatiently. "And then?"

"And will take B after all."

The Colonel stood rapt in unpleasant meditation for the space of five seconds.

"God bless my soul!" he cried. "I see what you mean. Confound it, of course he'll go for Carnmore. Lord, this is a puzzle. I must see Macpherson at once. Are you sure you're right, Nettie?"

"I'm not in the least sure. We've only a choice of uncertainties, and must gamble. But, as far as I see, if we must plump for one we should plump for Carnmore."

Colonel Raden departed from his study, after summoning Macpherson to that shrine of the higher thought, and Janet Raden, after one or two brief domestic interviews, collected her two terriers and set out for her morning walk. The morning was as fresh and bright as April, the rain in the night had set every burn singing, and the thickets and lawns were still damp where the sun had not penetrated. Her morning walk was wont to be a scamper, a thing of hops, skips, and jumps, rather than a sedate progress; but on this occasion, though two dogs and the whole earth invited to hilarity, she walked slowly and thoughtfully. The mossy broken tops of Carnbeg showed above a wood of young firs, and to the right rose the high blue peaks of the Carnmore ground. On which of these on the morrow would John Macnab begin his depredations? He had two days for his exploit; probably he would make his effort on the second day, and devote the first to confusing the minds of the defence. That meant that the problem would have to be thought out anew each day, for the alert intelligence of John Macnab—she now pictured him as a sort of Sherlock Holmes in knicker-bockers—would not stand still. The prospect exhilarated, but it also alarmed her; the desire to win a new hunter was now a fixed resolution; but she wished she had a colleague. Agatha was no use, and her father, while admirable in tactics, was weak in strategy; she longed more than ever for the help of that frail vessel, Sir Archie.

Her road led her by a brawling torrent through the famous Glenraden beechwood to the spongy meadows of the haugh, beyond which could be seen the shining tides of the Raden sweeping to the high-backed bridge across which ran the road to Carnmore. The haugh was all bog-myrtle and heather and bracken, sprinkled with great boulders which the river during the ages had brought down from the hills. Half a mile up it stood the odd tumulus called the Piper's Ring, crowned with an ancient gnarled fir, where reposed, according to the elder Bandicott, the dust of that dark progenitor, Harald Blacktooth. If Mr Bandicott proposed to excavate there he had his work cut out; the place was encumbered with giant stones since a thousand floods had washed its sides since it first received the dead Viking. Great birch woods from both sides of the valley descended to the stream, thereby making the excellence of the Home beat, for the woodland stag is a heavier beast than his brother of the high tops.

Close to the road, in a small hollow where one of the rivulets from the woods cut its way though the haugh, she came on an ancient cart resting on its shafts, an ancient horse grazing on a patch of turf among the peat, and a small boy diligently whittling his way through a pile of heather roots. The urchin sprang to his feet and saluted like a soldier.

"Please, lady," he explained in a high falsetto whine, "I've gotten permission from Mr Macpherson to make heather besoms on this muir. He's aye been awfu' kind to me, lady."

"You're the boy who sells fish? I've seen you on the road."

"Aye, lady, I'm Fish Benjie. I sell my fish in the mornin's and evenin's, and I've a' the day for other jobs. I've aye wanted to come here, for it's the grandest heather i' the country-side; and Mr Macpherson, he kens I'll do nae harm, and I've promised no to kindle a fire."

The child with the beggar's voice looked at her with such sage and solemn eyes that Janet, who had a hopeless weakness for small boys, sat down on a sun-warmed hillock and stared a him, while he turned resolutely to business.

"If you're hungry, Benjie," she said, "and they won't let you make a fire, you can come up to the Castle and get tea from Mrs Fraser. Tell her I sent you."

"Thank you, lady, but if *you* please, I was gaun to my tea at Mrs Macpherson's. She's fell fond o' my haddies, and she tell't me to tak a look in when I stoppit work. I'm ettlin' to be here for a guid while."

"Will you come every day?"

"Aye, every day about eight o'clock, and bide till maybe five in the afternoon when I go down to the cobles at Inverlarrig."

"Now, look here, Benjie. When you're sitting quietly working here I want you to keep your eyes open, and if you see any strange man, tell Mr Macpherson. By strange man I mean somebody who doesn't belong to the place. We're rather troubled by poachers just now."

Benjie raised a ruminant eye from his besom.

"Aye, lady. I seen a queer man already this mornin'. He cam up the road and syne started off over the bog. He was sweatin' sore, and there was twa men from Strathlarrig wi' him carryin' picks and shovels. . . . Losh, there he is comin' back."

Following Benjie's pointing finger Janet saw, approaching her from the direction of the Piper's Ring, a solitary figure which laboured heavily among the peat- bogs. Presently it was revealed as an elderly man wearing a broad grey wide-awake and a suit of flannel knickerbockers. His enormous horn spectacles clearly did not help his eyesight, for he had almost fallen over the shafts of the fish-cart before he perceived Janet Raden. He removed his hat, bowed with an antique courtesy, and asked permission to recover his breath.

"I was on my way to see your father," he said at length. "This morning I have prospected the barrow of Harald Blacktooth, and it is clear to me that I can make no progress unless I have Colonel Raden' s permission to use explosives. Only the very slightest use, I promise you. I have located, I think, the ceremonial entrance, but it is blocked with boulders which it would take a gang of navvies to raise with crowbars. A discreet application of dynamite would do the work in half an hour. I cannot think that Colonel Raden would object to my using it when I encounter such obstacles. I assure you it will not spoil the look of the barrow."

"I'm sure papa will be delighted. You're certain the noise won't frighten the deer? You know the Piper's Ring is in the forest."

"Not in the least, my dear young lady. The reports will be very slight, scarcely louder than a rifle-shot. I ought to tell you that I am an old hand at explosives, for in my young days I mined in Colorado, and recently I have employed them in my Alaska researches. . . ."

"If we go home now," said Janet, rising, "we'll just catch papa before he goes out. You're very warm, Mr Bandicott, and I think you would be the better for a rest and a drink."

"I certainly should, my dear. I was so eager to begin that I bolted my breakfast, and started off before Junius was ready. He proposes to meet me here."

Benjie, left alone, wrought diligently at his heather roots, whistling softly to himself, and every now and then raising his head to scan the haugh and the lower glen. Presently a tall young man appeared, who was identified as the younger American, and who was duly directed to follow his father to the Castle. The two returned in a little while, accompanied by Agatha Raden, and, while the elder Mr Bandicott hastened to the Piper's Ring, the young people sauntered to the Raden bridge and appeared to be deep in converse. "Thae twa's weel agreed," was Benjie's comment. A little before one o'clock the party adjourned to the Castle, presumably for luncheon, and Benjie, whose noon-tide meal was always sparing, nibbled a crust of bread and a rind of cheese. In the afternoon Macpherson and one of the gillies strolled past, and the head-stalker proved wonderfully gracious, adjuring him, as Janet had done, to keep his eyes open and report the presence of any stranger. "There'll be the three folk from Strathlarrig howkin' awa there, but if ye see anybody else, away up to the house and tell the wife. They'll no be here for any good." Benjie promised fervently. "I've grand een, Mr Macpherson, sir, and though they was to be crawlin' like a serpent I'd be on them." The head-stalker observed that he was a "gleg one," and went his ways.

Despite his industry Benjie was remarkably observant that day, but he was not looking for poachers. He had suddenly developed an acute interest in the deer. His unaided eyes were as good as the ordinary man's telescope, and he kept a keen watch on the fringes of the great birch woods. The excavation at the Piper's Ring kept away any beasts from the east side of the haugh, but on the west bank of the stream he saw two lots of hinds grazing, with one or two young stags among them, and even on the east bank, close in to the edge of the river, he saw hinds with calves. He concluded that on the fringes of the Raden the feeding must be extra good, and, as a steady west wind was blowing, the deer there would not be alarmed by Mr

67

Bandicott's quest. Just after he had finished his bread and cheese he was rewarded with the spectacle of a hummel, a great fellow of fully twenty stone, who rolled in a peat hole and then stood blowing in the shallow water as unconcerned as if he had been on the top of Carnmore. Later in the afternoon he saw a good ten-pointer in the same place, and a little later an eight-pointer with a damaged horn. He concluded that that particular hag was a favourite mud-bath for stags, and that with the wind in the west it was no way interfered with by the activities at the Piper's Ring.

About four o'clock Benjie backed the old horse into the shafts, and jogged up the beech-avenue to Mrs Macpherson's, where he was stayed with tea and scones. There was a gathering outside the door of Macpherson himself and the two gillies, and a strange excitement seemed to have fallen on that stolid community. Benjie could not avoid—indeed, I am not sure that he tried to avoid—hearing scraps of their talk. "I've been a' round Carnmore," said Alan, "and I seen some fine beasts. They're mostly in a howe atween the two tops, and a man at the Grey Beallach could keep an eye on all the good ground." "Aye, but there's the Carn Moss, and the burnheads—there will be beasts there too," said James Fraser. "There will have to be a man there, for him at the Grey Beallach would not ken what was happening." "And what about Corrie Gall?" asked Macpherson fiercely. "Ye canna post men on Carnmore—they will have to keep moving; it is that awful broken ground." Well, there's you and me and James," said Alan, "and there's Himself." "And that's the lot of us, and every man wanted," said Macpherson. "It's what I was always saying—ye will need every man for Carnmore, and must let Carnbeg alone, or ye can watch Carnbeg and not go near Carnmore. We're far ower few." "I wass thinking," said James Fraser, "that the youngest leddy might be watching Carnbeg." "Aye, James"—this satirically from Macpherson—"and how would the young leddy be keeping a wild man from killing a stag and getting him away?" "'Deed, I don't ken," said the puzzled James, "without she took a gun with her and had a shot at him."

Benjie drove quietly to Inverlarrig for his supply of fish, and did not return to his head-quarters in the Wood of Larrigmore till nearly seven o'clock. At eight, having cooked and eaten his supper, he made a simple toilet, which consisted in washing the fish-scales and the stains of peat from his hands, holding his head in the river, parting his damp hair with a broken comb, and putting over his shoulders a waterproof cape, which had dropped from some passing conveyance and had been found by him on the road. Thus accoutred, he crossed the river and by devious paths ascended to Crask.

He ensconced himself in the stable, where he was greeted sourly by the Bluidy Mackenzie, who was tied up in one of the stalls. There he occupied himself in whistling strathspeys and stuffing a foul clay pipe with the stump of a cigar which he had picked up in the yard. Benjie smoked not for pleasure, but from a sense of duty, and a few whiffs were all he could manage with comfort. The gloaming had fallen before he heard his name called, and Wattie Lithgow appeared. "Ye're there, ye monkey? The gentlemen are askin' for ye. Quick and follow me. They're in an awfu' ill key the nicht and maunna be keepit waitin'."

There certainly seemed trouble in the smoking-room when Benjie was ushered in. Lamancha was standing on the hearth-rug with a letter crumpled in his hand, and Sir Archie, waving a missive, was excitedly confronting him. The other two sat in arm-chairs with an air of protest and dejection.

"I forgot all about the infernal thing till I got Montgomery's letter. The 4th of September! Hang it, my assault on old Claybody is timed to start on the 5th. How on earth can I get to Muirtown and back and deliver a speech, and be ready for the 5th? Besides, it betrays my presence in this part of the world. It simply can't be done . . . and yet I don't know how on earth to get out of it? Apparently the thing was arranged months ago."

"You're for it all right, my son," cried Sir Archie, "and so am I. Here's the beastly announcement. '*A Great Conservative Meeting will be held in the Town Hall, Muirtown, on Thursday, September 4th, to be addressed by the Right Hon. the Earl of*

Lamancha, M.P., His Majesty's Secretary of State for the Dominions. The chair will be taken at 3 p.m. by His Grace the Duke of Angus, K.G. Among the speakers will be Colonel Wavertree, M.P., the Hon. W. J. Murdoch, Ex-Premier of New Caledonia, and Captain Sir Archibald Roylance, D.S.O., prospective Conservative candidate for Wester Ross.' Oh, will he? Not by a long chalk! Catch me going to such a fiasco, with Charles hidin' here and the show left to the tender mercies of two rotten bad speakers and a prosy chairman."

"Did you forget about it too?" Leithen asked.

" 'Course I did," said Archie wildly. "How could I think of anything with you fellows turnin' my house into a den of thieves? I forgot about it just as completely as Charles, only it doesn't matter about me, and it matters the devil of a lot about him. I don't stand an earthly chance of winnin' the seat, if, first of all, I mustn't canvass because of smallpox, and, second, my big meetin', on which all my fellows counted, is wrecked by Charles playin' the fool."

Lamancha's dark face broke into a smile.

"Don't worry, old chap. I won't let you down. But it looks as if I must let down John Macnab, and just when I was gettin' keen about him. . . . Hang it, no! There must be a way. I'm not going to be beaten either by Claybody or this damned Tory rally. Ned, you slacker, what's your advice?"

"Have a try at the double event," Leithen drawled. "You'll probably make a mess of both, but it's a sporting proposition."

Archie's face brightened. "You don't realise how sportin' a proposition it is. The Claybodys will be there, and they'll be all over you—brother nobleman, you know, and you goin' to poach their stags next day! Hang it, why shouldn't you turn the affair into camouflage? 'Out of my stony griefs Bethel I'll raise,' says the hymn. . . . We'll have to think the thing out ve-ry carefully.—Anyway, Charles, you've got to help me with my speech. I don't mind so much lyin' doggo here if I can put in a bit of good work on the 5th. . . . Now, Benjie my lad, for your report."

Benjie, not without a certain shyness, cleared his throat and

70

began. He narrated how, following his instructions, he had secured Macpherson's permission to cut heather for besoms on the Raden haugh. He had duly taken up his post there, had remained till four o'clock, and had seen such and such people and heard this and that talk. He recounted what he could remember of the speeches of Macpherson and the gillies.

"They've got accustomed to the sight of you, I suppose," Palliser-Yeates said at length.

"Aye, they're accustomed right enough. Both the young lady and Macpherson was tellin' me to keep a look-out for poachers." Benjie chuckled.

"Then to-morrow you begin to move up to the high ground by the Carnmore peat-road. Still keep busy at your besoms. You understand what I want you for, Benjie? If I kill a stag I have to get it off Glenraden land, and your old fish-cart won't be suspected."

"Aye, I see that fine. But I've been thinkin' that there's maybe a better way."

"Go ahead, and let's have it."

Benjie began his speech nervously, but he soon warmed to it, and borrowed a cigar-box and the fire-irons to explain his case. The interest of his hearers kindled, until all four men were hanging on his words. When he concluded and had answered sundry questions, Sir Archie drew a deep breath and laughed excitedly.

"I suppose there's nothing in that that isn't quite cricket. . . . I thought I knew something about bluff, but this—this absolutely vanquishes the band. Benjie, I'm goin' to have you taught poker. You've the right kind of mind for it."

5

THE ASSAULT ON GLENRADEN

SHORTLY after midnight of the 28th day of August three men foregathered at the door of Macpherson's cottage, and after a few words took each a different road into the dark wastes of wood and heather. Macpherson contented himself with a patrol of the low ground in the glen, for his legs were not as nimble as they once had been and his back had a rheumaticky stiffness. Alan departed with great strides for the Carnbeg tops, and James Fraser, the youngest and the leanest, set out for Carnmore, with the speed of an Indian hunter. . . . Darkness gave place to the translucence of early dawn: the badger trotted home from his wanderings: the hill-fox barked in the cairns to summon his household: sleepy pipits awoke: the peregrine who lived above the Grey Beallach drifted down into the glens to look for breakfast: hinds and calves moved up from the hazel shaws to the high fresh pastures: the tiny rustling noises of night disappeared in that hush which precedes the awakening of life: and then came the flood of morning gold from behind the dim eastern mountains, and in an instant the earth had wheeled into a new day. A thin spire of smoke rose from Mrs Macpherson's chimney, and presently the three wardens of the marches arrived for breakfast. They reported that the forest was still unviolated, that no alien foot had yet entered its sacred confines. Herd-boys, the offspring of Alan and James Fraser, had taken up their post at key-points, so that if a human being was seen on the glacis of the fort the fact would at once be reported to the garrison.

"I'm thinkin' he'll no come to-day," said Macpherson after his third cup of tea. "It will be the morn. The day he will be tryin' to confuse our minds, and that will no be a difficult job wi' you, Alan, my son."

"He'll come in the da-ark," said Alan crossly.

"And how would he be gettin' a beast in the dark? The Laird was sayin' that this man John Macnab was a gra-and sportsman. He will not be shootin' at any little staggie, but takin' a sizeable beast, and it's not a howlet could be tellin' a calf from a stag in these da-ark nights. Na, he will not shoot in the night, but he might be travellin' in the night and gettin' his shot in the early mornin'."

"What for," Alan asked, "should he not be havin' his shot in the gloamin' and gettin' the beast off the ground in the da-ark?"

"Because we will be watchin' all hours of the day. Ye heard what the Laird said, Alan Macdonald, and you, James Fraser. This John Macnab is not to shoot a Glenraden beast at all, at all, but if he shoots one he is not to move it one foot. If it comes to fightin', you are young lads and must break the head of him. But the Laird said for God's sake you was to have no guns, but to fight like honest folk with your fists, and maybe a wee bit stick. The Laird was sayin' the law was on our side, except for shootin'. . . . Now, James Fraser, you will take the outer marches the day, and keep an eye on the peat-roads from Inverlarrig, and you, Alan, will watch Carnbeg, and I will be takin' the woods myself. The Laird was sayin' that it would be Carnmore the man Macnab would be tryin', most likely at skreigh of day the morn, and he would be hidin' the beast, if he got one, in some hag, and waitin' till the da-ark to shift him. So the morn we will all be on Carnmore, and I can tell you the Laird has the ground planned out so that a snipe would not be movin' without us seein' him."

The early morning broadened into day, and the glen slept in the windless heat of late August. Janet Raden, sauntering down from the Castle towards the river about eleven o'clock, thought that she had never seen the place so sabbatically peaceful. To her unquiet soul the calm seemed unnatural, like a thick cloak covering some feverish activity. All the household were abroad since breakfast—her father on a preliminary reconnaissance of Carnmore, Agatha and Mr Junius Bandicott on a circuit of Carnbeg, while the gillies and their youthful allies sat perched with telescopes on eyries surveying every approach to the forst. The plans seemed perfect, but the dread of John Macnab, that dark conspirator, would not be exorcised. It was she who had devised the campaign, based on her reading of the enemy's mind; but had she fathomed it, she asked herself? Might he not even now be preparing some master-stroke which would crumble their crude defences? Horrible stories which she had read of impersonation and the shifts of desperate characters recurred to her mind. Was John Macnab perhaps old Mr Bandicott disguised as an archaeologist? Or was he one of the Strathlarrig workmen?

She walked over the moor to the Piper's Ring and was greeted by a mild detonation and a shower of earth. Old Mr Bandicott, very warm and stripped to his shirt, was desperately busy and most voluble about his task. There was no impersonation here, nor in the two fiery-faced labourers who were burrowing their way towards the resting-place of Harald Blacktooth. Nevertheless, her suspicion was not allayed, she felt herself in the antechamber of plotters, and looked any moment to see on the fringes of the wood or on the white ribbon of road a mysterious furtive figure which she would know for a minion of the enemy.

But the minion did not appear. As Janet stood on the rise before the bridge of Raden with her hat removed to let the faint south-west wind cool her forehead, she looked upon a scene of utter loneliness and peace. The party at the Piper's Ring were hidden, and in all the green amphitheatre nothing stirred but the stream. Even Fish Benjie and his horse had been stricken into carven immobility. He had moved away from the road a few hundred yards into the moor, not far from the waterside, and his little figure, as he whittled at his brooms, appeared from where Janet stood to be as motionless as a boulder, while the old grey pony mused upon three legs as rapt and lifeless as an Elgin marble. The two seemed to have become one with

74

nature, and to be as much part of the sleeping landscape as the clump of birches whose leaves did not even shimmer in that bright silent noontide.

The quiet did something to soothe Janet's restlessness, but after luncheon, which she partook of in solitary state, she found it returning. A kind of *folie de doute* assailed her, not unknown to generals in the bad hours which intervene between the inception and execution of a plan. She had a strong desire to ride up to Crask and have a talk with Sir Archie, and was only restrained by the memory of that young man's last letter, and the hint it contained of grave bodily maladies. She did not know whether to believe in these maladies or not, but clearly she could not thrust her company upon one who had shown a marked distaste for it. . . . Yet she had her pony saddled and rode slowly in the direction of Strathlarrig, half hoping to see a limping figure on the highway. But not a soul was in sight on the long blinding stretch or at the bridge where the Crask road started up the hill. Janet turned homeward with a feeling that the world had suddenly become dispeopled. She did not turn her head once, and so failed to notice first one figure and then another, which darted across the high road, and disappeared in the thick coverts of the Crask hill-side.

At the Castle she found Agatha and Junius Bandicott having tea, and presently her father arrived in a state of heat and exhaustion. Stayed with a whisky-and-soda, Colonel Raden became communicative. He had been over the high tops of Carnmore, had visited the Carn Moss, and Corrie Gall, had penetrated the Grey Beallach, had heard the tales of the gillies and of the herd-boys in their eyries, and his report was "all clear." The deer were undisturbed, according to James Fraser, since the morning. Moreover, the peat-road from Inverlarrig had relapsed owing to recent rains into primeval bog which no wheeled vehicle and few ponies could traverse. The main fortress seemed not only unassailed but unassailable, and Colonel Raden viewed the morrow with equanimity.

The Carnbeg party had a different story to tell, or rather the main members of it had no story at all. Agatha and Junius

Bandicott appeared to have sauntered idly into the pleasant wilderness of juniper and heather which lay between the mossy summits, to have lunched at leisure by the famous Cailleach's Well, and to have sauntered home again. They reported that it had been divine weather, for a hill breeze had tempered the heat, and that they had observed the Claybodys' yacht far out at the entrance of Loch Larrig. Also Junius had seen his first blue hare, which he called a "jack rabbit." Of anything suspicious there had been neither sign nor sound.

But at this moment a maid appeared with the announcement that "Macpherson was wanting to see the Colonel," and presently the head stalker arrived in what John Bunyan calls a "pelting heat." Generally of a pale complexion which never tanned, he was now as red as a peony, and his grey beard made a startling contrast with his flamboyant face. Usually he was an embarrassed figure inside the Castle, having difficulties in disposing of his arms and legs, but now excitement made him bold.

"I've seen him, Cornel," he panted. "Seen him crawlin' like an adder and runnin' like a sta-ag!"

"Seen who? Get your breath, Macpherson!"

"Him—the man—Macnab. I beg your pardon for my pechin', sir, but I came down the hill like I was a rollin' stone . . . . It was up on the backside of Craig Dhu near the old sheep-fauld. I seen a man hunkerin' among the muckle stones, and I got my glass on him, and he was a sma' man that I've never seen afore. I was wild to get a grip of him, and I started runnin' to drive him to the Cailleach's Well, where Miss Agatha and the gentleman was havin' their lunch. He seen me, and he took the road I ettled, and I thought I had him, for, thinks I, the young gentleman is soople and lang in the leg. But he seen the danger and turned off down the burn, and I couldna come near him. It would have been all right if I could have made the young gentleman hear, but though I was roarin' like a stot he was deafer than a tree. Och, it is the great peety."

"Agatha, what on earth were you doing?" Janet asked severely.

Junius Bandicott blushed hotly. "I never heard a sound," he said. "There must be something funny about the acoustics of that place."

Colonel Raden, who knew the power of his stalker's lungs, looked in a mystified way from one to the other.

"Didn't you see Macpherson, Agatha?" he asked. "He must have been in view coming over the shoulder of Craig Dhu."

It was Agatha's turn to blush, which she did with vigour, and, to Mr Bandicott's eyes, with remarkable grace.

"Ach, I was in view well enough," went on the tactless Macpherson, "and I was routin' like a wild beast. But the twa of them was that busy talking they never lifted their eyes, and the man, as I tell you, slippit off down the burn. It is a gre-at peety, whatever."

"What did you do then?" the Colonel demanded.

"I followed him till I lost him in that awful rough corrie. . . . But I seen him again—aye, I seen him again, away over on the Maam above the big wud. Standin', as impident as ye please, on the sky-line."

"How long after you lost him in the corrie?" Janet asked.

"Maybe half an hour."

"Impossible," she said sharply. "No living man could cover three miles of that ground in half an hour."

"I was thinkin' the body was the Deevil."

"You saw a second man. John Macnab has an accomplice."

Macpherson scratched his shaggy head. "I wouldn't say but ye're right, Miss Janet. Now I think of it, it was a bigger man. He didn't bide a moment after I caught sight of him, but I got my glass on him, and he was a bigger man. Aye, a bigger man, and, maybe, a younger man."

"This is very disturbing," said Colonel Raden, walking to the window and twisting his moustache. "What do you make of it, Nettie?"

"I think the affair is proceeding, as generals say about their battles, 'according to plan.' We didn't know before that John Macnab had a confederate, but of course he was bound to have one. There was nothing against it in the terms of the wager."

"Of course not, of course not. But what the devil was he doing on Carnbeg? There was no shot, Macpherson?"

"There was no shot, and there will be no shot. There wass no beasts the side they were on, and Alan is up there now with one of James's laddies."

"It's exactly what we expected," said Janet. "It proves that we were right in guessing that John Macnab would take Carnmore. He came here to-day to frighten us about Carnbeg—make us think that he was going to try there, and get us to mass our forces. To-morrow he'll be on Carnmore, and then he'll mean business. I hoped this would happen, and I was getting nervous when Agatha and Mr Bandicott came home looking as blank as the Babes in the Wood. But I wish I knew which was really John Macnab—the little one or the tall one."

"What does that matter?" her parent asked.

"Because I should be happier if he were tall. Little men are far more cunning."

Junius Bandicott, having recovered his composure, chose to be amused. "I take that as a personal compliment, Miss Janet. I'm pretty big, and I can't say I want to be thought cunning."

"Then John Macnab will get his salmon," said Janet with decision.

Junius laughed. "You bet he won't. I've gotten the place watched like the Rum Fleet at home. A bird can't hardly cough without its being reported to me. My fellows are on to the game, and John Macnab will have to be a mighty clever citizen to come within a mile of the Strathlarrig water. Nobody is allowed to fish it but myself till the 3rd of September is past. I reckon angling just now is the forbidden fruit in this neighbourhood. I've seen but the one fellow fishing in the last three days—on the bit of slack water five hundred yards below the bridge. It belongs to Crask, I think."

Janet nodded. "No good except with a worm after a spate. Crask has no fishing worth the name."

"I saw him from the automobile early this morning," Junius continued. "Strange sight he was, too—dressed in pyjamas and rubbers—flogging away at the most helpless stretch you can imagine—dead calm, not a ripple, He had out about fifty yards of line, and when I passed he made a cast which fell with a flop about his ears. Who do you suppose he was? Somebody from Crask?"

Janet, who was the family's authority on Crask, agreed. "Probably some English servant who came down before breakfast just to say he had fished for salmon."

After tea Janet went down into the haugh. She met old Mr Bandicott returning from the Piper's Ring, a very grubby old gentleman, and a little dashed in spirits, for he had as yet seen no sign of Harald Blacktooth's coffin. "Another day's work," he announced, "and then I win or lose. I thought I had struck it this afternoon, but it was the solid granite. If the fellow is there he's probably in a rift of the rock. That has been known to happen. The Vikings found a natural fissure, stuck their dead chief in it, and heaped earth above to make a barrow. . . ."

Down near the stream she met Benjie, who appeared to have worked late at his besoms, bumping over the moor to the road. He and his old pony made a more idyllic picture than ever in the mellow light of evening, almost too conventionally artistic to be real, she thought, till Benjie's immobile figure woke to life at the sight of her and he pulled his lint-white forelock. "A grand nicht, lady," he crooned, and jogged on into the beeches' shade. . . . She sat on the bridge and watched the Raden waters pass from gold to amethyst and from amethyst to purple, and then sauntered back through the sweet-smelling dusk. Visions of John Macnab filled her mind, now a tall bravo with a colonial accent, now a gnarled Caliban of infinite cunning and gnome-like agility. Where in this haunted land was he ensconced—in some hazel covert, or in some clachan but-and-ben, or miles distant in a populous hotel, ready to speed in a swift car to the scene of action? . . . Anyhow, in twenty-four hours she would know if she had defeated this insolent challenger. On the eve of battle she had forgotten all about the stakes and her new hunter; it was the honour of Glenraden that was concerned, that little stone castle against the world.

Night fell, cool and cloudless, and the gillies went on their patrols. Carnmore was their only beat, and they returned one at a time to snatch a few hours' rest. At dawn they went out again—with the Colonel, but without Alan, who was to follow after he had had his ration of sleep. It was arranged that the two girls and Junius Bandicott should spend the day on Carnbeg by way of extra precaution, though if a desperate man made the assault there it was not likely that Junius, who knew nothing of deer and had no hill-craft, would be able to stop him.

Janet woke in low spirits, and her depression increased as the morning advanced. She was full of vague forebodings, and of an irritable unrest to which her steady nerves had hitherto been a stranger. She wished she were a man and could be now on Carnmore, for Carnbeg, she was convinced, was out of danger. Junius, splendid in buckskin breeches and a russet sweater, she regarded with disfavour; he was a striking figure, but out of keeping with the hills, the obvious amateur, and she longed for the halting and guileful Sir Archie. Nor was her temper improved by the conduct of her companions. Agatha and Junius seemed to have an inordinate amount to say to each other, and their conversation was idiotic to the ears of a third party. Their eyes were far more on each other than on the landscape, and their telescopes were never in use. But it mattered little, for Carnbeg slept in a primordial peace. Only pipits broke the silence, only a circling merlin made movement in a spell-bound world. There were some hinds on the west side of Craig Dhu, but no stag showed—as was natural, the girl reflected, for in this weather and thus early in the season the stags would be on the highest tops. John Macnab had chosen rightly if he wanted a shot, but there were three gillies and her father to prevent him getting his beast away.

At luncheon, which was eaten by the Cailleach's Well, Junius took to quoting poetry and Agatha to telling, very charmingly, the fairy tales of the glens. To Janet it all seemed wrong; this was not an occasion for literary philandering, when the credit of Glenraden was at stake. But even she was

80

forced to confess that nothing was astir in the mossy wilderness. She climbed to the top of Craig Dhu and had a long spy, but, except for more hinds and one small knobber, living thing there was none. As the afternoon drew on, she drifted away from the two, who, being engrossed with each other, did not notice her departure.

She wandered through the deep heather of the Maam to where the great woods began that dipped to the Raden glen. It was pleasant walking in the cool shade of the pines on turf which was half thyme and milkwort and eyebright, and presently her spirits rose. Now and then, on some knuckle of blaeberry-covered rock which rose above the trees, she would halt, and, stretched at full length, would spy the nooks of the Home beat. There was no lack of deer there. She picked up one group and then another in the aisles and clearings of the woods, and there were shootable stags among them.

A report like a rifle-shot suddenly startled her. Then she remembered old Mr Bandicott down in the haugh, and, turning her glance in that direction, saw a thin cloud of blue smoke floating away from the Piper's Ring.

Slowly she worked her way down-hill, aiming at the haugh about a mile upstream from the excavators. Once a startled hind and calf sprang up from her feet, and once an old fox slipped out of a pile of rocks and revived thoughts of Warwickshire and her problematical hunter. Soon she was not more than three hundred feet above the stream level, and found a bracken-clad hillock where she could lie and watch the scene. There was a roebuck feeding just below her, a roebuck with fine horns, and it amused her to see the beast come nearer and nearer, since the wind was behind him. He got within five yards of the girl, who lay mute as a stone; then some impulse made him look up and meet her eye, and in a second he had streaked into cover.

Amid that delicious weather and in that home of peace Janet began to recapture her usual mirthfulness. She had been right; Carnmore was the place John Macnab would select, unless his heart had failed him, and on Carnmore he would get a warm

81

reception. There was no need to worry any longer about John Macnab. . . . Her thoughts went back to Agatha. Clearly Junius Bandicott was in love with her, and probably she would soon be in love with Junius Bandicott. No one could call it anything but a most suitable match, but Janet was vaguely unhappy about it, for it meant a break in their tiny household and the end of a long and affectionate, if occasionally tempestuous, comradeship. She would be very lonely at Glenraden without Agatha, and what would Agatha do when transplanted to a foreign shore—Agatha, for whom the world was bounded by her native hills? She began to figure to herself what America was like, and, as her pictures had no basis of knowledge, they soon became fantastic, and merged into dreams. The drowsy afternoon world laid its spell upon the girl, and she fell asleep.

She awoke half an hour later with the sound of a shot in her ear. It set her scrambling to her feet till she remembered the excavators at the Piper's Ring, who were out of sight of the knoll on which she stood, somewhat on her right rear. Reassured, she lazily scanned the sleeping haugh, with the glittering Raden in the middle distance, and beyond the wooded slopes of the other side of the glen. She noticed a small troop of deer splashing through the shallows. Had they been scared by Mr Bandicott's explosion? That was odd, for the report had been faint and they were up-wind from it.

They were badly startled, for they raced through the river and disappeared in a few breathless seconds in the farther woods. . . . Suddenly a thought made her heart beat wildly, and she raked the ground with her glass. . . .

There was something tawny on a patch of turf in a little hollow near the stream. A moment of anxious spying showed her that it was a dead stag. The report had not been Mr Bandicott's dynamite, but a rifle.

Down the hill-side like a startled hind went Janet. She was choking with excitement, and had no clear idea in her head except a determination that John Macnab should not lay hand on the stricken beast. If he had pierced their defences, and got his shot, he would at any rate not get the carcass of the ground. No thought of the stakes and her hunter occurred to her—only of Glenraden and its inviolate honour.

Almost at once she lost sight of the place where the stag lay. She was now on the low ground of the haugh, in a wilderness of bogs and hollows and overgrown boulders, with half a mile of rough country between her and her goal. Soon she was panting hard: presently she had a stitch in her side; her eyes dimmed with fatigue, and her hat flew off and was left behind. It was abominable ground for speed, for there were heather-roots to trip the foot, and mires to engulf it, and noxious stones over which a runner must go warily or break an ankle. On with bursting heart went Janet, slipping, floundering, more than once taking wild tosses. Her light shoes grew leaden, her thin skirts a vast entangling quilt; her side ached and her legs were fast numbing. . . . Then, from a slight rise, she had a glimpse of the Raden water, now very near, and the sight of a moving head. Her speed redoubled, and miraculously her aches ceased—the fire of battle filled her, as it had burned in her progenitors when they descended on their foes through the moonlit passes.

Suddenly she was at the scene of the dark deed. There lay the dead stag, and beside it a tall man with his shirt-sleeves turned up and a knife in his hand. That the miscreant should be calmly proceeding to the gralloch was like a fiery stimulant to Janet's spirit. Gone was every vestige of fatigue, and she descended the last slope like a maenad.

"Stop!" she sobbed. "Stop, you villain!"

The man started at her voice, and drew himself up. He saw a slim dishevelled girl, hatless, her fair locks fast coming down, who, in the attitude of a tragedy queen, stood with uplifted and accusing hand. She saw a tall man, apparently young, with a very ruddy face, a thatch of sandy hair, and ancient, disreputable clothes.

"You are beaten, John Macnab," cried the panting voice. "I forbid you to touch that stag. I . . ."

The man seemed to have grasped the situation, for he shut

the knife and slipped it back in his pocket. Also he smiled. Also he held both hands above his head.

"*Kamerad!*" he said. "I acknowledge defeat, Miss Raden."

Then he picked up his rifle and his discarded jacket, and turned and ran for it. She heard him splashing through the river, and in three minutes he was swallowed up in the farther woods.

The victorious Janet sank gasping on the turf. She wanted to cry, but changed her mind and began to laugh hysterically. After that she wanted to sing. She and she alone had defeated the marauder, while every man about the place was roosting idly on Carnmore. Now at last she remembered that hunter which would carry her in the winter over the Midland pastures. That was good, but to have beaten John Macnab was better. . . . And then just a shade of compunction tempered her triumph. She had greatly liked the look of John Macnab. He was a gentleman—his voice bore witness to the fact, and the way he had behaved. *Kamerad!* He must have fought in the war and had no doubt done well. Also, he was beyond question a sportsman. The stag was just the kind of beast that a sportsman would kill—a switch-horn, going back in condition—and he had picked him out of a herd of better beasts. The shot was a workmanlike one—through the neck... . And the audacity of him! His wits had beaten them all, for he had chosen the Home beat which everyone had dismissed as inviolable. Truly a foeman worthy of her steel, whom like all good fighters after victory she was disposed to love.

Crouched beside the dead stag, she slowly recovered her breath. What was the next move to be? If she left the beast might not John Macnab return and make off with it? No, he wouldn't. He was a gentleman, and would not go back on his admission of defeat. But she was anxious to drain the last drops of her cup of triumph, to confront the idle garrison of Carnmore on its return with the tangible proof of her victory. The stag should be lying at the Castle door, and she herself waiting beside it to tell her tale. She might borrow Mr Bandicott's men to move it.

84

Hastily doing up her hair, she climbed out of the hollow to the little ridge which gave a prospect over the haugh. There before her, not a hundred yards distant, was the old cart and the white pony of Fish Benjie, looking as if it had been part of the landscape since the beginning of time.

Benjie had wormed his way far into the moss, for he was more than half a mile from the road. It appeared that he had finished his day's work on the besoms, for his pony was in the shafts, and he himself was busy loading the cart with the fruits of his toil. She called out to him, but got no reply, and it was not till she stood beside him that he looked up from his work.

"Benjie," she said, "come at once. I want you to help me. Have you been here long?"

"Since nine this mornin', lady." Benjie's face was as impassive as a stump of oak.

"Didn't you hear a shot?"

"I heard a gude wheen shots. The auld man up at the Piper's Ring has been blastin' awa."

"But close to you? Didn't you see a man—not five minutes ago?"

"Aye, I seen a man. I seen him crossin' the water. I thought he was a gentleman from the Castle. He had a gun wi' him."

"It was a poacher, Benjie," said Janet dramatically. "The poacher I wanted you to look out for. He has killed a stag, too, but I drove him away. You must help me to get the beast home. Can you get your cart over that knowe?"

"Fine, lady."

Without more words Benjie took the reins and started the old pony. The cart floundered a little in a wet patch, tittuped over the tussocks, and descended with many jolts to the neighbourhood of the stag—Janet dancing in front of it like an Israelitish priest before the Ark of the Covenant.

The late afternoon was very hot, for down in the haugh the wind had died away. The stag weighed not less than fifteen stone, and before they finished Janet would have called them tons. Yet the great task of transhipment was accomplished. The pony was taken out of the shafts and the cart tilted, and,

85

after some strenuous minutes, the carcase was heaved and pushed and levered on to its floor. Janet, hanging on to the shafts, with incredible exertions pulled them down, while Benjie—a tiny Atlas—prevented the beast from slipping back by bearing its weight on his shoulders. The backboard was put in its place, the mass of brooms and heather piled on the stag, the pony restored to the shafts, and the cortege was ready for the road. Benjie had his face adorned with a new scratch and a quantity of deer's blood, Janet had nobly torn her jumper and one stocking; but these were trivial casualties for so great an action.

"Drive straight to the Castle and tell them to leave the beast before the door. You understand, Benjie? Before the door—not in the larder. I'm going to strike home through the woods, for I'm an awful sight."

"Ye look very bonny, lady," said the gallant Benjie as he took up the reins.

Janet watched the strange outfit lumber from the hollow and nearly upset over a hidden boulder. It had the appearance of a moving peat-stack, with a solitary horn jutting heavenwards like a withered branch. Once again the girl subsided on the heather and laughed till she ached.

.   .   .   .   .

The highway by the Larrrig side slept in the golden afternoon. Not a conveyance had disturbed its peace save the baker's cart from Inverlarrig, which had passed about three o'clock. About half-past five a man crossed it—a man who had descended from the hill and used the stepping-stones where Sir Archibald Roylance had come to grief. He was a tall man with a rifle, hatless, untidy and very warm, and he seemed to desire to be unobserved, for he made certain that the road was clear before he ventured on it. Once across, he found shelter in a clump of broom, whence he could command a long stretch of the highway, almost from Glenraden gates to the Bridge of Larrig.

Mr Palliser-Yeates, having reached sanctuary—for behind him lay the broken hillsides of Crask—mopped his brow and lit a pipe. He did not seem to be greatly distressed at the result of the afternoon. Indeed, he laughed—not wildly like Janet, but quietly and with philosophy. "A very neat hold-up," he reflected. "Gad, she came on like a small destroying angel. . . . That's the girl Archie's been talking about . . . a very good girl. She looked as if she'd have taken on an army corps. . . . Jolly romantic ending—might have come out of a novel. Only it should have been Archie, and a prospect of wedding bells—what? . . . Anyway, we'd have won out all right but for the girl, and I don't mind being beaten by her. . . ."

His meditations were interrupted by the sound of furious wheels on the lone highway, and he cautiously raised his head to see an old horse and an older cart being urged towards him at a canter. The charioteer was a small boy, and above the cart sides projected a stag's horn.

Forgetting all precautions, he stood up, and at the sight of him Benjie, not without difficulty, checked the ardour of his much-belaboured beast, and stopped before him.

"I've gotten it," he whispered hoarsely. "The stag's in the cairt. The lassie and me histed him in, and she tell't me to drive to the Castle. But when I was out o' sicht o' her, I took the auld road through the wud and here I am. We've gotten the stag off Glenraden ground and we can hide him up at Crask, and I'll slip doun i' the cairt afore mornin' and leave him ootbye the Castle wi' a letter from John Macnab. Fegs, it was a near thing!"

Benjie's voice rose into a shrill paean, his disreputable face shone with unholy joy. And then something in Palliser-Yeates's eyes cut short his triumph.

"Benjie, you little fool, right about turn at once. I'm much obliged to you, but it can't be done. It isn't the game, you know. I chucked up the sponge when Miss Raden challenged me, and I can't go back on that. Back you go to Glenraden and hand over the stag. Quick, before you're missed. . . . And look here—you're a first-class sportsman, and I'm enormously grateful to you. Here is something for your trouble."

Benjie's face grew very red as he swung his equipage round. "I see," he said. "If ye like to be beat by a lassie, dinna blame me. I'm no wantin' your money."

The next moment the fish-cart was clattering in the other direction.

To a mystified and anxious girl, pacing the gravel in front of the Castle, entered the fish-cart. The old horse seemed in the last stages of exhaustion, and the boy who drove it was a dejected and sparrow-like figure.

"Where in the world have you been?" Janet demanded.

"I was run awa wi', lady," Benjie whined. "The auld powny didna like the smell o' the stag. He bolted in the wud, and I didna get him stoppit till verra near the Larrig Bridge."

"Poor little Benjie! Now you're going to Mrs Fraser to have the best tea you ever had in your life, and you shall also have ten shillings."

"Thank you kindly, lady, but I canna stop for tea. I maun awa down to Inverlarrig for my fish." But his hand closed readily on the note, for he had no compunction in taking money from one who had made him to bear the bitterness of incomprehensible defeat.

6

THE RETURN OF HARALD BLACKTOOTH

MISS JANET RADEN had a taste for the dramatic, which that night was nobly gratified. The space in front of the great door of the Castle became a stage of which the sole furniture was a deceased stag, but on which event succeeded event with a speed which recalled the cinema rather than the legitimate drama.

First, about six o'clock, entered Agatha and Junius Bandicott from their casual wardenship of Carnbeg. The effect upon the young man was surprising. Hitherto he had only half believed in John Macnab, and had regarded the defence of Glenraden as more or less of a joke. It seemed to him inconceivable that, even with the slender staffing of the forest, one man could enter and slay and recover a deer. But when he heard Janet's tale he became visibly excited, and his careful and precise English, the bequest of his New England birth, broke down into college slang.

"The man's a crackerjack," he murmured reverentially. "He has us all rocketing around the mountain tops, and then takes advantage of my dad's blasting operations and raids the front yard. He can pull the slick stuff all right, and we at Strathlarrig had better get cold towels round our heads and do some thinking. Our time's getting short, too, for he starts at midnight the day after to-morrow. . . . What did you say the fellow was like, Miss Janet? Young, and big, and behaved like a gentleman? It's a tougher proposition than I thought, and I'm going home right now to put old Angus through his paces."

With a deeply preoccupied face Junius, declining tea, fetched his car from the stableyard and took his leave.

At seven-fifteen Colonel Raden, bestriding a deer pony,

emerged from the beech avenue, and waved a cheerful hand to his daughters.

"It's all right, my dears. Not a sign of the blackguard. The men will remain on Carnmore till midnight to be perfectly safe, but I'm inclined to think that the whole thing is a fiasco. He has been frightened away by our precautions. But it's been a jolly day on the high tops, and I have the thirst of all creation."

Then his eyes fell on the stag. "God bless my soul," he cried, "what is that?"

"That," said Janet, "is the stag which John Macnab killed this afternoon."

The Colonel promptly fell off his pony.

"Where—when?" he stammered.

"On the Home beat," said Janet calmly. The situation was going to be quite as dramatic as she had hoped. "I saw it fall, and ran hard and got up to it just when he was starting the gralloch. He was really quite nice about it."

"What did he do?" her parent demanded.

"He held up his hands and laughed and cried *'Kamerad!'* Then he ran away."

"The scoundrel showed a proper sense of shame."

"I don't think he was ashamed. Why should he be, for we accepted his challenge. You know, he's a gentleman, papa, and quite young and good looking."

Colonel Raden's mind was passing through swift stages from exasperation to unwilling respect. It was an infernal annoyance that John Macnab should have been suffered to intrude on the sacred soil of Glenraden, but the man had played the boldest kind of hand, and he had certainly not tailored his beast. Besides, he had been beaten—beaten by a girl, a daughter of the house. The honour of Glenraden might be considered sacrosanct after all.

A long drink restored the Colonel's equanimity, and the thought of their careful preparations expended in the void moved him to laughter.

" 'Pon my word, Nettie, I should like to ask the fellow to dinner. I wonder where on earth he is living. He can't be far off, for he is due at Strathlarrig very soon. What did young Bandicott say the day was?"

"Midnight, the day after to-morrow. Mr Junius feels very solemn after to-day, and has hurried home to put his house in order."

"Nettie," said the Colonel gravely, "I am prepared to make the modest bet that John Macnab gets his salmon. Hang it all, if he could outwit us—and he did it, confound him—he is bound to outwit the Bandicotts. I tell you what, John Macnab is a very remarkable man—a man in a million, and I'm very much inclined to wish him success."

"So am I," said Janet; but Agatha announced indignantly that she had never met a case of grosser selfishness. She announced, too, that she was prepared to join in the guarding of Strathlarrig.

"If you and Junius are no more use than you were on Carnbeg to-day, John Macnab needn't worry," said Janet sweetly.

Agatha was about to retort when there was a sudden diversion. The elder Bandicott appeared at a pace which was almost a run, breathing hard, and with all the appearance of strong excitement. Fifty yards behind him could be seen the two Strathlarrig labourers, making the best speed they could under the burden of heavy sacks. Mr Bandicott had no breath left to speak, but he motioned to his audience to give him time and permit his henchmen to arrive. These henchmen he directed to the lawn, where they dropped their sacks on the grass. Then, with an air which was almost sacramental, he turned to Colonel Raden.

"Sir," he said, "you are privileged—_we_ are privileged— to assist in the greatest triumph of modern archaeology. I have found the coffin of Harald Blacktooth with the dust of Harald Blacktooth inside it."

"The devil you have!" said the Colonel. "I suppose I ought to congratulate you, but I'm bound to say I'm rather sorry. I feel as if I had violated the tomb of my ancestors."

"You need have no fear, sir. The dust has been reverently

91

restored to its casket, and to-morrow the Piper's Ring will show no trace of the work. But within the stone casket there were articles which, in the name of science, I have taken the liberty to bring with me, and which will awaken an interest among the learned not less, I am convinced, than Schliemann's discoveries at Mycenae. I have found, sir, incredible treasures."

"Treasures!" cried all three of his auditors, for the word has not lost its ancient magic.

Mr Bandicott, with the air of one addressing the Smithsonian Institution, signalled to his henchmen, who thereupon emptied the sacks on the lawn. A curious jumble of objects lay scattered under the evening sun—two massive torques, several bowls and flagons, spear-heads from which the hafts had long since rotted, a sword-blade, and a quantity of brooches, armlets, and rings. A dingy enough collection they made to the eyes of the onlookers as Mr Bandicott arranged them in two heaps.

"These," he said, pointing to the torques, armlets, and flagons, "are, so far as I can judge, of solid gold."

The Colonel called upon his Maker to sanctify his soul. "Gold! These are great things! They must be prodigiously valuable. Are they mine, or yours, or whose?"

"I am not familiar with the law of Scotland on the matter of treasure trove, but I assume that the State can annex them, paying you a percentage of their value. For myself, I gladly waive all claims. I am a man of science, sir, not a treasure-hunter. . . . But the merit of the discovery does not lie in those objects, which can be paralleled from many tombs in Scotland and Norway. No, sir, the tremendous, the epoch-making value is to be found in these." And he indicated some bracelets and a necklace which looked as if they were made of queerly-marked and very dirty shells.

Mr Bandicott lifted one and fingered it lovingly.

"I have found such objects in graves as far apart as the coast of Labrador and the coast of Rhode Island, and as far inland as the Ohio basin. These shells were the common funerary adjunct of the primitive inhabitants of my country, and they are peculiar to the North American continent. Do you see what follows, sir?"

The Colonel did not, and Mr Bandicott, his voice thrilling with emotion, continued:

"It follows that Harald Blacktooth obtained them from the only place he could obtain them, the other side of the Atlantic. There is historical warrant for believing that he voyaged to Greenland; and now we know that he landed upon the main North American continent. The legends of Eric the Red and Leif the Lucky are verified by archaeology. In you, sir, I salute, most reverently salute, the representative of a family to whom belongs the credit hitherto given to Columbus."

Colonel Raden plucked feebly at his moustache, and Janet, I regret to say, laughed. But her untimely merriment was checked by Mr Bandicott, who was pronouncing a sort of benediction.

"I rejoice that it has been given to me, an American, to solve this secular riddle. When I think that the dust which an hour ago I touched, and which has lain for centuries under that quiet mound, was once the man who, first of Europeans, trod our soil, my imagination staggers. Colonel Raden, I thank you for having given me the greatest moment of my not uneventful life."

He took off his hat, and the Colonel rather shame-facedly removed his. The two men stood looking solemnly at each other till practical considerations occurred to the descendant of the Viking.

"What are you going to do with the loot?" he asked.

"With your permission, I will take it to Strathlarrig, where I can examine and catalogue it at my leisure. I propose to announce the find at once to the world. To-morrow I will return with my men and remove the traces of our excavation."

Mr Bandicott departed in his car, sitting erect at the wheel in a strangely priest-like attitude, while the two men guarded the treasure behind. He had no eyes for the twilight landscape, or he would have seen in the canal-like stretch of the Larrig belonging to Crask, which lay below the rapids and was universally condemned as hopeless for fish, a solitary angler, who, as the car passed, made a most bungling amateurish cast, but who, when the coast was once more clear, flung a line of surprising delicacy. He could not see the curious way in which that angler placed his fly, laying it with a curl a yard above a moving fish, and then sinking it with a dexterous twist: nor did he see, a quarter of an hour later, the same angler land a fair salmon from water in which in the memory of man no salmon had ever been taken before.

Colonel Raden and his daughters stood watching the departing archaeologist, and as his car vanished among the beeches Janet seized her sister and whirled her into a dance. "Such a day," she cried, when the indignant Agatha had escaped and was patting her disordered hair. "Losses—one stag, which was better dead. Gains—defeat of John Macnab, fifty pounds sterling, a share of unknown value in Harald Blacktooth's treasure, and the annexation of America by the Raden family."

"You'd better say that America has annexed us," said the still flustered Agatha. "They've dug up our barrow, and this afternoon Junius Bandicott asked me to marry him."

Janet stopped in her tracks. "What did you say?"

"I said 'No' of course. I've only known him a week." But her tone was such as to make her sister fear the worst.

Mr Bandicott was an archaeologist, but he was also a business man, and he was disposed to use the whole apparatus of civilisation to announce his discovery to the world. With a good deal of trouble he got the two chief Scottish newspapers on the telephone, and dictated to them a summary of his story. He asked them to pass the matter on to the London press, and he gave them ample references to establish his good faith. Also he prepared a sheaf of telegrams and cables—to learned societies in Britain and America, to the great New York daily of which he was the principal owner, to the British Museum, to the Secretary for Scotland, and to friends in the same line of scholarship. Having left instructions that these messages should be despatched from Inverlarrig at dawn, he went to bed in a state of profound jubilation and utter fatigue.

Next morning, while his father was absorbed in the remains of Harald Blacktooth, Junius summoned a council of war. To it there came Angus, the head-keeper, a morose old man near six-foot-four in height, clean-shaven, with eyebrows like a penthouse; Lennox, his second-in-command, whom Leithen had met on his reconnaissance; and two youthful watchers, late of Lovat's Scouts, known as Jimsie and Davie. There were others about the place who could be mobilised if necessary, including the two chauffeurs, an under-footman and a valet; but, as Junius looked at this formidable quartet, and reflected on the narrow limits of the area of danger, he concluded that he had all the man-power he needed.

"Now, listen to me, Angus," he began. "This poacher Macnab proposes to start in to-morrow night at twelve o'clock, and according to his challenge he has forty-eight hours to get a fish in—up till midnight on the 3rd of September. I want your advice about the best way of checkmating him. You've attended to my orders, and let nobody near the river during the past week?"

"Aye, sir, and there's nobody socht to gang near it," said Angus. "The country-side has been as quiet as a grave."

"Well, it won't be after to-morrow night. You've probably heard that this Macnab killed a stag on Glenraden yesterday—killed it within half a mile of the house, and would have got away with it but for the younger Miss Raden."

They had heard of it, for the glen had talked of nothing else all night, but they thought it good manners to express amazement. "Heard ye ever the like?" said one. "Macnab maun be a fair deevil," said another. "If I had just a grip of him," sighed the blood-thirsty Angus.

"It's clear we're up against something quite out of the common," Junius went on, "and we daren't give him the faintest outside chance. Now, let's consider the river. You say you've seen nobody near it."

"There hasn't been a line cast in the watter forbye your own, sir," said Angus.

"I just seen the one man fishin' a' week," volunteered Jimsie. "It was on the Crask water below the brig. I jaloused that he was one of the servants from Crask, and maybe no very right in the heid. He had no notion of it at all, at all."

"Well, that's so far good. Now what about the river outside the park? Our beat runs from the Larrig Bridge—what's it like between the bridge and the lodge? You've never taken me fishing there."

"Ye wad need to be dementit before you went fishin' there," said Angus grimly. "There's the stretch above the brig that they ca' the Lang Whang. There was never man killed a saumon in it, for the fish dinna bide, but rin through to the Wood Pule. There's fish in the Wood Pule, but the trees are that thick that ye canna cast a flee. Though I'll no say," he added meditatively, "that ye couldna cleek a fish out of it. I'd better put a watcher at the Wood Pule."

"You may rule that out, for the bargain says 'legitimate means,' and from all I know of Macnab he's a sportsman and keeps his word. Well, then, we come to the park, where we've five pools—the Duke's, the Black Scour, Davie's Pot, Lady Maisie's, and the Minister's. We've got to keep our eyes skinned there. . . . What about the upper water?"

"There's no a fish in it," said Lennox. "They canna get past the linn above the Minister's. There was aye talk o' makin' a salmon ladder, but naething was done, and there's nocht above the Minister's but small broon troot."

"That makes it a pretty simple proposition," said Junius. "We've just the five pools to guard. For the form of the thing we'll keep watchers on all night, but we may take it that the danger lies only in the thirty-four hours of daylight. Now, remember, we're taking no chances. Not a soul is to be allowed to fish on the Strathlarrig water till after midnight on the 3rd of September. Not even I or my father. Macnab's a foxy fellow and I wouldn't put it past him to disguise himself as Mr Bandicott or myself. Do you understand? If you see a man near the river, kick him out. If he has a rod in his hand, lock him up in the garage and send for me. . . . No, better still. Nobody's to be allowed inside the gates—except Colonel Raden and his daughters. You'd better tell the lodge-keeper, Angus. If anybody comes to call, they must come back another day. These are my orders, you understand, and I fire anyone who disobeys them. If the 3rd of September passes without accident there's twenty dollars—I mean to say, five pounds—for each of you. That's all I've got to say."

"Will we watch below the park, sir?" Angus asked.

"Watch every damned foot of the water from the bridge to the linns."

Thus it came about that when Janet Raden took her afternoon ride past the Wood of Larrigmore she beheld a man patrolling the bog like a policeman on point duty, and when she entered the park for a gallop on the smooth turf she observed a picket at each pool. "Poor John Macnab!" she sighed. "He hasn't the ghost of a chance. I'm rather sorry my family discovered America."

Next day, the 1st of September, the Scottish Press published a short account of Mr Bandicott's discovery, and *The Scotsman* had a leader on it. About noon a spate of telegrams began, and the girl who carried them on a bicycle from Inverlarrig had a weary time of it. The following morning the Press of Britain spread themselves on the subject. *The Times* had a leader and an interview with a high authority at the British Museum; the *Daily Mail* had a portrait of Mr Bandicott and a sketch of his past career, a photograph of what purported to be a Viking's tomb in Norway, and a chatty article on the law of treasure-trove. The *Morning Post* congratulated the discoverer in the name of science, but lamented in the name of patriotism that the honour should have fallen to an alien—views which led to an interminable controversy in its pages with the secretary of the Pilgrims' Club and the president of the American Chamber of Commerce. The evening papers had brightly written articles on Strathlarrig, touching on the sport of deer-stalking, Celtic mysticism, the crofter question, and the law dealing with access to mountains. The previous evening, too, the special correspondents had begun to arrive from all points of the compass, so that the little inn of Inverlarrig had people sleeping in its one bathroom and under its dining-room table. By the morning of the 2nd of September the glen had almost doubled its male population.

The morning, after some rain in the night, broke in the thin fog which promised a day of blazing heat. Sir Edward Leithen, taking the air after breakfast, decided that his attempt should be made in the evening, for he wanted the Larrig waters well warmed by the sun for the type of fishing he proposed to follow. Benjie had faithfully reported to him the precautions which the Bandicotts had adopted, and his meditations were not cheerful. With luck he might get a fish, but only by a miracle could he escape unobserved. His plan depended upon the Lang Whang being neglected by the watchers as not worthy of their vigilance, but according to Benjie's account even the Lang Whang had become a promenade. He had now lost any half-heartedness in the business, and his obstinate soul was as set on victory as ever it had been the case in the Law Courts. For the past four days he had thought of nothing else,—his interest in Palliser-Yeates's attack on Glenraden had been notably fainter than that of the others; every energy he had of mind and body was centred upon killing a fish that night and carrying it off. With some amusement he reflected that he had dissipated the last atom of his ennui, and he almost regretted that apathy had been exchanged for this violent preoccupation.

Presently he turned his steps to the arbour to the east of the garden, which forms at once a hiding-place and a watch-tower. There he found his host busied about the preparation of his speech, with the assistance of Lamancha, who was also engaged intermittently in the study of the ordnance map of Haripol.

"It's a black look-out for you, Ned," said Sir Archie. "I hear

98

the Bandicotts have taped off every yard of their water, and have got a man to every three. Benjie says the place only wants a piper or two to be like the Muirtown Highland Gathering. What are you going to do about it?"

"I'm going to have a try this evening. I can't chuck in my hand, but the thing's a stark impossibility. I hoped old Bandicott would be so excited at unearthing the Viking that he would forget about precautions, but he's as active as a beaver."

"That's the young 'un. He don't give a damn for Vikings, but he's out to protect his fish. You've struck the American business mind, my lad, and it's an awful thing for us casual Britons. I suppose you won't let me come down and watch you. I'd give a lot to see a scrap between you and that troglodyte Angus."

At that moment Benjie, wearing the waterproof cape of ceremony, presented himself at the arbour door. He bore a letter which he presented to Sir Archie. The young man read it with a face which was at once perplexed and pleased.

"It's from old Bandicott. He says he has got some antiquarian swell—Professor Babwater I think the name is—coming to stay, and he wants me to dine tonight—says the Radens are coming too. . . . This is the devil. What had I better do, Charles?"

"Stay at home. You'll put your foot in it somehow if you go. The girl who held up old John will be there, and she's bound to talk about John Macnab, and you're equally bound to give the show away."

"But I haven't any sort of excuse. Americans are noted for their politeness, and here have I been shutting the door in the face of the poor old chap when he toiled up the hill. He won't understand it, and people will begin to talk, and that's the quickest way to blow the gaff. Besides, I've got to give up this lie about my ill-health if I'm to appear at Muirtown the day after to-morrow. What do *you* say, Ned?"

"I think you'd better go," Leithen answered. "We can't have the neighbourhood thinking you are plague-stricken. You'll be drinking port, while I'm being carted by the gillies into the coal-hole. But for Heaven's sake, Archie, go canny. That Raden girl will turn you inside out, if you give her a chance. And don't you try and be clever, whatever happens. If there's a row and you see me being frog-marched into captivity, don't trouble to create a diversion. Behave as if you had never seen me in your life before. . . . You hadn't heard of John Macnab except from Miss Raden, and you're desperately keen to hear more, you understand. Play the guileless innocent and rack your brains to think who he can be. Start any hare you like—that he's D'Annunzio looking for excitement . . . or the Poet Laureate . . . or an escaped lunatic. And keep it up that you are in delicate health. Oh, and talk politics—they're safe enough. Babble about the Rally, and how the great Lamancha's coming up for it all the way from the Borders."

Archie nodded, with a contented look in his eyes. "I'm goin' to take your advice. Where did you get this note, Benjie? From Mactavish at the lodge? All right, I'll give you a line to take back with you. . . . By the way, Ned, what's your get-up tonight? I'd better know beforehand in case of accidents."

"I'm going to look the basest kind of poaching tramp. I've selected my costume from the combined wardrobes of this household, and I can tell you it's pretty dingy. Mrs Lithgow is at present engaged in clouting the oldest pair of Wattie's breeks for me. . . . My only chance is to be a regular ragamuffin, and the worst I need fear then is a rough handling from the gillies. Bandicott, I take it, is not the sort of fellow to want to prosecute. If I'm caught—which is fairly certain—I'll probably get a drubbing and spend the night in a cellar and be given my breakfast next morning and kicked out. It's a different matter for you, Charles, with the legally minded Claybody."

"What odds are you offerin'?" Sir Archie asked. "John backed himself and I took a tennner off him. What about an even fiver?"

"I'll give you three to one in five-pound notes that I win," said Leithen grimly. "But that's pride, not conviction."

100

"Done with you, my lad," said Sir Archie, and departed to write an acceptance of the invitation to dinner.

Fish Benjie remained behind, and it was clear that he had something to communicate. He caught Lamancha's eye, who gave him the opening he sought by asking what was the news from Strathlarrig. Benjie had the instinct of the ballad-maker, and would begin his longer discourses with an epic flourish of the "Late at e'en drinkin' the wine" style.

"It was at fower o'clock this mornin' they started," he announced, "and they're still comin'."

"Coming? Who?" Leithen asked.

"Jornalists. The place is crawlin' wi' them. I seen six on bicycles and five in cawrs and twa in the Inverlarrig dowgcairt. They're a' wantin' to see auld Bandicott, but auld Bandicott will no see them. Mactavish stops them at the lodge, and speirs what they want, and they gie him cairds wi' their names prentit, and he sends them up to the hoose, but he'll no let them enter. Syne the message comes back that the maister will see them the day after the morn, but till then naebody maun put a fit inside the gates."

"What happened then?" Leithen asked with acute interest.

"It hasna happened—it's still happenin'! I never in my life heard sic a lot o' sweer words. Says ane, 'Does the auld dotterel think he can defy the British Press? We'll mak his life no worth leevin'.' Says another, 'I've come a' the gait frae London and I'll no budge till I've seen the banes o' that Viking!' One or twa went back to Inverlarrig, but the feck o' them just scattered like paitricks. They clamb the wall, and they waded up the water, and they got in by the top o' the linns. In half an hour there was half a dizzen o' them inside the Strathlarrig policies. Man"—here he fixed his glowing eye on Leithen—"if ye had been on the Lang Whang this mornin' ye could have killed a fish and naebody the wiser."

"Good Lord! Are they there still?"

"Na. They were huntit oot. Every man aboot the place was hunting' them, and Angus was roarin' like a bull. The young Laird thocht they were Bolshies and cam doun wi' a gun. Syne the auld man appeared and spoke them fair and told them he was terribly sorry, but he couldna see them for twa days, and if they contentit themselves that lang he would hae them a' to their denner and show them everything. After that they gaed awa, but there's aye mair arrivin' and I'm expectin' mair riots. They're forritsome lads, thae jornalists, and a dour crop to shift. But they're kind folk, and gie'd me a shilling' a-piece for advisin' them."

"What did you advise?"

"I advised them to gang doun to Glenraden," said Benjie with a goblin smile. "I said they should gang and howk in the Piper's Ring and they would maybe find mair treasure. Twa-three o' them got spades and picks and startit off. I'm thinkin' Macpherson will be after them wi' a whup."

Leithen's brows were puckered in thought. "It looks as if my bet with Archie wasn't so crazy after all. This invasion is bound to confuse Bandicott's plans. And you say it's still going on? The gillies will be weary men before night."

"They will that," Benjie assented. "And there's no a man o' them can rin worth a docken, except Jimsie. Thae jornalists was far soopler."

"More power to the Press. Benjie, back you go and keep an eye on Strathlarrig, and stir up the journalists to a sense of their rights. Report here this afternoon at four, for we should be on the move by six, and I've a lot to say to you."

In the course of the morning Leithen went for a walk among the scaurs and dingles of Crask Hill. He followed a footpath which took him down the channel of a tiny burn and led to a little mantelpiece of a meadow from which Wattie Lithgow drew a modest supply of bog-hay. His mind was so filled with his coming adventure that he walked with his head bent and at a turn of the path nearly collided with a man.

Murmuring a gruff "Fine day," he would have passed on, when he became aware that the stranger had halted. Then, to his consternation, he heard his name uttered, and had perforce to turn. He saw a young man, in knickerbockers and heavy

102

nailed boots, who smiled diffidently as if uncertain whether he would be recognised.

"Sir Edward Leithen, isn't it?" he said. "I once had the pleasure of meeting you, sir, when you lunched with the Lobby journalists. I was then on the Lobby staff of the *Monitor*. My name is Crossby."

"Of course, of course. I remember perfectly. Let's sit down, Mr Crossby, unless you're in a hurry. Where are you bound for?"

"Simply stretching my legs. I was climbing rocks at Sligachan when my paper wired me to come on here. The Press seem to have gone mad about this Viking's tomb—think they've got hold of a second Tutankhamen. So I got a fisherman to take me and my bicycle over to the mainland and pedalled the rest of the road. I thought I had a graft with old Bandicott, for I used to write for his paper—*The New York Bulletin,* you know—but it appears there's nothing doing. Odd business, for you don't often find Americans shy of the Press. But I think I've found out the reason, and that makes a good enough story in itself. Perhaps you've heard it?"

"No," said Leithen, "but I'd like to, if you don't mind. I'm not a journalist, so I won't give you away. Let's have it."

He stole a glance at his companion, and saw a pleasant, shrewd, boyish face, with the hard sunburnt skin of one in the prime of physical condition. Like many others of his type, Leithen liked journalists as much as he disliked men of letters—the former had had their corners smoothed by a rough life, and lacked the vanity and spiritual pride of the latter. Also he had acquired from experience a profound belief in the honour of the profession, for at various times in his public career he had put his reputation into their hands and they had not failed him. It was his maxim that if you tried to bamboozle them they were out for your blood, but that if you trusted them they would see you through.

"Let's hear it, Mr Crossby," he repeated. "I'm deeply interested."

"Well, it's a preposterous tale, but the natives seem to

believe it. They say that some fellow, who calls himself John Macnab, has dared the magnates in these parts to prevent his killing a stag or a salmon in their preserves. He has laid down pretty stiff conditions for himself, for he has to get his beast off their ground and hand it back to them. They say he has undertaken to pay £500 to any charity the owner names if he succeeds and £1,000 if he fails—so he must have money to burn, and it appears that he has already paid the £500. He started on Glenraden, and the old Highland chief there had every man and boy for three days watching the forest. Then on the third day, when everybody was on the mountain-tops, in sails John Macnab and kills a stag under the house windows. He reckoned on the American's dynamite charges in his search for the Viking to hide his shot. And he would have got away with it too, if one of the young ladies hadn't appeared on the scene and cried 'Desist!' So what does this bandit do but off with his hat, makes his best bow, and says 'Madame, your servant,' and vanishes, leaving the chief richer by a thousand pounds. It's Bandicott's turn to-day and to-morrow, and the Strathlarrig household is squatting along the river banks, and the hard-working correspondent is chivvied away till the danger is past. I'm for Macnab myself. It warms my heart to think that there's such a sportsman left alive. It's pure Robin Hood."

Leithen laughed. "I back him too. Are you going to publish that story?"

"Yes, why not? I've written most of it and it goes by the afternoon post." Mr Crossby pulled out a note-book and fluttered the leaves.

"I call it 'The Return of Harald Blacktooth.' Rather neat, I think. The idea is that when they started to dig up the old fellow his spirit reincarnated itself in John Macnab. I hope to have a second instalment, for something's bound to happen at Strathlarrig to-day or to-morrow. Are you holidaying here, Sir Edward? Crask's the name of this place, isn't it? They told me that that mad fellow Roylance owned it."

Leithen nodded. He was bracing himself for another

decision of the same kind as he had taken when he met Fish Benjie. Providence seemed to be forcing him to preserve his incognito only by sharing the secret.

"But, of course," Mr Crossby went on, "my main business here is the Viking, and I'm keen to find some way to get over Bandicott's reticence. I don't want to wait till the day after tomorrow and then come in with the ruck. I wonder . . . would it be too much to ask you to give me a leg up? I expect you know the Bandicotts?"

"Curiously enough, I don't. I am not sure how far I can help you, Mr Crossby, but I rather think you can help me. Are you by any happy chance a long-distance runner?"

The journalist opened his eyes. "Well, I used to be. South London Harriers, you know. And I'm in fairly good condition at present after ten days on the Coolin rocks."

"Well, if I can't give you a story, I think I can put you in the way of an adventure. Will you come up to Crask to luncheon and we'll talk it over?"

7

THE OLD ETONIAN TRAMP

SIR ARCHIE got himself into the somewhat ancient dress-coat which was the best he had at Crask, and about half-past seven started his Hispana (a car in which his friends would not venture with Archie as driver) down the long hill to the gates of Strathlarrig. He was aware that somewhere in the haugh above the bridge was Leithen, but the only figure visible was that of Jimsie, the Strathlarrig gillie, who was moodily prowling about the upper end. As he passed the Wood of Larrigmore Benjie's old pony was grazing at tether, and the old cart rested on its shafts; the embers of a fire still glowed among the pine-needles, but there was no sign of Benjie. He was admitted after a parley by Mactavish the lodge-keeper, and when he reached the door of the house he observed a large limousine being driven off to the back premises by a very smart chauffeur. Only Haripol was likely to own such a car, and Sir Archie reflected with amusement that the host of John Macnab was about to attend a full conclave of the Enemy.

The huge, ugly drawing-room looked almost beautiful in the yellow light of evening. A fire burned on the hearth after the fashion of Highland houses even in summer, and before it stood Mr Acheson Bandicott, with a small clean-shaven man, who was obviously the distinguished Professor in whose honour the feast was given, and Colonel Raden, a picturesque figure in kilt and velvet doublet, who seemed hard put to it to follow what was clearly a technical colloquy. Agatha and Junius were admiring the sunset in the west window, and Janet was talking to a blond young man who seemed possessed of a singularly penetrating voice.

Sir Archie was unknown to most of the company, and when

his name was announced everyone except the Professor turned towards him with a lively curiosity. Old Mr Bandicott was profuse in his welcome, Junius no less cordial, Colonel Raden approving, for indeed it was not in human nature to be cold towards so friendly a being as the Laird of Crask. Sir Archie was apologetic for his social misfeasances, congratulatory about Harald Blacktooth, eager to atone for the past by an exuberant neighbourliness. "Been havin' a rotten time with the toothache," he told his host. "I roost up alone in my little barrack and keep company with birds . . . . Bit of a naturalist, you know. . . . Yes, sir, quite fit again, but my leg will never be much to boast of."

Colonel Raden appraised the lean, athletic figure. "You've been our mystery man, Sir Archibald. I'm almost sorry to meet you, for we lose our chief topic of discussion. You're fond of stalking, they tell me. When are you coming to kill a stag at Glenraden?"

"When will you ask me?" Sir Archie laughed. "I'm still fairly good on the hill, but just now I'm sittin' indoors all day tuggin' at my hair and tryin' to compose a speech."

Colonel Raden's face asked for explanations.

"Day after to-morrow in Muirtown. Big Unionist meetin', and I've got to start the ball. It's jolly hard to know what to talk about, for I've a pretty high average of ignorance about everything. But I've decided to have a shot at foreign policy. You see, Charles—" Sir Archie stopped in a fright. He had been within an ace of giving the show away.

"Of course. 'Pon my soul I had forgotten that you were our candidate. It's an uphill fight I'm afraid. The people in these parts, sir, are the most obstinate reactionaries on the face of the globe; but they've been voting Liberal ever since the days of John Knox."

Mr Bandicott regarded Sir Archie with interest.

"So you're standing for Parliament," he said. "Few things impress me more in Great Britain than the way young men take up public life as if it were the natural coping-stone to their education. We have no such tradition, and we feel the absence of it. Junius would as soon think of running for Congress as of keeping a faro-saloon. Now I wonder, Sir Archibald, what induced you to take this step?"

But Sir Archie was gone, for he had seen the beckoning eyes of Janet Raden. That young woman, ever since she had heard that the Laird of Crask was coming to dinner, had looked forward to this occasion as her culminating triumph. He had been her confidant about the desperate John Macnab, and from her he must learn the tale of her victory. Her pleasure was increased by the consciousness that she was looking her best, for she knew that her black gown was a good French model and well set off her delicate colouring. She looked with eyes of friendship on him as he limped across the room, and noted his lean distinction. No other country, she thought, produced this kind of slim, graceful, yet weathered and hard-bitten youth.

"Do you know Mr Claybody?"

Mr Claybody said he was delighted to meet his neighbour again. "It's years," he said, "since we met at Ronham. I spend my life in the train now, and never get more than a few days at a time at Haripol. But I've managed to secure a month this year to entertain my friends. I was looking forward in any case to seeing you at Muirtown on the 4th. I've been helping to organise the show, and I consider it a great score to have got Lamancha. This place had never been properly worked, and with a little efficient organisation we ought to put you in right enough. There's no doubt Scotland is changing, and you'll have the tide to help you."

Mr Claybody was a very splendid person. He looked rather like a large edition of the great Napoleon, for he had the same full fleshy face, and his head was set on a thickish neck. His blond hair was beautifully sleek and his clothes were of a perfection uncommon in September north of the Forth. Not that Mr Claybody was either fat or dandified; he was only what the ballad calls "fair of flesh," and he employed a good tailor and an assiduous valet. His exact age was thirty-two, and he did not look older, once the observer had got over his curiously sophisticated eyes.

108

But Sir Archie was giving scant attention to Mr Claybody.

"Have you heard?" Janet broke out. "John Macnab came, saw, and didn't conquer."

"I've heard nothing else in the last two days."

"And I was right! He is a gentleman."

"No? Tell me all about the fellow." Sir Archie's interest was perhaps less in the subject than in the animation which it woke in Janet's eyes.

But the announcement that dinner was served cut short the tale, though not before Sir Archie had noticed a sudden set of Mr Claybody's jaw and a contraction of his eyebrows. "Wonder if he means to stick to his lawyer's letter," he communed with himself. "In that case it's quod for Charles."

The dining-room at Strathlarrig was a remnant of the old house which had been enveloped in the immense sheath of the new. It had eighteenth-century panelling unchanged since the days when Jacobite chiefs in lace and tartan had passed their claret glasses over the water, and the pictures were all of forbidding progenitors. But the ancient narrow windows had been widened, and Sir Archie, from where he sat, had a prospect of half a mile of the river, including Lady Maisie's Pool, bathed in the clear amber of twilight. He was on his host's left hand, opposite the Professor, with Agatha Raden next to him: then came Junius: while Janet was between Johnson Claybody and the guest of the occasion.

Mr Claybody still brooded over John Macnab.

"I call the whole thing infernal impertinence," he said in his loud, assured voice. "I confess I have ceased to admire undergraduate 'rags.' He threatens to visit us, and my father intends to put the matter into the hands of the police."

"That would be very kind," said Janet sweetly. "You see, John Macnab won't have the slightest trouble in beating the police."

"It's the principle of the thing, Miss Raden. Here is an impudent attack on private property, and if we treat it as a joke it will only encourage other scoundrels. If the man is a gentleman, as you say he is, it makes it more scandalous."

"Come, come, Mr Claybody, you're taking it too seriously." Colonel Raden could be emphatic enough on the rights of property, but no Highlander can ever grow excited about trespass. "The fellow has made a sporting offer and is willing to risk a pretty handsome stake. I rather admire what you call his impudence. I might have done the same thing as a young man, if I had had the wits to think of it."

Mr Claybody was quick to recognise an unsympathetic audience. "Oh, I don't mean that we're actually going to make a fuss. We'll give him a warm reception if he comes—that's all. But I don't like the spirit. It's too dangerous in these unsettled times. Once let the masses get into their heads that landed property is a thing to play tricks with, and you take the pin out of the whole system. You must agree with me, Roylance?"

Sir Archie, remembering his part, answered with guile. "Rather! Rotten game for a gentleman, I think. All the same, the chap seems rather a sportsman, so I'm in favour of letting the law alone and dealing with him ourselves. I expect he won't have much of a look in on Haripol."

"I can promise you he won't," said Mr Claybody shortly.

Professor Babwater observed that it would be difficult for a descendant of Harald Blacktooth to be too hard on one who followed in Harald's steps. "The Celt," he said, "has always sought his adventures in a fairy world. The Northman was a realist, and looked to tangible things like land and cattle. Therefore he was a conqueror and a discoverer on the terrestial globe, while the Celt explored the mysteries of the spirit. Those who, like you, sir"—he bowed to Colonel Raden—"have both strains in their ancestry, should have successes in both worlds."

"They don't mix well," said the Colonel sadly. "There was my grandfather, who believed in Macpherson's *Ossian* and ruined the family fortunes in hunting for Gaelic manuscripts on the continent of Europe. And his father was in India with Clive, and thought about nothing except blackmailing native chiefs till he made the place too hot to hold him. Look at my daughters, too. Agatha is mad about poetry and such-like, and Janet is a bandit. She'd have made a dashed good soldier, though."

"Thank you, papa," said the lady. She might have objected to the description had she not seen that Sir Archie accepted it with admiring assent.

"I suppose," said old Mr Bandicott reflectively, "that the war was bound to leave a good deal of unsettlement. Junius missed it through being too young—never got out of a training camp—but I have noticed that those who fought in France find it difficult to discover a groove. They are energetic enough, but they won't 'stay put', as we say. Perhaps this Macnab is one of the unrooted. In your country, where everybody was soldiering, the case must be far more common."

Mr Claybody announced that he was sick of hearing the war blamed for the average man's deficiencies. "Every waster," he said, "makes an excuse of being shell-shocked. I'm very clear that the war twisted nothing in a man that wasn't twisted before."

Sir Archie demurred. "I don't know. I've seen some pretty bad cases of fellows who used to be as sane as a judge, and came home all shot to bits in their mind."

"There are exceptions, of course. I'm speaking of the general rule. I turn away unemployables every day—good soldiers, maybe, but unemployable—and I doubt if they were ever anything else."

Something in his tone annoyed Janet.

"You saw a lot of service, didn't you?" she asked meekly.

"No—worse luck! They made me stick at home and slave fourteen hours a day controlling cotton. It would have been a holiday for me to get into the trenches. But what I say is, a sane man usually remained sane. Look at Sir Archibald. We all know what a hectic time he had, and he hasn't turned a hair."

"I'd like you to give me that in writing," Sir Archie grinned. "I've known people who thought I was rather cracked."

"Anyhow, it made no difference to your nerves," said Colonel Raden.

"I hope not. I expect that was because I enjoyed the beastly thing. Perhaps I'm naturally a bit of a bandit—like Miss Janet."

111

"Perhaps you're John Macnab," said that lady.

"Well, you've seen him and can judge."

"No. I'll be a witness for the defence if you're ever accused. But you mustn't be offended at the idea. I suppose poor John Macnab is now crawling round Strathlarrig trying to find a gap between the gillies to cast a fly."

"That's about the size of it," Junius laughed. "And there's twenty special correspondents in the neighbourhood cursing his name. If they get hold of him, they'll be savager than old Angus."

Mr Bandicott, after calling his guests' attention to the merits of a hock which he had just acquired—it was a Johannisberg with the blue label—declared that in his belief the war would do good to English life, when the first ferment had died away.

"As a profound admirer of British institutions," he said, "I have sometimes thought that they needed a little shaking up and loosening. In America our classes are fluid. The rich man of to-day began life in a shack, and the next generation may return to it. It is the same with our professions. The man who starts in the law may pass to railway management, and end as the proprietor of a department store. Our belief is that it doesn't matter how often you change your trade before you're fifty. But an Englishman, once he settles in a profession, is fixed in it till the Day of Judgment, and in a few years he gets the mark of it so deep that he'd be a fish out of water in anything else. You can't imagine one of your big barristers doing anything else. No fresh fields and pastures new for them. It would be a crime against Magna Carta to break loose and try company-promoting or cornering the meat trade for a little change."

Professor Babwater observed that in England they sometimes—in his view to the country's detriment—became politicians.

"That's the narrowest groove of all," said Mr Bandicott with conviction. "In this country, once you start in on politics you're fixed in a class and members of a hierarchy, and you've got to go on, however unfitted you may be for the job, because it's sort of high treason to weaken. In America a man tries politics as he tries other things, and if he finds the air of Washington uncongenial he quits, or tries newspapers, or Wall Street, or oil."

"Or the penitentiary," said Junius.

"And why not?" asked his father. "I deplore criminal tendencies in any public man, but the possibility of such a downfall keeps the life human. It is very different in England. The respectability of your politicians is so awful that, when one of them backslides, every man of you combines to hush it up. There would be a revolution if the people got to suspect. Can you imagine a Cabinet Minister in the police court on a common vulgar charge?"

Professor Babwater said he could well imagine it—it was where most of them should be; but Colonel Raden agreed that the decencies had somehow to be preserved, even at the cost of a certain amount of humbug. "But, excuse me," he added, "if I fail to see what good an occasional sentence of six months hard would do to public life."

"I don't want it to happen," said his host, who was inspired by his own Johannisberg, "but I'd like to think it *could* happen. The permanent possibility of it would supple the minds of your legislators. It would do this old country a power of good if now and then a Cabinet Minister took to brawling and went to jail."

It was a topic which naturally interested Sir Archie, but the theories of Mr Bandicott passed by him unheeded. For his seat at the table gave him a view of the darkening glen, and he was aware that on that stage a stirring drama was being enacted. His host could see nothing, for it was behind him; the Professor would have had to screw his head round; to Sir Archie alone was vouchsafed a clear prospect. Janet saw that he was gazing abstractedly out of the window, but she did not realise that his eyes were strained and every nerve in him excitedly alive. . . .

For suddenly into his field of vision had darted a man. He was on the far side of the Larrig, running hard, and behind him, at a distance of some forty yards, followed another. At first he thought it was Leithen, but even in the dusk it was plain that it was a shorter man—younger, too, he looked, and of a notable activity. He was gaining on his pursuers, when the chase went out of sight. . . . Then Sir Archie heard a far-away whistling, and would have given much to fling open the window and look out. . . .

Five minutes passed and again the runner appeared— this time dripping wet and on the near side. Clearly not Leithen, for he wore a white sweater, which was a garment unknown to the Crask wardrobe. He must have been headed off up-stream, and had doubled back. That way lay danger, and Sir Archie longed to warn him, for his route would bring him close to the peopled appendages of Strathlarrig House. . . . Even as he stared he saw what must mean the end, for two figures appeared for one second on the extreme left of his range of vision, and in front of the fugitive. He was running into their arms!

Sir Archie seized his glass of the blue-labelled Johannisberg, swallowed the wine the wrong way, and promptly choked.

When the Hispana crossed the Bridge of Larrig His Majesty's late Attorney-General was modestly concealed in a bush of broom on the Crask side, from which he could watch the sullen stretches of the Lang Whang. He was carefully dressed for the part in a pair of Wattie Lithgow's old trousers much too short for him, a waistcoat and jacket which belonged to Sime the butler and which had been made about the year 1890, and a vulgar flannel shirt borrowed from Shapp. He was innocent of a collar, he had not shaved for two days, and as he had forgotten to have his hair cut before leaving London his locks were of a disreputable length. Last, he had a shocking old hat of Sir Archie's from which the lining had long since gone. His hands were sun-burned and grubby, and he had removed his signet-ring. A light ten-foot greenheart rod lay beside him, already put up, and to the tapered line was fixed a tapered cast ending in a strange little cocked fly. As he waited he was busy oiling fly and line.

His glass showed him an empty haugh, save for the figure of Jimsie at the far end close to the Wood of Larrigmore. The sun-warmed waters of the river drowsed in the long dead stretches, curled at rare intervals by the faintest western breeze. The banks were crisp green turf, scarcely broken by a boulder, but five yards from them the moss began—a wilderness of hags and tussocks. Somewhere in its depths he knew that Benjie lay coiled like an adder, waiting on events.

Leithen's plan, like all great strategy, was simple. Everything depended on having Jimsie out of sight of the Lang Whang for half an hour. Given that, he believed he might kill a salmon. He had marked out a pool where in the evening fish were usually stirring, one of those irrational haunts which no piscatorial psychologist has ever explained. If he could fish fine and far, he might cover it from a spot below a high bank where only the top of his rod would be visible to watchers at a distance. Unfortunately, that spot was on the other side of the stream. With such tackle, landing a salmon would be a critical business, but there was one chance in ten that it might be accomplished; Benjie would be at hand to conceal the fish, and he himself would disappear silently into the Crask thickets. But every step bristled with horrid dangers. Jimsie might be faithful to his post—in which case it was hopeless; he might find the salmon dour, or a fish might break him in the landing, or Jimsie might return to find him brazenly tethered to forbidden game. It was no good thinking about it. On one thing he was decided: if he were caught, he would not try to escape. That would mean retreat in the direction of Crask, and an exploration of the Crask coverts would assuredly reveal what must at all costs be concealed. No. He would go quietly into captivity, and trust to his base appearance to be let off with a drubbing.

As he waited, watching the pools turn from gold to bronze, as the sun sank behind the Glenraden peaks, he suffered the inevitable reaction. The absurdities seemed huge as mountains, the difficulties innumerable as the waves of the sea. There remained less than an hour in which there would be sufficient light to fish—Jimsie was immovable (he had just lit his pipe and was sitting in meditation on a big stone)—every moment

115

the Larrig waters were cooling with the chill of evening. Leithen consulted his watch, and found it half-past eight. He had lost his wrist-watch, and had brought his hunter, attached to a thin gold chain. That was foolish, so he slipped the chain from his button-hole and drew it through the arm-hole of his waistcoat.

Suddenly he rose to his feet, for things were happening at the far side of the haugh. Jimsie stood in an attitude of expectation—he seemed to be hearing something far up-stream. Leithen heard it too, the cry of excited men. . . . Jimsie stood on one foot for a moment in doubt; then he turned and doubled towards the Wood of Larrigmore. . , . The gallant Crossby had got to business and was playing hare to the hounds inside the park wall. If human nature had not changed, Leithen thought, the whole force would presently join the chase—Angus and Lennox and Jimsie and Dave and doubtless many volunteers. Heaven send fleetness and wind to the South London Harrier, for it was his duty to occupy the interest of every male in Strathlarrig till such time as he subsided with angry expostulation into captivity.

The road was empty, the valley was deserted, when Leithen raced across the bridge and up the south side of the river. It was not two hundred yards to his chosen stand, a spit of gravel below a high bank at the tail of a long pool. Close to the other bank, nearly thirty yards off, was the shelf where fish lay of an evening. He tested the water with his hand, and its temperature was at least 60^0. His theory, which he had learned long ago from the aged Bostonian, was that under such conditions some subconscious memory revived in salmon of their early days as parr when they fed on surface insects, and that they could be made to take a dry fly.

He got out his line to the required length with half a dozen casts in the air, and then put his fly three feet above the spot where a salmon was wont to lie. It was a curious type of cast, which he had been practising lately in the early morning, for by an adroit check he made the fly alight in a curl, so that it floated for a second or two with the leader in a straight line away from

116

it. In this way he believed that the most suspicious fish would see nothing to alarm him, nothing but a hapless insect derelict on the water.

Sir Archie had spoken truth in describing Leithen to Wattie Lithgow as an artist. His long, straight, delicate casts were art indeed. Like thistledown the fly dropped, like thistledown it floated over the head of the salmon, but like thistledown it was disregarded. There was indeed a faint stirring of curiosity. From where he stood Leithen could see that slight ruffling of the surface which means an observant fish. . . .

Already ten minutes had been spent in this barren art. The crisis craved other measures.

His new policy meant a short line, so with infinite stealth and care Leithen waded up the side of the water, sometimes treading precarious ledges of peat, sometimes waist deep in mud and pond-weed, till he was within twenty feet of the fishing-ground. Here he had not the high bank for a shelter, and would have been sadly conspicuous to Jimsie, had that sentinel remained at his post. He crouched low and cast as before with the same curl just ahead of the chosen spot.

But now his tactics were different. So soon as the fly had floated past where he believed the fish to be, he sank it with a dexterous twist of the rod-point, possible only with a short line. The fly was no longer a winged thing; drawn away under water, it roused in the salmon early memories of succulent nymphs. . . . At the first cast there was a slight swirl, which meant that a fish near the surface had turned to follow the lure. The second cast the line straightened and moved swiftly upstream.

Leithen had killed in his day many hundreds of salmon—once in Norway a notable beast of fifty-five pounds. But no salmon he had ever hooked had stirred in his breast such excitement as this modest fellow of eight pounds. " ' 'Tis not so wide as a church-door,' " he reflected with Mercutio, " 'but 'twill suffice'—if I can only land him." But a dry-fly cast and a ten-foot rod are a frail wherewithal for killing a fish against time. With his ordinary fifteen-footer and gut of

117

moderate strength he could have brought the little salmon to grass in five minutes, but now there was immense risk of a break, and a break would mean that the whole enterprise had failed. He dared not exert pressure; on the other hand, he could not follow the fish except by making himself conspicuous on the greensward. Worst of all, he had at the best ten minutes for the job.

Thirty yards off an otter slid into the water. Leithen wished he was King of the Otters, as in the Highland tale, to summon the brute to his aid.

The ten minutes had lengthened to fifteen—nine hundred seconds of heart-disease—when, wet to the waist, he got his pocket-gaff into the salmon's side and drew it on to the spit of gravel where he had started fishing. A dozen times he thought he had lost, and once when the fish ran straight up the pool his line was carried out to its last yard of backing. He gave thanks to high Heaven, when, as he landed it, he observed that the fly had all but lost its hold and in another minute would have been free. By such narrow margins are great deeds accomplished.

He snapped the cast from the line and buried it in mud. Then cautiously he raised his head above the bank. The gloaming was gathering fast, and so far as he could see the haugh was still empty. Pushing his rod along the ground, he scrambled on to the turf.

Then he had a grievous shock. Jimsie had reappeared, and he was in full view of him. Moreover, there were two men on bicycles coming up the road, who, with the deplorable instinct of human nature, would be certain to join in any pursuit. He was on turf as short as a lawn, cumbered with a tell-tale rod and a poached salmon. The friendly hags were a dozen yards off, and before he could reach them his damning baggage would be noted.

At this supreme moment he had an inspiration, derived from the memory of the otter. To get out his knife, cut a ragged wedge from the fish, and roll it in his handkerchief was the work of five seconds. To tilt the rod over the bank so that it lay in the deep shadow was the work of three more. . . . Jimsie had

118

seen him, for a wild cry came down the stream, a cry which brought the cyclists off their machines and set them staring in his direction. Leithen dropped his gaff after the rod, and began running towards the Larrig bridge—slowly, limpingly, like a frightened man with no resolute purpose of escape. And as he ran he prayed that Benjie from the deeps of the moss had seen what had been done and drawn the proper inference.

It was a bold bluff, for he had decided to make the salmon evidence for, not against him. He hobbled down the bank, looking over his shoulder often as if in terror, and almost ran into the arms of the cyclists, who, warned by Jimsie's yells, were waiting to intercept him. He dodged them, however, and cut across to the road, for he had seen that Jimsie had paused and had noted the salmon lying blatantly on the sward, a silver splash in the twilight. Leithen doubled up the road as if going towards Strathlarrig, and Jimsie, the fleet of foot, did not catch up with him till almost on the edge of the Wood of Larrigmore. The cyclists, who had remounted, arrived at the same moment to find a wretched muddy tramp in the grip of a stalwart but breathless gillie.

"I tell ye I was daein' nae harm," the tramp whined. "I was walkin' up the water-side—there's nae law to keep a body frae walkin' up a water-side when there's nae fence—and I seen an auld otter killin' a saumon. The fish is there still to prove I'm no leein'."

"There is a fush, but you wass thinkin' to steal the fush, and you would have had it in your breeks if I hadna seen you. That is poachin', ma man, and you will come up to Strathlarrig. The master said that anyone goin' near the watter was to be lockit up, and you will be lockit up. You can tell all the lees you like in the mornin'."

Then a thought struck Jimsie. He wanted the salmon, for the subject of otters in the Larrig had been a matter of dispute between him and Angus, and here was evidence for his own view.

"Would you two gentlemen oblige me by watchin' this man while I rin back and get the fush? Bash him on the head if he offers to rin."

119

The cyclists, who were journalists out to enjoy the evening air, willingly agreed, but Leithen showed no wish to escape. He begged a fag in a beggar's whine, and, since he seemed peaceable, the two kept a good distance for fear of infection. He stood making damp streaks in the dusty road, a pitiable specimen of humanity, for his original get-up was not improved by the liquefaction of his clothes and a generous legacy of slimy peat. He seemed to be nervous, which indeed he was, for if Benjie had not seized his chance he was utterly done, and if Jimsie should light upon his rod he was gravely compromised.

But when Jimsie returned in a matter of ten minutes he was empty-handed.

"I never kenned the like," he proclaimed. "That otter has come back and gotten the fush. Ach, the maleecious brute!"

The rest of Leithen's progress was not triumphant. He was conducted to the Strathlarrig lodge, where Angus, whose temper and wind had alike been ruined by the pursuit of Crossby, laid savage hands upon him, and frog-marched him to the back premises. The head-keeper scarcely heeded Jimsie's tale. "Ach, ye poachin' va-aga-bond. It is the jyle ye'll get," he roared, for Angus was in a mood which could only be relieved by violence of speech and action. Rumbling Gaelic imprecations, he hustled his prisoner into an outhouse, which had once been a larder and was now a supplementary garage, slammed and locked the door, and, as a final warning, kicked it viciously with his foot, as if to signify what awaited the culprit when the time came to sit on his case.

Sir Archie, if not a skeleton at the feast, was no better than a shadow. The fragment of drama which he had witnessed had rudely divorced his mind from the intelligent conversation of Mr Bandicott, he was no longer slightly irritated by Mr Claybody, he forgot even the attractions of Janet. What was going on in that twilit vale? Lady Maisie's Pool had still a shimmer of gold, but the woods were now purple and the waterside turf a dim amethyst, the colour of the darkening sky.

120

All sound had ceased except the rare cry of a bird from the hill, and the hoot of a wandering owl. . . . Crossby had beyond doubt been taken, but where was Leithen?

He was recalled to his surroundings by Janet's announcement that Mr Bandicott proposed to take them all in his car to the meeting at Muirtown.

"Oh, I say," he pleaded, "I'd much rather you didn't. I haven't a notion how to speak—no experience, you see—only about the third time I've opened my mouth in public. I'll make an awful ass of myself, and I'd much rather my friends didn't see it. If I know you're in the audience, Miss Janet, I won't be able to get a word out."

Mr Bandicott was sympathetic. "Take my advice, and do not attempt to write a speech and learn it by heart. Fill yourself with your subject, but do not prepare anything except the first sentence and the last. You'll find the words come easily when you once begin—if you have something you really want to say."

"That's the trouble—I haven't. I'm goin' to speak about foreign policy, and I'm dashed if I can remember which treaty is which, and what the French are making a fuss about, or why the old Boche can't pay. And I keep on mixing up Poincaré and Mussolini. . . . I'm goin' to write it all down, and if I'm stuck I'll fish out the paper and read it. I'm told there are fellows in the Cabinet who do that when they're cornered."

"Don't stick too close to the paper," the Colonel advised. "The Highlander objects to sermons read to him, and he may not like a read speech."

"Whatever he does I'm sure Sir Archibald will be most enlightening," Mr Bandicott said politely. "Also I want to hear Lord Lamancha. We think rather well of that young man in America. How do you rate him here?"

Mr Claybody, as a habitant of the great world, replied. "Very high in his own line. He's the old-fashioned type of British statesman, and people trust him. The trouble about him and his kind is that they're a little too far removed from the ordinary man—they've been too cosseted and set on a pedestal

121

all their lives. They don't know how to handle democracy. You can't imagine Lamancha rubbing shoulders with Tom, Dick and Harry."

"Oh, come!" Sir Archie broke in. "In the war he started as a captain in a yeomanry regiment, and he commanded a pretty rough Australian push in Palestine. His men fairly swore by him."

"I daresay," said the other coldly. "The war doesn't count for my argument, and Australians are not quite what I mean."

The butler, who was offering liqueurs, was seen to speak confidentially to Junius, who looked towards his father, made as if to speak, and thought better of it. The elder Mr Bandicott was once more holding the table.

"My archaeological studies," he said, "and my son's devotion to sport are apt to circumscribe the interest of my visits to this country. I do not spend more than a couple of days in London, and when I am there the place is empty. Sometimes I regret that I have not attempted to see more of English society in recent years, for there are many figures in it I would like to meet. There are some acquaintances, too, that I should be delighted to revive. Do you know Sir Edward Leithen, Mr Claybody? He was recently, I think, the British Attorney-General."

Mr Claybody nodded. "I know him very well. We have just briefed him in a big case."

"Sir Edward Leithen visited us two years ago as the guest of our Bar Association. His address was one of the most remarkable I have ever listened to. It was on John Marshall—the finest tribute ever paid to that great man, and one which I venture to say no American could have equalled. I had very little talk with him, but what I had impressed me profoundly with the breadth of his outlook and the powers of his mind. Yes, I should like to meet Sir Edward Leithen again."

The company had risen and were moving towards the drawing-room.

"Now I wonder," Mr Claybody was saying. "I heard that Leithen was somewhere in Scotland. I wonder if I could get him up for a few days to Haripol. Then I could bring him over here."

An awful joy fell upon Sir Archie's soul. He realised anew the unplumbed preposterousness of life.

Ere they reached the drawing-room Junius took Agatha aside.

"Look here, Miss Agatha, I want you to help me. The gillies have been a little too active. They've gathered in some wretched hobo they found looking at the river, and they've annexed a journalist who stuck his nose inside the gates. It's the journalist that's worrying me. From his card he seems to be rather a swell in his way—represents the *Monitor* and writes for my father's New York paper. He gave the gillies a fine race for their money, and now he's sitting cursing in the garage and vowing every kind of revenge. It won't do to antagonise the Press, so we'd better let him out and grovel to him, if he wants apologies. . . . The fact is, we're not in a very strong position, fending off the newspapers from Harald Blacktooth because of this ridiculous John Macnab. If you could let the fellow out it would be casting oil upon troubled waters. You could smooth him down far better than me."

"But what about the other? A hobo, you say! That's a tramp, isn't it?"

"Oh, tell Angus to let him out too. Here are the keys of both garages. I don't want to turn this place into a lock-up. Angus won't be pleased, but we have to keep a sharp watch for John Macnab to-morrow, and it's bad tactics in a campaign to cumber yourself with prisoners."

The two threaded mysterious passages and came out into a moonlit stable-yard. Junius handed the girl a great electric torch. "Tell the fellow we eat dirt for our servants' officiousness. Offer him supper, and—I tell you what—ask him to lunch the day after to-morrow. No, that's Muirtown day. Find out his address and we'll write to him and give him first chop at the Viking. Blame it all on the gillies."

Agatha unlocked the door of the big garage and to her surprise found it brilliantly lit with electric light. Mr Crossby was sitting in the driver's seat of a large motor-car, smoking a pipe and composing a story for his paper. At the sight of Agatha he descended hastily.

"We're so sorry," said the girl. "It's all been a stupid mistake. But, you know, you shouldn't have run away. Mr Bandicott had to make rules to keep off poachers, and you ought to have stopped and explained who you were."

To this charming lady in the grass-green gown Mr Crossby's manner was debonair and reassuring.

"No apology is needed. It wasn't in the least the gillies' blame. I wanted some exercise, and I had my fun with them. One of the young ones has a very pretty turn of speed. But I oughtn't to have done it—I quite see that—with everybody here on edge about this John Macnab. Have I your permission to go?"

"Indeed you have. Mr Bandicott asked me to apologise most humbly. You're quite free unless—unless you'd like to have supper before you go."

Mr Crossby excused himself, and did not stay upon the order of his going. He knew nothing of the fate of his colleague, and hoped that he might pick up news from Benjie in the neighbourhood of the Wood of Larrigmore.

The other garage stood retired in the lee of a clump of pines—a rude, old-fashioned place, which generally housed the station lorry. Agatha, rather than face the disappointed Angus, decided to complete the task of jail-delivery herself. She had trouble with the lock, and when the door opened she looked into a pit of darkness scarcely lightened by the outer glow of moonshine. She flashed the torch into the interior and saw, seated on a stack of petrol tins, the figure of the tramp.

Leithen, who had been wondering how he was to find a bed in that stony place, beheld the apparition with amazement. He guessed that it was one of the Miss Radens, for he knew that they were dining at Strathlarrig. As he stood sheepishly before her his wits suffered a dislocation which drove out of his head the remembrance of the part he had assumed.

"Mr Bandicott sent me to tell you that you can go away," the girl said.

"Thank you very much," said Leithen in his ordinary voice.

Now in the scramble up the river bank and in the rough handling of Angus his garments had become disarranged, and his watch had swung out of his pocket. In adjusting it in the garage he had put it back in its normal place, so that the chain showed on Sime's ancient waistcoat. From it depended one of those squat little gold shields which are the badge of athletic prowess at a famous school. As he stood in the light of her torch Agatha noted this shield, and knew what it signified. Also his tone when he spoke had startled her.

"Oh," she cried, "you were at Eton?"

Leithen was for a moment nonplussed. He thought of a dozen lies, and then decided on qualified truth.

"Yes," he murmured shamefacedly. "Long ago I was at Eton."

The girl flushed with embarrassed sympathy.

"What—what brought you to this?" she murmured.

"Folly," said Leithen, recovering himself. "Drink and such-like. I have had a lot of bad luck but I've mostly myself to blame."

"You're only a tramp now?" Angels might have envied the melting sadness of her voice.

"At present. Sometimes I get a job, but I can't hold it down." Leithen was warming to his work, and his tones were a subtle study in dilapidated gentility.

"Can't anything be done?" Agatha asked, twining her pretty hands.

"Nothing," was the dismal answer. "I'm past helping. Let me go, please, and forget you ever saw me."

"But can't papa . . . won't you tell me your name or where we can find you?"

"My present name is not my own. Forget about me, my dear young lady. The life isn't so bad. . . . I'm as happy as I deserve to be. I want to be off, for I don't like to stumble upon gentlefolks."

She stood aside to let him pass, noting the ruin of his clothes, his dirty unshaven face, the shameless old hat that he raised to her. Then, melancholy and reflective, she returned to Junius. She could not give away one of her own class, so, when Junius asked her about the tramp, she only shrugged her white shoulders. "A miserable creature. I hope Angus wasn't too rough with him. He looked as if a puff of wind would blow him to pieces."

.　　.　　.　　.　　.　　.

Ten minutes later Leithen, having unobtrusively climbed the park wall and so escaped the attention of Mactavish at the lodge, was trotting at a remarkable pace for a tramp down the road to the Larrig Bridge. Once on the Crask side, he stopped to reconnoitre. Crossby called softly to him from the covert, and with Crossby was Benjie.

"I've gotten the saumon," said the latter, "and your rod and gaff too. Hae ye the bit you howkit out o' the fush?"

Leithen produced his bloody handkerchief.

"Now for supper, Benjie, my lad," he cried. "Come along, Crossby, and we'll drink the health of John Macnab."

The journalist shook his head. "I'm off to finish my story. The triumphant return of Harald Blacktooth is going to convulse these islands to-morrow."

8

SIR ARCHIE IS INSTRUCTED IN
THE CONDUCT OF LIFE

EARLY next morning, when the great door of Strathlarrig House was opened, and the maids had begun their work, Oliphant, the butler—a stately man who had been trained in a ducal family—crossed the hall to reconnoitre the outer world. There he found an under-housemaid nursing a strange package which she averred she had found on the doorstep. It was some two feet long, swathed in brown paper, and attached to its string was a letter inscribed to Mr Junius Bandicott.

The parcel was clammy and Oliphant handled it gingerly. He cut the cord, disentangled the letter, and revealed an oblong of green rushes bound with string. The wrapping must have been insecure, for something forthwith slipped from the rushes and flopped on the marble floor, revealing to Oliphant's disgusted eyes a small salmon, blue and stiff in death.

At that moment Junius, always an early bird, came whistling downstairs. So completely was he convinced of the inviolability of the Strathlarrig waters that the spectacle caused him no foreboding.

"What are you flinging fish about for, Oliphant?" he asked cheerfully.

The butler presented him with the envelope. He opened it and extracted a dirty half sheet of notepaper, on which was printed in capitals "With the compliments of John Macnab."

Amazement, chagrin, amusement followed each other on Junius's open countenance. Then he picked up the fish and marched out-of-doors shouting "Angus" at the top of a notably powerful voice. The sound brought the scared face of Professor Babwater to his bedroom window.

Angus, who had been up since four, appeared from Lady

Maisie's Pool, where he had been contemplating the waters. His vigil had not improved his appearance or his temper, for his eye was red and choleric and his beard was wild as a mountain goat's. He cast one look at the salmon, surmised the truth, and held up imploring hands to Heaven.

"John Macnab!" said Junius sternly. "What have you got to say to that?"

Angus had nothing audible to say. He was handling the fish with feverish hands and peering at its jaws, and presently under his fingers a segment fell out.

"That fush was cleekit," observed Lennox, who had come up. "It was never catched with a flee."

"Ye're a leear," Angus roared. "Just tak a look at the mouth of it. There's the mark of the huke, ye gommeril. The fush was took wi' a rod and line."

"You may reckon it was," observed Junius. "I trust John Macnab to abide by the rules of the game."

Suddenly light seemed to break in on Angus's soul. He bellowed for Jimsie, who was placidly making his way towards the group at the door, lighting his pipe as he went.

"Look at that, James Mackenzie. Aye, look at it. Feast your een on it. You wass tellin' me there wass otters in the Larrig and I said there wass not. You wass tellin' me there wass an otter had a fush last night at the Lang Whang. There's your otter and be damned to ye!"

Jimsie, slow of comprehension, rubbed his eyes.

"Where wass you findin' the fush? Aye, it's the one I seen last night. That otter must be wrang in the heid."

"It is not wrang in the heid. It's you that are wrang in the heid, James Mackenzie. The otter is a ver-ra clever man, and its name will be John Macnab." Slowly enlightenment dawned on Jimsie's mind.

"He wass the tramp," he ingeminated. "He wass the tramp."

"And he's still lockit up," Angus cried joyfully. "Wait till I get my hands on him." He was striding off for the garage when a word from Junius held him back.

"You won't find him there. I gave orders last night to let him go. You know, Angus, you told me he was only a tramp that had been seen walking up the river."

"We will catch him yet," cried the vindictive head-keeper. "Get you on your bicycle, Jimsie, and away after him. He'll be on the Muirtown road. . . . There's just the one road he can travel."

"No, you don't," said Junius. "I don't want him here. He has beaten us fairly in a match of wits, and the business is finished."

"But the thing's no possible," Jimsie moaned. "The skeeliest fisher would not take a saumon in the Lang Whang with a flee. . . . And I wasna away many meenutes. . . . And the tramp was a poor shilpit body—not like a fisher or any kind of gentleman at all—at all. . . . And he hadna a rod. . . . The thing's no possible."

"Well, who else could it be?"

"I think it was the Deevil."

Jimsie, cross-examined, went over the details of his evening's experience.

"The journalist may have been in league with him—or he may not," Junius reflected. "Anyway, I'll tackle Mr Crossby. I want to find out what I can about this remarkable sportsman."

"You will not find out anything at all, at all," said Angus morosely. "For I tell ye, sir, Jimsie is right in one thing—Macnab is not a man—he is the Deevil."

"Then we needn't be ashamed of being beat by him. . . . Look here, you men. We've lost, but you've had an uncomforable time these last twenty-four hours. And I'm going to give you what I promised you if we won out. I reckon the market price of salmon is not more than fifty cents a pound. Macnab has paid about thirty dollars a pound for this fish, so we've a fair margin on the deal."

Mr Acheson Bandicott received the news with composure, if not with relief. Now he need no longer hold the correspondents at arm's length but could summon them to his presence and enlarge on Harald Blacktooth. His father's equanimity cast whatever balm was needed upon Junius's wounded pride, and presently he saw nothing in the affair but comedy. His thoughts turned to Glenraden. It might be well for him to announce in person that the defences of Strathlarrig had failed.

On his way he called at the post-office where Agatha had told him that Crossby was lodging. He wanted a word with the journalist, who clearly must have been *particeps criminis,* and as he could offer as bribe the first full tale of Harald Blacktooth (to be unfolded before the other correspondents arrived for luncheon) he hoped to acquire a story in return. But, according to the post-mistress, Mr Crossby had gone. He had sat up most of the night writing, and, without waiting for breakfast, had paid his bill, strapped on his ruck-sack and departed on his bicycle.

Junius found the Raden family on the lawn, and with them Archie Roylance.

"Got up early to go over my speech for to-morrow," the young man explained. "I'm gettin' the dashed thing by heart—only way to avoid regrettable incidents. I started off down the hill repeatin' my eloquence, and before I knew I was at Glenraden gates, so I thought I'd come in and pass the time of day. . . . Jolly interestin' dinner last night, Bandicott. I liked your old Professor. . . . Any news of John Macnab?"

"There certainly is. He has us beat to a frazzle. This morning there was a salmon on the doorstep presented with his compliments."

The effect of this announcement was instant and stupendous. The Colonel called upon his gods. "Not killed fair? It's a stark impossibility, sir. You had the water guarded like the Bank of England." Archie expressed like suspicions; Agatha was sad and sympathetic, Janet amused and covertly joyful.

"I reckon it was fair enough fishing," Junius went on. "I've been trying to puzzle the thing out, and this is what I made of it. Macnab was in league with one of those pressmen, who started out to trespass inside the park and drew off all the watchers in

130

pursuit, including the man at the Lang Whang. He had them hunting for about half an hour, and in that time Macnab killed his fish. . . . He must be a dandy at the game, too, to get a salmon in that dead water. . . . Jimsie—that's the man who was supposed to watch the Lang Whang—returned before he could get away with the beast, so what does the fellow do but dig a bit out of the fish and leave it on the bank, while he lures Jimsie to chase him. Jimsie saw the fish and put it down to an otter, and by and by caught the man up the road. There must have been an accomplice in hiding, for when Jimsie went back to pick up the salmon it had disappeared. The fellow, who looked like a hobo, was shut up in a garage, and after dinner we let him go, for we had nothing against him, and now he is rejoicing somewhere at our simplicity. . . . It was a mighty clever bit of work, and I'm not ashamed to be beaten by that class of artist. I hoped to get hold of the pressman and find out something, but the pressman seems to have leaked out of the landscape."

"Was that tramp John Macnab?" Agatha asked in an agitated voice.

"None other. You let him out, Miss Agatha. What was he like? I can't get proper hold of Jimsie's talk."

"Oh, I should have guessed," the girl lamented. "For, of course, I saw he was a gentleman. He was in horrible old clothes, but he had an Eton shield on his watch-chain. He seemed to be ashamed to remember it. He said he had come down in the world—through drink!"

Archie struggled hard with the emotions evoked by this description of an abstemious personage currently believed to be making an income of forty thousand pounds.

"Then we've both seen him," Janet cried. "Describe him, Agatha. Was he youngish and big, and fair-haired, and sunburnt? Had he blue eyes?"

"No-o. He wasn't like that. He was about papa's height, and rather slim, I think. He was very dirty and hadn't shaved, but I should say he was sallow, and his eyes—well, they were certainly not blue."

"Are you certain? You only saw him in the dark."

"Yes, quite certain. I had a big torch which lit up his whole figure. Now I come to think of it, he had a striking face—he looked like somebody very clever—a judge perhaps. That should have made me suspicious, but I was so shocked to see such a downfall that I didn't think about it."

Janet looked wildly around her. "Then there are two John Macnabs."

"Angus thinks he is the Devil," said Junius.

"It looks as if he were a syndicate," said Archie, who felt that some remark was expected of him.

"Well, I'm not complaining," said Junius. "And now we're off the stage, and can watch the play from the boxes. I hope you won't be shocked, sir, but I wouldn't break my heart if John Macnab got the goods from Haripol."

"By Gad, no!" cried the Colonel. "'Pon my soul, if I could get in touch with the fellow I'd offer to help him—though he'd probably be too much of a sportsman to let me. That young Claybody wants taking down a peg or two. He's the most insufferably assured young prig I ever met in my life."

"He looked the kind of chap who might turn nasty," Sir Archie observed.

"How do you mean?" Junius asked. "Get busy with a gun—that sort of thing?"

"Lord, no. The Claybodys are not likely to start shootin'. But they're as rich as Jews, and they're capable of hirin' prize-fighters or puttin' a live wire round the forest. Or I'll tell you what they might do—they might drive every beast on Haripol over the marches and keep 'em out for three days. It would wreck the ground for the season, but they wouldn't mind that—the old man can't get up the hills and the young 'un don't want to."

"Agatha, my dear," said her father, "we ought to return the Claybody's call. Perhaps Mr Junius would drive us over there in his car this afternoon. For, of course, you'll stay to luncheon, Bandicott—and you, too, Roylance."

Sir Archie stayed to luncheon; he also stayed to tea; and

between these meals he went through a surprising experience. For, after the others had started for Haripol, Janet and he drifted aimlessly towards the Raden bridge and then upward through the pinewoods on the road to Carnmore. The strong sun was tempered by the flickering shade of the trees, and, as the road wound itself out of the crannies of the woods to the bare ridges, light wandering winds cooled the cheek, and, mingled with the fragrance of heather and the rooty smell of bogs, came a salty freshness from the sea. The wide landscape was as luminous as April—a bad presage for the weather, since the Haripol peaks, which in September should have been dim in a mulberry haze, stood out sharp like cameos. The two did not talk much, for they were getting beyond the stage where formal conversation is felt to be necessary. Sir Archie limped along at a round pace, which was easily matched by the girl at his side. Both would instinctively halt now and then, and survey the prospect without speaking, and both felt that these pregnant silences were bringing them very near to one another.

At last the track ran out in screes, and from a bald summit they were looking down on the first of the Carnmore corries. Janet seated herself on a mossy ledge of rock and looked back into the Raden glen, which from that altitude had the appearance of an enclosed garden. The meadows of the lower haugh lay green in the sun, the setting of pines by some freak of light was a dark and cloudy blue, and the little castle rose in the midst of the trees with a startling brightness like carven marble. The picture was as exquisite and strange as an illumination in a missal.

"Gad, what a place to live in!" Sir Archie exclaimed.

The girl, who had been gazing at the scene with her chin in her hands, turned on him eyes which were suddenly wistful and rather sad. As contrasted with her sister's, Janet's face had a fine hard finish which gave it a brilliancy like an eager boy's. But now a cloud-wrack had been drawn over the sun.

"We've lived there," she said, "since Harald Black-tooth—at least papa says so. But the end is very near now. We are the last of the Radens. And that is as it should be, you know."

133

"I'm hanged if I see that," Sir Archie began, but the girl interrupted.

"Yes, it is as it should be. The old life of the Highlands is going, and people like ourselves must go with it. There's no reason why we should continue to exist. We've long ago lost our justification."

"D'you mean to say that fellows like Claybody have more right to be here?"

"Yes. I think they have, because they're fighters and we're only survivals. They will disappear, too, unless they learn their lesson. . . . You see, for a thousand years we have been going on here, and other people like us, but we only endured because we were alive. We have the usual conventional motto on our coat of arms—*Pro Deo et Rege*—a Heralds' College invention. But our Gaelic motto was very different—it was 'Sons of Dogs, come and I will give you flesh.' As long as we lived up to that we flourished, but as soon as we settled down and went to sleep and became *rentiers* we were bound to decay. . . . My cousins at Glenaicill were just the same. Their motto was 'What I have I hold,' and while they remembered it they were great people. But when they stopped holding they went out like a candle, and the last of them is now living in St Malo and a Lancashire cotton-spinner owns the place. . . . When we had to fight hard for our possessions all the time, and give flesh to the sons of dogs who were our clan, we were strong men and women. There was a Raden with Robert Bruce—he fell with Douglas in the pilgrimage to the Holy Sepulchre—and a Raden died beside the King at Flodden—and Radens were in everything that happened in the old days in Scotland and France. But civilisation killed them—they couldn't adapt themselves to it. Somehow the fire went out of the blood, and they became vegetables. Their only claim was the right of property, which is no right at all."

"That's what the Bolsheviks say," said the puzzled Sir Archie.

"Then I'm a Bolshevik. Nobody in the world to-day has a right to anything which he can't justify. That's not politics, it's the way nature works. Whatever you've got—rank or power or fame or money—you've got to justify it, and keep on justifying it, or go under. No law on earth can buttress up a thing which nature means to decay."

"D'you know that sounds to me pretty steep doctrine?"

"No, it isn't. It isn't doctrine, and it isn't politics, it's common sense. I don't mean that we want some silly government redistributing everybody's property. I mean that people should realise that whatever they've got they hold under a perpetual challenge, and they are bound to meet that challenge. Then we'll have living creatures instead of mummies."

Sir Archie stroked his chin thoughtfully. "I daresay there's a lot in that. But what would Colonel Raden say to it?"

"He would say I was a bandit. And yet he would probably agree with me in the end. Agatha wouldn't, of course. She adores decay—sad old memories and lost causes and all the rest of it. She's a sentimentalist, and she'll marry Junius and go to America, where everybody is sentimental, and be the sweetest thing in the Western hemisphere, and live happy ever after. I'm quite different. I believe I'm kind, but I'm certainly hard-hearted. I suppose it's Harald Blacktooth coming out."

Janet had got off her perch, and was standing a yard from Sir Archie, her hat in her hand and the light wind ruffling her hair. The young man, who had no skill in analysing his feelings, felt obscurely that she fitted most exquisitely into the picture of rock and wood and water, that she was, in very truth, a part of his clean elemental world of the hill-tops.

"What about yourself?" she asked. "In the words of Mr Bandicott, are you going to make good?"

She asked the question with such an air of frank comradeship that Sir Archie was in no way embarrassed. Indeed he was immensely delighted.

"I hope so," he said. "But I don't know. . . . I'm a bit of a slacker. There doesn't seem much worth doing since the war."

"What nonsense! You find a thousand things worth doing, but they're not enough—and they're not big enough. Do you

135

mean to say you want to hang up your hat at your age and go to sleep? You need to be challenged."

"I expect I do," he murmured.

"Well, *I* challenge you. You're fit and you're young, and you did extraordinarily well in the war, and you've hosts of friends, and—and—you're well off, aren't you?"

"Pretty fair. You see, I had a long minority, and—oh yes, I've far more money than I want."

"There you are. I challenge you. You're bound to justify what you've got. I won't have you idling away your life till you end as the kind of lean brown old gentleman in a bowler hat that one sees at Newmarket. It's a very nice type, but it's not good enough for you, and I won't have it. You must not be a dilettante pottering about with birds and a little sport and a little politics."

Sir Archie had been preached at occasionally in his life, but never quite in this way. He was preposterously pleased and also a little solemnised.

"I'm quite serious about politics."

"I wonder," said Janet, smiling. "I don't mean scraping into Parliament, but real politics—putting the broken pieces together, you know. Papa and the rest of our class want to treat politics like another kind of property in which they have a vested interest. But it won't do—not in the world we live in to-day. If you're going to do any good you must feel the challenge and be ready to meet it. And then you must become yourself a challenger. You must be like John Macnab."

Sir Archie stared.

"I don't mean that I want you to make poaching wagers like John. You can't live in a place and play those tricks with your neighbours. But I want you to follow what Mr Bandicott would call the 'John Macnab proposition.' It's so good for everybody concerned. Papa has never had so much fun out of his forest as in the days he was repelling invasion, and even Mr Junius found a new interest in the Larrig. . . . I'm all for property, if you can defend it; but there are too many fatted calves in the world."

136

Sir Archie suddenly broke into loud laughter.

"Most people tell me I'm too mad to do much good in anything. But you say I'm not mad enough. Well, I'm all for challengin' the fatted calves, but I don't fancy that's the road that leads to the Cabinet. More like the jail, with a red flag firmly clenched in my manly hand."

The girl laughed too. "Papa says that the man who doesn't give a damn for anybody can do anything he likes in the world. Most people give many damns for all kinds of foolish things. Mr Claybody, for example—his smart friends, like Lord Lamancha and the Attorney-General—what is his name?— Leithen?—and his silly little position, and his father's new peerage. But you're not like that. I believe that all wisdom consists in caring immensely for the few right things and not caring a straw about the rest."

Had anyone hinted to Sir Archie that a young woman on a Scots mountain could lecture him gravely on his future and still remain a ravishing and adorable thing he would have dismissed the suggestion with incredulity. At the back of his head he had that fear of women as something mysterious and unintelligible which belongs to a motherless and sisterless childhood, and a youth spent almost wholly in the company of men. He had immense compassion for a sex which seemed to him to have a hard patch to hoe in the world, and this pitifulness had always kept him from any conduct which might harm a woman. His numerous fancies had been light and transient like thistledown, and his heart had been wholly unscathed. Fear that he might stumble into marriage had made him as shy as a woodcock—a fear not without grounds, for a friend had once proposed to write a book called *Lives of the Hunted*, with a chapter on Archie. Wherefore, his hour having come, he had cascaded into love with desperate completeness, and with the freshness of a mind unstaled by disillusion. . . . All he knew was that a miraculous being had suddenly flooded his world with a new radiance, and was now opening doors and inviting him to dazzling prospects. He felt at once marvellously confident, and supremely humble. Never had mistress a more docile pupil.

They wandered back to the house, and Janet gave him tea in a room full of faded chintzes and Chinese-Chippendale mirrors. Then, when the sun was declining behind the Carnmore peaks, Sir Archie at last took his leave. His head was in a happy confusion, but two ideas rose above the surge—he would seize the earliest chance of asking Janet to marry him, and by all his gods he must not make a fool of himself at Muirtown. She had challenged him, and he had accepted the challenge; he must make it good before he could become in turn a challenger. It may be doubtful if Sir Archie had any very clear notions on the matter, but he was aware that he had received an inspiration, and that somehow or other everything was now to be different. . . . First for that confounded speech. He strove to recollect the sentences which had followed each other so trippingly during his morning's walk. But he could not concentrate his mind. Peace treaties and German reparations and the recognition of Russia flitted from him like a rapid film, to be replaced by a "close-up" of a girl's face. Besides, he wanted to sing, and when song flows to the lips consecutive thought is washed out of the brain.

In this happy and exalted mood, dedicate to great enterprises of love and service, Sir Archie entered the Crask smoking-room, to be brought heavily to earth by the sordid business of John Macnab.

Leithen was there, reading a volume of Sir Walter Scott with an air of divine detachment. Lamancha, very warm and dishevelled, was endeavouring to quench his thirst with a large whisky-and-soda; Palliser-Yeates, also the worse for wear, lay in an attitude of extreme fatigue on a sofa; Crossby, who had sought sanctuary at Crask, was busy with the newspapers which had just arrived, while Wattie Lithgow stood leaning on his crook staring into vacancy, like a clown from some stage Arcadia.

"Where on earth have you been all day, Archie?" Lamancha asked sternly.

"I walked over to Glenraden and stayed to luncheon.

They're all hot on your side there—Bandicott too. There's a general feelin' that young Claybody wants takin' down a peg."

"Much good that will do us. John and Wattie and I have been crawling all day round the Haripol marches. It's pretty clear what they'll do—you think so, Wattie?"

"Alan Macnicol is not altogether a fule. Aye, I ken fine what they'll dae."

"Clear the beasts off the ground?" Archie suggested.

"No," said Lamancha. "Move them into the Sanctuary, and the Sanctuary is in the very heart of the forest—between Sgurr Mor and Sgurr Dearg at the head of the Reascuill. It won't take many men to watch it. And the mischief is that Haripol is the one forest where it can be done quite simply. It's so infernally rough that if the deer were all over it I would back myself to get a shot with a fair chance of removing the beast, but if every stag is inside an inner corral it will be the devil's own business to get within a thousand yards of them—let alone shift the carcass."

"If the wind keeps in the west," said Wattie, "It is a manifest impossibeelity. If it was in the north there would be a verra wee sma' chance. All other airts are hopeless. We maun just possess our souls in patience, and see what the day brings forth. . . . I'll awa and mak arrangements for the morn."

Lamancha nodded after the retreating figure.

"He is determined to go to Muirtown to-morrow. Says you promised that he should be present when you made your first bow in public, and that he has arranged with Shapp to drive him in the Ford. . . . But about Haripol. This idea of Wattie's—and I expect it's right—makes the job look pretty desperate. I had worked out a very sound scheme to set my Lord Claybody guessing—similar to John's Glenraden plan but more ingenious; but what's the use of bluff if every beast is snug in an upper corrie with a cordon of Claybody's men round it? Wattie says that Haripol is fairly crawling with gillies."

Crossby raised his head from his journalistic researches. "The papers have got my story all right, I see. The first one, I

139

mean—the 'Return of Harald Blacktooth.' They've featured it well, too, and I expect the evening papers are now going large on it. But it's nothing to what the second will be to-morrow morning. I'm prepared to bet that our Scottish Tutankhamen drops out of the running, and that the Press of this land thinks of nothing for a week except the salmon Sir Edward got last night, It's the silly season, remember!"

Lamancha's jaw dropped. "Crossby, I don't want to dash your natural satisfaction, but I'm afraid you've put me finally in the cart. If the public wakes up and takes an interest in Haripol, I may as well chuck in my hand."

"I wasn't such an ass as to mention Haripol," said the correspondent.

"No, but of course it will get out. Some of your journalistic colleagues will hear of it at Strathlarrig, and, finding that the interest has departed from Harald Blacktooth, will make a bee-line for Haripol. Your success, which I don't grudge you, will be my ruin. In any case the Claybodys will be put on their mettle, for, if they are beaten by John Macnab, they know they'll be a public laughing-stock. . . . What sort of fellow is young Claybody, Archie?"

"Bit shaggy about the heels. Great admirer of yours. Ask Ned—he said he knew Ned very well."

Leithen raised his eyes from *Redgauntlet*. "Never heard of the fellow in my life."

"Oh yes, you have. He said he had briefed you in a big case."

"Well, you can't expect me to know all my clients any more than John knows the customers of his little bank." Leithen relapsed into Sir Walter.

"I'm going to have a bath." Lamancha rose and cautiously relaxed his weary limbs. "I seem to be in for the most imbecile escapade in history with about one chance in a billion. That's Wattie's estimate, and he knows what a billion is, which I don't."

"What about dropping it?" Archie suggested; for, though he was sworn to the "John Macnab proposition," he was growing very nervous about this particular manifestation. "Young

140

Claybody is an ugly customer, and we don't want the thing to end in bad blood. Besides, you're cured already—you told me so yesterday."

"That's true," said Lamancha, who was engaged in tossing with Palliser-Yeates for the big bath. "I'm cured. I never felt keener in my life. I'm so keen that there's nothing on earth you could offer me which would keep me away from Haripol. . . . You win, John. Gentlemen of the Guard, fire first, and don't be long about it. I can't stretch myself in that drain-pipe that Archie calls his second bathroom."

Dinner was a cheerful meal, for Mr Crossby had much to say, Lamancha was in high spirits, and Leithen had the benignity of the successful warrior. But the host was silent and abstracted. He managed to banish Haripol from his mind, but he thought of Janet, he thought of Janet's sermon, and in feverish intervals he tried to think of his speech for the morrow. A sense of a vast insecurity had come upon him, of a shining goal which grew brighter the more he reflected upon it, but of some awkward hurdles to get over first.

Afterwards, when the talk was of Haripol, he turned to the newspapers to restore him to the world of stern realities. He did not read that masterpiece of journalism, Crossby's story, but he found a sober comfort in *The Times'* leading articles and in the political notes. He felt himself a worker among *flâneurs*.

"Here's something about you, Charles," he said. "This paper says that political circles are looking forward with great interest to your speech at Muirtown. Says it will be the first important utterance since Parliament rose, and that you are expected to deal with Poincaré's speech at Rheims and a letter by a Boche whose name I can't pronounce."

"Political circles will be disappointed," said Lamancha, "for I haven't read them. Montgomery is taking all the boxes and I haven't heard from the office for three weeks. I can't be troubled with newspapers in the Highlands."

"Then what are you goin' to say to-morrow?" Archie demanded anxiously.

"I'll think of some rot. Don't worry, old fellow. Muirtown is a second-class show compared to Haripol."

Archie was really shocked. He was envious of a man who could treat thus cavalierly a task which affected him with horrid forebodings, and also scandalised at the levity of his leaders. It seemed to him that Lamancha needed some challenging. Finding no comfort in his company, he repaired to bed, where healthful sleep was slow in visiting him. He repeated his speech to himself, but it would persist in getting tangled up with Janet's sermon and his own subsequent reflections, so that, when at last he dropped off, it was into a world of ridiculous dreams where a dreadful composite figure—Poincarini or Mussolinaré—sat heavily on his chest.

9

SIR ARCHIE INSTRUCTS HIS COUNTRYMEN

CROSSBY was right in his forecast. The sudden interest in the Scottish Tutankhamen did not survive the revelation of Harald Blacktooth's reincarnation as John Macnab. The twenty correspondents, after lunching heavily with Mr Bandicott, had been shown the relics of the Viking and had heard their significance expounded by their host and Professor Babwater; each had duly despatched his story, but before night-fall each was receiving urgent telegrams from his paper clamouring for news, not of Harald, but of Harald's successor. Crossby's tale of the frustrated attempt on the Glenraden deer had intrigued several million readers—it was the silly season, remember—and his hint of the impending raid on the Strathlarrig salmon had stirred a popular interest vowed to any lawless mystery and any competitive sport. In the doings of John Macnab were blended the splendid uncertainty of a well-matched prize fight and the delicious obscurity of crime. Next morning the news of John's victory at Strathlarrig was received by the several million readers with an enthusiasm denied to the greater matters of public conduct. John Macnab became a slogan for the newsboy, a flaming legend for bills and headlines, a subject of delighted talk at every breakfast-table. Never had there been a more famous eight-pound salmon since fish first swam in the sea.

It was a cold grey morning when Lamancha and Archie left Crask in the Hispana, bound for the station of Bridge of Gair, fifty miles distant by indifferent hill-roads. Lamancha, who had written for clothes, was magnificently respectable below his heavy ulster—a respectability which was not his usual habit but a concession to the urgent demand for camouflage. He was also in a bad temper, for his legs were still abominably stiff, and, though in need of at least ten hours' sleep, he had been allowed precisely six. At long last, too, his speech had begun to weigh upon him. "Shut up, Archie," he had told his host. "I must collect what's left of my wits, or I'll make an exhibition of myself. You say we get the morning's papers at Bridge of Gair? They may give me a point or two. Lord, it's like one of those beastly mornings in Switzerland when they rake you up at two to climb Mount Blanc and you wish you had never been born."

Sir Archie had no inclination to garrulity, for black fear had settled on his soul. In a few hours' time he would be doing what he had never done before, standing before a gaping audience which was there to be amused and possibly instructed. He had a speech in his pocket, carefully fashioned in consultation with Lamancha, but he was miserably conscious that it had no relation to his native wood-notes. What was Poincaré to him, or he to Poincaré? Why on earth had he not chosen to speak about something which touched his interests—farming, for example, on which he held views, or the future of the Air Force—instead of venturing in the unknown deserts of foreign affairs? Well, he had burned his boats and must make the best of it. The great thing was to be sure that the confounded speech had been transferred from paper to his memory.

But as the miles slipped behind him he realised with horror that his memory was playing him false. He could not get the bits to fit in; what he had reeled off so smoothly twenty-four hours ago now came out in idiotic shreds and patches. He felt himself slipping into a worse funk than he had ever known in all his tempestuous days. . . . For a moment he thought of throwing up the sponge. He might engineer a breakdown—it would have to be a bad spill, for the day was yet young—and so deprive Muirtown of the presence of both Lamancha and himself. It was not the thought of the Conservative cause or his own political chances that made him reject this cowardly expedient. Two reasons dissuaded him: one, that though his friends continually prophesied disaster, he had never yet had a

144

smash with his car, and his pride was involved; the other, that such a course would reveal Lamancha's presence in his company too near the suspect neighbourhood and might expose the secret of John Macnab. . . . No, he had to go through with it, and, conning such wretched fragments of his oratory as he could dig out of his recollection, Sir Archie drove the Hispana over the bleak moorlands till he was looking down on the wide strath of the Gair, with the railway line scarring the heather and the hotel chimneys smoking beside a cold blue-grey river. He had glanced now and then at his fellow orator, whose professional apathy he profoundly envied, since for the last dozen miles Lamancha had been peacefully asleep.

They breakfasted at the hotel, and presently sought the station platform in the quest for papers. They were informed that papers came with the train for which they were waiting, and when the said train arrived, half an hour late, and Lamancha, according to arrangement, had sought a seat in the front while Archie favoured the rear, the latter secured a London evening paper of the previous day and that morning's *Scotsman*. The compartment in which he found himself was crowded with sleepy and short-tempered people who had made the night journey from the south. So on a pile of three gun-cases in the corridor Archie sat himself and gave his attention to the enlightened Press of his country.

He rubbed his eyes to make certain that he was not dreaming. For there, in conspicuous print on a prominent page of a respected newspaper, was the name of John Macnab. There was other news: of outrages in Mexico and earthquakes in the Pacific, of the disappearance of a solicitor and the arrival in London of a cinema star, but all seemed dwarfed and paled by Crossby's story. There was news of Harald Blacktooth, too, and authentic descriptions of the treasure-trove, but this was in an unconsidered corner. Cheek by jowl with the leading article was what clearly most interested the editor out of all the events on the surface of the globe—the renascence of Harald Blacktooth phoenix-like from his ashes, and the capture of the Strathlarrig salmon.

145

Archie read the thing confusedly without taking much of it in. Then he turned to the London evening paper. It was a journal which never objected to breaking up its front page for spicy news, and there on the front page was a summary of the Strathlarrig exploit. Moreover, there was a short hastily compiled article on the subject and a number of stimulating notes. John Macnab was becoming a household name, and the gaze of Britain was being centred on his shy personality. The third act in the drama would be played under bright light to a full gallery. . . . Archie's eyes caught the end of the first *Scotsman* leader, which contained a reference to the Muirtown meeting, and a speculation as to what the Secretary of State for the Dominions would say. Archie, too, speculated as to what Lamancha was saying at that moment at the other end of the train.

This new complexity did something to quiet his nerves and take his mind off his approaching ordeal. There was no word in the papers of the coming raid on Haripol—Crossby had had that much sense—but, of course, whatever happened at Haripol would be broadcast through the land. The Claybodys, if they defeated John Macnab, would be famous; ridiculous, if they were beaten; and, while the latter fate might be taken with good humour by the Bandicotts, it would be gall and wormwood to a young gentleman with strong notions on the rights and dignities of landed property. It was mathematically certain that Johnson Claybody, as soon as he saw the newspapers, would devote all the powers of a not insignificant mind and the energies of a stubborn temper to the defence of Haripol. That was bad enough, but the correspondents at Strathlarrig were likely to have heard by this time of the third of John Macnab's wagers, and the attempt might have to be made under their argus-eyed espionage. Altogether, things were beginning to look rather dark for John, and incidentally for Sir Archie.

These morose reflections occupied him till the train stopped at Frew, the ticket-station for Muirtown. Here, according to plan, Sir Archie descended, for he could not arrive at the

146

terminus in Lamancha's company. There was a cold gusty wind from the north-west which promised rain, the sky was overcast, and the sea, half a mile distant across the sand-dunes, was grey and sullen. Sir Archie, having two hours to fill before the official luncheon, resolved to reject the ancient station fly and walk. . . . Once again the shadow of his speech descended on him. He limped along the shore road, trying to see the words as he had written them down, trying especially to get the initial sentence clear for each paragraph, for he believed that if he remembered these the rest would follow. The thing went rather better now. Parts came in a cascade of glibness, and he remembered Lamancha's injunction not to be too dapper or too rapid. The peroration was all right, and so was the exordium; only one passage near the middle seemed to offer a snag. He devoted the rest of his walk exclusively to this passage, till he was assured that he had it by heart.

He reached Muirtown within an hour, and decided to kill time by visiting some of his friends among the shopkeepers. The gunmaker welcomed him cordially, and announced his intention of coming to hear him that afternoon. But politics had clearly been ousted from that worthy's head by the newspaper which lay on his counter. "What about this John Macnab, Sir Erchibald," he asked.

"What about him? I'm hanged if I know what to think."

"If Mr Tarras wasn't deid in Africa I would ken fine what to think. The man will likely be a gentleman, and he must be a grand fisher. I ken that bit o' the Larrig, and to get a salmon in it wants a fair demon at the job. Crask is no three miles away. D'ye hear nothing at Crask?"

It was the same wherever he went. The fishmonger pointed to a fish on his slabs, and observed that it would be about the size of the one taken at Strathlarrig. The bookseller, who knew his customer's simple tastes in letters, regretted that no contemporary novel of his acquaintance promised such entertainment as the drama now being enacted in Wester Ross. Tired of needless lying, Sir Archie forsook the shops and went for a stroll beside the harbour. But even there John Macnab

147

seemed to pursue him. Wherever he saw a man with a paper he knew what he was reading, the people at the street corners were no doubt discussing the same subject—nay, he was sure he heard the very words spoken as he passed. . . . The sight of a blue poster with his name in large letters reminded him of his duties, and he turned his steps towards the Northern Club.

He was greeted by his host, a Baillie of the town (the Provost belonged to the enemy camp), and was presented to the other guests. "This is our candidate for Wester Ross, my lord," and Archie was introduced to Lamancha, who smiled urbanely and remarked that he had had the pleasure of meeting Sir Archibald Roylance before. The Duke of Angus would not arrive till the hour of meeting, but Colonel Wavertree was there, a dapper red-faced gentleman who had an interest in breweries, and Mr Murdoch of New Caledonia—immense, grizzled and bearded, who had left the Lews as a child of three for the climes which had given him fortune. Also there was Lord Claybody, who came forward at once to renew his acquaintance.

"Very glad to see you, Sir Archibald. This is your first big meeting, isn't it? Good luck to you. A straight-forward declaration of principles is what we want from our future member, and I've no doubt we'll get it from you. Johnson sent his humblest apologies. He drove me in this morning, but unfortunately a troublesome bit of business took him back at once."

Sir Archie thought he knew what that business was. He had always rather liked old Claybody, and now that he had leisure to study him the liking was confirmed. There was much of the son's arrogance about the eyes and mouth, but there was humour, too, which was lacking in Johnson, and his voice had a pleasant Midland burr. But he looked horribly competent and wide-awake. One would, thought Sir Archie, if one had made a great fortune oneself, and he concluded that the owner of Haripol was probably a bad man to get up against.

At luncheon they should have talked of the state of the nation and the future of their party; instead they talked of John

148

Macnab. It was to be noted that Lord Claybody did not contribute much to the talk; he pursed his lips when the name was mentioned, and he did not reveal the challenge to Haripol. Patently he shared his son's views on the matter. But the others made no secret of their interest. Colonel Wavertree, who had come in from a neighbouring grouse-moor, was positive that the ruffian's escapades were not over. "He'll go round the lot of us," he said, "and though it costs him fifty pound a time, I daresay he gets his money's worth. I believe he is paid by the agents to put up the price of Highland places, for if he keeps on it will mean money in the pocket of every sporting tenant, besides the devil of a lot of fun." Mr Murdoch said it reminded him of the doings of one Pink Jones in New Caledonia forty years ago, and told a long and pointless tale of that hero. As for Lamancha, he requested to be given the whole story, and made very good show of merriment. "A parcel of under-graduates, I suppose," he said.

But the Baillie, who gave him the information, was a serious man and disapproved. "It will get the country-side a bad name, my lord. It is a challenge to law and order. There's too many Bolsheviks about as it is, without this John Macnab aidin' and abettin' them."

"Most likely the fellow is a sound Tory," said Lamancha; but the Ballie ventured respectfully to differ. "If your lordship will forgive me, there's some things too serious for jokin'," he concluded sententiously.

It was a dull luncheon, but to Archie the hours passed like fevered seconds. Agoraphobia had seized him once more, and he felt his tongue dry and his stomach hollow with trepidation. Food did not permit itself to be swallowed, so he contented himself with drinking two whisky-and-sodas. Towards the close of the meal that wild form of valour which we call desperation was growing in him. He could do nothing more about his infernal speech, and must fling himself on fortune.

As they left the table the Baillie claimed him. "Your agent is here, Sir Archibald. He wanted a word with you before the meeting."

A lean, red-haired man awaited them in the hall.

"Hullo, Mr Brodie. How are you? Glad to see you. Well, what's the drill for this afternoon?"

"It's that I was wantin' to see ye about, sir. The arrangement was that you should speak first, then Lord Lamancha, then Colonel Wavertree, and Mr Murdoch to finish off. But Baillie Dorrit thinks Lord Lamancha should open, him bein' a Cabinet Minister, and that you should follow."

"Right-o, Brodie! I'm game for anything you like. I've been a slack candidate up to now, and I don't profess to know the job like you." Sir Archie spoke with a jauntiness which made his heart sink, but the agent was impressed.

"Fine, sir. I can see ye're in grand fettle. Ye'll have a remarkable audience. There's been a demand for tickets far beyond the capacity o' the hall, and I hear of folk comin' from fifty mile round."

Every word was like a knell to the wretched Archie, but with his spirits in the depths his manner took on a ghastly exhilaration. He lit a cigar with shaking fingers, patted Brodie on the back, linked his arm with the Baillie's, and in the short walk to the hall chattered like a magpie. So fevered was his behaviour that, as they entered the building by a side-door, Lamancha whispered in his ear, "Steady, old man. For God's sake, keep your head," and Archie turned on him a face like a lost soul's.

"I'm goin' over the top," he said.

The Town Hall of Muirtown, having been built originally for the purpose of a drill-hall, was capable of holding inside its bare walls the better part of two thousand people. This afternoon it was packed to the door, presumably with voters, for the attendants had ruthlessly turned away all juvenile politicians. As Sir Archie took his seat on the platform, while a selection from the Muirtown Brass Band rendered "Annie Laurie," he seemed to be looking down as from an aeroplane on a strange, unfeatured country. The faces might have been tomb-stones for all the personality they represented. Some of his friends were there, no doubt, but he could no more have recognised them than he could have picked out the starling which haunted the Crask lawn from a flock seen next day on the hill. The place swam in a mist, like a corrie viewed in the morning from the hill-tops, and he knew that the mist came out of his own quaking soul. He had heard of stage-fright, but had never dreamed that it could be such a blackness of darkness.

The Duke of Angus was very old, highly respected, and almost wholly witless. He had never been very clever—Disraeli, it was said, had refused him the Thistle on the ground that he would eat it—and of late years his mind had retired into a happy vacuity. As a chairman he was mercifully brief. He told a Scots story, at which he shook with laughter, but the point of which he unfortunately left out; he repeated very loudly the names of the speakers—Sir Archie started at the sound of his own like a scared fawn; in a tone which was almost a bellow he uttered the words "Lord Lamancha," and then he sat down.

Lamancha had the reputation which is always accorded to a man whose name is often in the newspapers. Most of the audience had never seen him in the flesh, and human nature is grateful for satisfied curiosity. Presently he had them docile under the spell of his charming voice. He never attempted oratory in the grand style, but he possessed all the lesser accomplishments. He had nothing new to say, but he said the old things with a pleasant sincerity and that simplicity which is the result only of a long-practised art. It was the kind of speech of which he had made hundreds and would make hundreds more; there was nothing in it to lay hold of, but it produced an impression of being at once weighty and spontaneous, flattering to the audience and a proof of the speaker's easy mastery of his trade. There was a compliment to the Duke, a warm tribute to Sir Archie, a bantering profession of shyness on the part of a Borderer speaking north of the Forth. Then, by an easy transition, he passed to Highland problems— land, emigration, the ex-service men—and thence to the prime economic needs of Britain since 1918, the relation of these needs to world demands, the necessity of meeting them by using the full assets of an Empire which had been a unit in war and should be a unit in peace. There was little to inspire, but little to question; platitudes were so artfully linked together as to give the impression of a rounded and stable creed. Here was one who spoke seriously, responsibly, and yet with optimism; there was character here, said the ordinary man, and yet obviously a mind as well. Even the stern critics on the back benches had no fault to find with a statement from which they could only dissent with respect. None recognised that it was the manner that bewitched them. Lamancha, who on occasion could be profound, was now only improvising. The matter was a mosaic of bits of old speeches and answers to deputations, which he put together cynically with his left hand. But the manner was superb—the perfect production of a fine voice, the cunning emphasis, the sudden halts, the rounded cadences, the calculated hesitations. He sat down after forty minutes amid a tempest of that applause which is the tribute to professional skill and has nothing to do with conviction.

Sir Archie had listened with awe. Knowing now from bitter experience the thorny path of oratory, he was dumbfounded by this spectacle of a perfection of which he had never dreamed. What a fiasco would his halting utterance be in such company! He glanced at the notes in his hand, but could not read them; he strove to remember his opening sentences, and discovered them elusive. Then suddenly he heard his name spoken, and found himself on his feet.

He was scarcely aware of the applause with which he was greeted. All he knew was that every word of his speech had fled from his memory and would never return. The faces below him were a horrid white blur at which he knew he was foolishly grinning. . . . In his pocket was an oration carefully written out. If he were to pluck it forth, and try to read it, he knew that he could not make sense of a word, for his eyes had lost the power of sight. . . . Profound inertia seized him; he must do something, but there was a dreadful temptation to do nothing, just to go on grinning, like a man in a nightmare who finds himself in the track of an express train.

Nevertheless, such automata are we, he was speaking. He did not know what he was saying, but as a matter of fact he was repeating the words with which the chairman had introduced him. "Ladies and gentlemen, we are fortunate in the privilege of having heard so stirring and statesmanlike an address as that which His Majesty's Secretary of State for the Dominions has just delivered. Now we are to hear what our gallant and enterprising friend, the prospective candidate for Wester Ross, has to say to us about the problems which confront the nation."

He repeated this exordium like a parrot. The audience scented a mild joke, and laughed. . . . Then in a twittering falsetto he repeated it again—this time in silence. There was a vague sense that something had gone wrong. He was about to repeat it a third time, and then the crash would have come, and he would have retired gibbering from the field.

The situation was saved by Wattie Lithgow. Seated at the back of the hall, Wattie saw that his master was in deadly peril, and took the only way to save him. He had a voice of immense compass, and he used it to the full.

"Speak up, man," he roared. "I canna hear a word ye're sayin'."

There were shouts of "Order," and the stewards glared angrily at Wattie, but the trick had been done. Sir Archie's eyes opened, and he saw the audience no longer like turnips in a field, but as living and probably friendly human beings. Above all, he saw Wattie's gnarled face and anxious eyes. Suddenly his brain cleared, and, had he desired it, he could have reeled off the speech in his pocket as glibly as he had repeated it in the solitude of Crask. But he felt that that was no longer possible. The situation required a different kind of speech, and he believed he could make it. He would speak direct to Wattie, as he had often lectured him in the Crask smoking-room.

"Ladies and gentlemen," he said—and his voice had become full and confident—"your 'gallant and enterprising friend' is not much of a hand at public speaking. I have still my job to learn, and with your help I hope soon to learn it. What I have

153

to say to you this afternoon is the outcome of my first amateurish study of public questions. You may take it that my views are honest and my own. I am not a gramophone."

In this last sentence he lied, for what he said was for the most part not his own; it was the sermon which Janet Raden had preached him the day before in the clear air of the Carnmore tops. Mixed up with it were fragments of old discourses of his own to Wattie, and reflections which had come to him in the last ten years of a variegated life. The manner was staccato, the style was slangy and inelegant, but it was not a lesson learned and recited, but words spoken direct to those into whose eyes he was looking. He had found touch with his audience, and he held their attention in a vice.

It was a strange, inconsequent speech, but it had a curious appeal in it—the appeal of youth and candour and courage. It was philosophy rather than politics, a ragged but arresting philosophy. He began by confessing that the war had left the world in a muddle, a muddle which affected his own mind. The only cure was to be honest with oneself, and to refuse to accept specious nonsense and conventional jargon. He told the story from Andersen of the Emperor's New Suit. "Our opponents call us Tories," he said; "they can call us anything they jolly well please. I am proud to be called a Tory. I understand that the name was first given by Titus Oates to those who disbelieved in his Popish Plot. What we want to-day is Toryism—the courage to give the lie to impudent rogues."

That was a memory of Leithen's table talk. The rest was all from Janet Raden. He preached the doctrine of Challenge; of no privilege without responsibility, of only one right of man—the right to do his duty; of all power and property held on sufferance. These were the thoughts which had been growing in his head since yesterday afternoon. He spoke of the changing face of the land—the Highlands ceasing to be the home of men and becoming the mere raw material of picture post-cards, the old gentry elbowed out and retiring with a few trinkets and pictures and the war medals of their dead to suburban lodgings. It all came of not meeting the

154

challenge. . . . What was Bolshevism but a challenge, perhaps a much-needed challenge, to make certain of the faith that was in a man? He had no patience with the timorous and whining rich. No law could protect them unless they made themselves worth protecting. As a Tory, he believed that the old buildings were still sound, but they must be swept and garnished, that the ancient weapons were the best, but they must be kept bright and shining and ready for use. So soon as a cause feared inquiry and the light of day that cause was doomed. The ostrich, hiding its head in the sand, left its rump a fatal temptation to the boot of the passer-by.

Sir Archie was not always clear, he was often ungrammatical, and he nobly mixed his metaphors, but he held his audience tight. He did more, when at the close of his speech he put his case in the form of an apologue—the apologue of John Macnab. The mention of the name brought laughter and loud cheering. John Macnab, he said, was abroad in the world to-day, like a catfish among a shoal of herrings. He had his defects, no doubt, but he was badly wanted, for he was at bottom a sportsman and his challenge had to be met. Even if the game went against them the challenged did not wholly lose, for they were stirred out of apathy into life.

No queerer speech was ever made by a candidate on his first public appearance. It had no kind of success with the Baillie, nor, it may be presumed, with Lord Claybody; indeed, I doubt if any of the distinguished folk on the platform quite approved of it, except Lamancha. But there was no question of its appeal to the audience, and the applause which had followed Lamancha's peroration was as nothing to that amid which Sir Archie resumed his seat.

At the back of the hall a wild-eyed man sitting near Wattie Lithgow had been vociferous in his plaudits. "He ca's himsel' a Tory. By God, it's the red flag that he'll be wavin' soon."

"If you say that again," said Wattie fiercely, "I'll smash your heid."

"Keep your hair on," was the reply. "I'm for the young ane, whatever he ca's himsel'."

155

Archie sat down with his brain in a whirl, for he had tasted the most delicious of joys—the sense of having moved a multitude. He had never felt happier in his life—or, let it be added, more truly amazed. A fiery trail was over, and brilliantly over. He had spoken straightforwardly to his fellow-mortals with ease and acceptance. The faces below him were no longer featureless, but human and friendly and interesting. He did not listen closely to Colonel Wavertree's remarks, which seemed to be mostly about taxation, or to the Ex-Premier of New Caledonia, who was heavily rhetorical and passionately imperial. Modest as he was, he had a pleased consciousness that, though he might have talked a good deal of rot, he had gripped his hearers as not even Lamancha had gripped them. He searched through the hall for faces to recognise. Wattie he saw, savagely content; the Colonel, too, who looked flushed and happy, and Junius, and Agatha. But there was no sign of Janet, and his failure to find her threw a dash of cold water on his triumph.

The next step was to compass an inconspicuous departure. Lamancha would be escorted in state to the four-forty-five train, and he must join it at Frew. While "God save the King" was being sung, Sir Archie escaped by a side-door, followed by an excited agent. "Man, ye went down tremendous," Brodie gasped. "Ye changed your mind—ye told me ye were goin' to deal wi' foreign policy. Anyway, ye've started fine, and there'll be no gettin' inside the hall the next time ye speak in Muirtown."

Archie shook him off, picked up a taxi-cab at the station, and drove to Frew. There, after lurking in the waiting-room, he duly entered a third-class carriage in the rear of the south-going train. At six o'clock he emerged on to the platform at Bridge of Gair, and waited till the train had gone before he followed Lamancha to the hotel. He found his friend thinking only of Haripol. "I had a difficult job to get rid of Claybody, and had to tell a lot of lies. Said I was going to stay with Lanerick and that my man had gone on there with my luggage. We'd better be off, for we've a big day before us to-morrow."

But, as the Hispana started up the road to the pass, Lamancha smiled affectionately on the driver and patted his shoulder. "I've often called you an idiot, Archie, but I'm bound to say to-day you were an inspired idiot. You may win this seat or not—it doesn't matter—but sooner or later you're going to make a howling success in that silly game."

Beyond the pass the skies darkened for rain, and it was in a deluge that the car, a little after eight o'clock, crossed the Bridge of Larrig. Archie had intended to go round by one of the peat-roads, but the wild weather had driven everyone to shelter, and it seemed safe to take the straight road up the hill. Shapp, who had just arrived in the Ford, took charge of the car, and Archie and Lamancha sprinted through the drizzle to the back-door.

To their surprise it was locked, and when, in reply to their hammering, Mrs Lithgow appeared, it was only after repeated questions through the scullery-window that she was convinced of their identity and permitted them to enter.

"We've been sair fashed wi' folk," was her laconic comment, as she retired hastily to the kitchen after locking the door behind them.

In the smoking-room they found the lamps lit, the windows shuttered, Crossby busy with the newspapers, Palliser-Yeates playing patience, and Leithen as usual deep in the works of Sir Walter Scott. "Well," was the unanimous question, "how did it go off?"

"Not so bad," said Archie. "Charles was in great form. But what on earth has scared Mrs Lithgow?"

Leithen laid down his book. "We've had the devil of a time. Our base has been attacked. It looks as if we may have a rearguard action to add to our troubles. We're practically besieged. Two hours ago I was all for burning our ciphers and retiring."

"Besieged? By whom?"

"By the correspondents. Ever since the early afternoon. I fancy their editors have been prodding them with telegrams.

157

Anyhow, they've forgotten all about Harald Blacktooth and are hot on the scent of John Macnab."

"But what brought them here?"

"Method of elimination, I suppose. Your journalist is a sharp fellow. They argued that John Macnab must have a base near by, and, as it wasn't Strathlarrig or Glenraden, it was most likely here. Also they caught sight of Crossby taking the air, and gave chase. Crossby flung them off—happily they can't have recognised him—but they had him treed in the stable loft for three hours."

"Did they see you?"

"No. Some got into the hall and some glued their faces to this window, but John was under the table and I was making myself very small at the back of the sofa. . . . Mrs Lithgow handled them like Napoleon. Said the Laird was away and wouldn't be back till midnight, but he'd see them at ten o'clock to-morrow. She had to promise that, for they are determined ruffians. They'd probably still be hanging about the place if it hadn't been for this blessed rain."

"That's not all," said Palliser-Yeates. "We had a visit from a lunatic. We didn't see him, for Mrs Lithgow lured him indoors and has him shut up in the wine-cellar."

"Good God! What kind of lunatic?" Sir Archie exclaimed.

"Don't know. Mrs Lithgow was not communicative. She said something about smallpox. Maybe he's a fellow-sufferer looking for Archie's company. Anyhow, he's in the wine-cellar for Wattie to deal with."

Sir Archie rose and marched from the room, and did not return till the party were seated at a late supper. His hair was harassed, and his eyes were wild.

"It wasn't the wine-cellar," he groaned, "it was the coal-hole. He's upstairs now having a bath and changing into a suit of my clothes. Pretty short in the temper, too, and no wonder. For Heaven's sake, you fellows, stroke him down when he appears. We've got to bank on his being a good chap and tell him everything. It's deuced hard luck. Here am I just makin' a promising start in my public career, and you've gone and

158

locked up the local Medical Officer of Health who came to inquire into a reputed case of smallpox."

10

IN WHICH CRIME IS ADDED TO CRIME

By the mercy of Providence Doctor Kello fulfilled Archie's
definition of a "good chap." He was a sandy-haired young
man from Dundee, who had been in the Air Force, and on his
native dialect had grafted the intricate slang of that service.
Archie had found him half-choked with coal-dust and wrath,
and abject apologies had scarcely mollified him. But a hot bath
and his host's insistence that he should spend the night at
Crask—Dr Kello knew very well that at the inn he would get
no more than a sofa—had worked a miracle, and he appeared
at the supper-table prepared to forgive and forget. He was a
little awed by the company in which he found himself, and
nervously murmured, "Pleased to meet ye" in response to the
various introductions. A good meal and Archie's Veuve
Clicquot put him into humour with himself and at ease with his
surroundings. He exchanged war reminiscences, and told
stories of his professional life—"Ye wouldn't believe, I tell ye,
what queer folk the Highlanders are"—and when later in the
evening Archie, speaking as to a brother airman, made a clean
breast of the John Macnab affair, he received the confession
with obstreperous hilarity. "It's the best stunt I ever heard tell
of," he roared, slapping his knee. "Ye may depend on me to
back ye up, too. Is it the journalists that's worrying ye? You
leave the merchants to me. I'll shut their mouths for them. Ten
o'clock to-morrow, is it? Well, I'll be there with a face as long
as my arm, and I'll guarantee to send them down the hill like a
kirk emptying."

All night it rained in bucketfuls, and the Friday morning
broke with the same pitiless deluge. Lamancha came down to

breakfast in a suit of clothes which would have been refused by a self-respecting tramp, but which, as a matter of fact, had been his stalking outfit for a dozen years. The Merklands were not a dressy family. He studied the barograph, where the needle was moving ominously downward, and considered the dissolving skies and the mist which rose like a wall beyond the terrace.

"It's no good," he told his host. "You might as well try to stalk Haripol in a snow blizzard. To-day must be washed out, and that leaves us only to-morrow. We'll have to roost indoors, and we're terribly at the mercy of that hive of correspondents."

The hive came at ten, a waterproofed army defying the weather in the cause of duty. But in front of the door they were met by Dr Kello, with a portentous face.

"Good morning, boys," he said. "Sir Archibald Roylance asked me to see ye on his behalf. My name's Kello—I'm Medical Officer of Health for this part of the world. I'm very sorry, but ye can't see Sir Archibald this morning. In fact, I want ye to go away and not come near the place at all."

He was promptly asked for his reason.

"The fact is that a suspected case of smallpox has been reported from Crask. That's why I'm here. I say 'suspected,' for, in my own opinion, it's nothing of the sort. But I'm bound to take every precaution, and, for your own sakes, I can't let a man-jack of ye a step nearer."

The news was received in silence, and added to the depression of the dripping weather. A question was asked.

"No, it's not Sir Archibald. He's as disappointed as you are at not being able to welcome ye. He says if ye come back in forty-eight hours—that's the time when I hope to give the place a clean bill of health—he would like to stand ye drinks and have a crack with ye."

Five minutes later the doctor returned to the smoking-room. "They're off like good laddies, and I don't think they'll trouble ye for the next two days. Gosh! They're as feared of infectious diseases as a Highlander. I'll give them a wee while to go down the hill, and then I'll start off home on my motor-bike. I'm very much obliged to you gentlemen for your good entertainment. . . . Ye may be sure I'll hold my tongue about the confidence ye've honoured me with. Not a cheep from me! But I can tell ye, I'll be keeping my ears open for word of John Macnab. Good luck to ye, gentlemen!"

The departure of Doctor Kello was followed by the appearance of Wattie Lithgow, accompanied by Benjie, whose waterproof cape of ceremony had now its uses.

"I've got bad news from this laddie," said the former, lugging Benjie forward by the ear. "He was at Haripol early this morning and a' the folk there was speakin' about it. Macnicol tell't him—"

"No, he didna," put in Benjie. "Macnicol's ower prood to speak to me. I heard it frae the men in the bothy and frae ane o' the lassies up at the big hoose."

"Weel, what a'body kens is maistly true. Ye'll no guess what yon auld Claybody is daein'. Ye ken he's a contractor, forbye ither things, and he's got the contrack for makin' the big dam at Kinlochbuie. There's maybe a thousand navvies workin' there, and he's bringin' ower a squad o' them—Benjie says mair nor a hundred—to guaird the forest."

"Ass!" exclaimed Palliser-Yeates. "He'll drive every beast into Caithness."

"Na, na. Macnicol is not entirely wantin' in sense. The navvies will no be allowed inside the forest. They'll be a guaird outside—what's that they ca' it?—an outer barrage. Macnicol will see that a' the deer are in the Sanctuary, and in this kind o' weather it will no be that deeficult. But it will be verra **deeficult** for his lordship to get inside the forest, and it will be **verra near** an impossibeelity to get a beast out."

Archie looked round the room. "Dashed unsportin' I call it. I bet it's the young 'un's idea."

"Look here, Charles," said Leithen. "Isn't it about time to consider whether you shouldn't cry off this Haripol affair? It was different at the start. John and I had a fair sporting chance. Our jobs were steep enough, but yours is absolutely perpendicular. . . . The Claybodys are not taking any

162

chances, and a hundred able-bodied navvies is a different-sized proposition to a few gillies. The confounded Press has blazoned the thing so wide that if you're caught you'll be a laughing-stock to the whole civilised world. Don't you see that you simply can't afford to lose, any more than the Claybodys? Then, to put the lid on it, our base is under a perpetual threat from those newspaper fellows. I'd rather have all Scotland Yard after me than the Press—you agree, Crossby? I'm inclined to think that John Macnab has done enough *pour chauffer la gloire.* It's insanity to go on."

Lamancha shook his head. "It's all very well for you—you won. I tell you frankly that nothing on earth will prevent me having a try at Haripol. All you say is perfectly true, but I don't choose to listen to it. This news of Wattie's only makes me more determined."

Leithen subsided into his book, observing—"I suppose that is because you're a great man. You're a sober enough fellow at most times, but you're able now and then to fling your hat over the moon. You can damn the consequences, which I suppose is one of the tests of greatness. John and I can't, but we admire you, and we'll bail you out."

It was Sir Archie, strangely enough, who now abetted Lamancha's obstinacy. "I grant you the odds are stiff," he declared, "but that only means that we must find some way to shorten them. Nothing's impossible after yesterday. There was I gibbering with terror and not a notion in my head, and yet I got on fairly well, didn't I, Wattie?"

"Ye made a grand speech, sir. There was some said it was the best speech they ever heard in a' their days. There was one man said ye was haverin', but"—fiercely—"he didna say it twice."

"We've the whole day to make a plan," Archie went on. "Hang it all, there must be some way to diddle the Claybodys. We've got a pretty good notion of the lie of the land, and Wattie's a perfect Red Indian at getting up to deer. We muster four and a half able-bodied men, counting me as half. And there's Benjie. Benjie, you're a demon at strategy. Have you anything to say?"

"Aye," said Benjie, "I've a plan. But ye're ower particular here, and maybe ye wadna like it." This with a dark glance at Palliser-Yeates, who was leaving the room to get more tobacco.

"We'll have it, all the same. Let's sit down to business. Stick the ordnance map on that table, Charles, and you, Ned, shut that book and give us the benefit of your powerful mind."

Leithen rose, yawning. "I've left my pipe in the dining-room. Wait a moment till I fetch it."

Now Dr Kello, on his departure, had left the front-door of the house open, and the steady downpour of rain blanketed all other sounds from outside. So it came to pass that when Archie's quick ear caught the noise of footsteps on the gravel and he bounded into the hall, he was confronted with the spectacle of Colonel Raden and his daughters already across the doorstep. Moreover, as luck would have it, at that moment Leithen from the dining-room and Palliser-Yeates from his bedroom converged on the same point.

"Hullo, Roylance," the Colonel cried. "This is a heathenish hour for a visit, but we had to have some exercise, and my daughters wanted to come up and congratulate you on your performance yesterday. A magnificent speech, sir! Uncommon good sense! What I—"

But the Colonel stopped short in mystification at the behaviour of his daughters, who were staring with wide eyes at two unknown figures who stood shamefacedly behind Sir Archie. This last, having no alternative, was trying to carry off things with a high hand.

"Let me introduce," he was proclaiming, "Sir Edward Leithen—Mr Palliser-Yeates—Miss Raden, Miss Janet Raden, Colonel—"

But he was unheeded. Agatha was looking at Leithen and Janet at Palliser-Yeates, and simultaneously the two ejaculated, "John Macnab!"

Archie saw that it was all up. Shouting for Mrs Lithgow, he helped his visitors to get out of their mackintoshes, and ordered his housekeeper to have these garments dried. Then he ushered them into the smoking-room where were Lamancha and Crossby and Benjie and a good peat-fire. Wattie, at the first sound of voices, had discreetly retired.

"Come along, Colonel, I'll explain. Very glad to see you—have that chair . . . what about dry stockings? . . ."

But his hospitable bustle was unheeded. The Colonel, hopelessly at sea, was bowing to a tall man who in profound embarrassment was clearing books and papers out of chairs.

"Yes, that's Lord Lamancha. You heard him yesterday. Charles, this is Colonel Raden, and Miss Agatha and Miss Janet. That is Mr Crossby, the eminent journalist. That little scallywag is Fish Benjie, whom I believe you know. . . . Sit down, please, all of you. We're caught out and are going to confess. Behold the lair of John Macnab."

Colonel Raden was recovering himself.

"I read in the papers," he said, "that John Macnab is the reincarnation of Harald Blacktooth. In that case we are related. With which of these gentleman have I the honour to claim kin?"

The words, the tone, convinced Sir Archie that the danger was past, and his nervousness fled.

"Properly speakin', you've found three new relatives. There they are. Not bad fellows, though they've been givin' me a hectic time. Now *I* retire—shoes off, feet fired, and turned out to grass. Ned, you've a professional gift of exposition. Fire away, and tell the whole story."

Sir Edward Leithen obeyed, and it may be said that the tale lost nothing in his telling. He described the case of three gentlemen, not wholly useless to their country, who had suddenly fallen into ennui. He told of a cure, now perfected, but of a challenge not yet complete. "I've been trying to persuade Lord Lamancha to drop the thing," he said, "but the Claybodys have put his back up, and I'm not sure that I blame him. It didn't matter about you or Bandicott, for you took it like sportsmen, and we should have felt no disgrace in being beaten by you. But Claybody is different."

"By Gad, sir, you are right," the Colonel shouted, rising to his feet and striding about the room. "He and his damned navvies are an insult to every gentleman in the Highlands. They're enough to make Harald Blacktooth rise from the dead. I should never think anything of Lord Lamancha again—and I've thought a devilish lot of him up to now—if he took this lying down. Do you know, sir"—turning to Lamancha—"that I served in the Scots Guards with your father—we called them the Scots Fusilier Guards in those days—and I am not going to fail his son."

Sir Edward Leithen was a philosopher, with an acute sense of the ironies of life, and as he reflected that here was a laird, a Tory, and a strict preserver of game working himself into a passion over the moral rights of the poacher, he suddenly relapsed into helpless mirth. Colonel Raden regarded him sternly and uncomprehendingly, but Janet smiled, for she too had an eye for comedy.

"I'm tremendously grateful to you," Lamancha said. "You know more about stalking than all of us put together, and we want your advice."

"Janet," commanded her parent, "you have the best brain in the family. I'll be obliged if you'll apply it to this problem."

For an hour the anxious conclave surrounded the spread-out ordnance-map. Wattie was summoned, and with a horny finger expounded the probable tactics of Macnicol and the presumable disposition of the navvy guard. At the end of the consultation Lamancha straightened his back.

"The odds are terribly steep. I can see myself dodging the navvies, and with Wattie's help getting up to a stag. But if Macnicol and the gillies are perched round the Sanctuary they are morally certain to spot us, and, if we have to bolt, there's no chance of getting the beast over the march. That's a hole I see no way out of."

"Janet," said the Colonel, "do you?"

Janet was looking abstractedly out of the window. "I think it is going to clear up," she observed, disregarding her father's question. "It will be a fine afternoon, and then, if I am any judge of the weather, it will rain cats and dogs in the evening."

"We had better scatter after luncheon," said Lamancha, "and each of us go for a long stride. We want to be in training for to-morrow."

After the Colonel had suggested half a dozen schemes, the boldness of which was only matched by their futility, the Radens rose to go. Janet signalled to Benjie, who slipped out after her, and the two spoke in whispers in the hall, while Archie was collecting the mackintoshes from the kitchen.

"I want you to be at Haripol this afternoon. Wait for me a little on this side of the lodge about half-past three."

Benjie grinned and nodded. "Aye, lady, I'll be there." He, too, had a plan for shortening the odds, and he had so great a respect for Janet's sagacity that he thought it probable that she might have reached his own conclusion.

As Janet had foretold, it was a hot afternoon. The land steamed in the sun, but every hill-top was ominously clouded. While the inhabitants of Crask were engaged in taking stealthy but violent exercise among the sinuousities of Sir Archie's estate, Janet Raden mounted her yellow pony and rode thoughtfully towards Haripol by way of Inverlarrig and the high road. There were various short-cuts, suitable for a wild-cat like Benjie, but after the morning's torrential rains she had no fancy for swollen bogs and streams. She found Benjie lurking behind a boulder near the lodge, and in the shelter of a clump of birches engaged him in earnest conversation. Then she rode decorously through the gates and presented herself at the castle door.

Haripol was immense, new, and, since it had been built by a good architect out of good stone, not without its raw dignity. Janet found Lady Claybody in a Tudor hall which had as much connection with a Scots castle as with a Kaffir kraal. There was a wonderful jumble of possessions —tapestries which included priceless sixteenth-century Flemish pieces, and French fakes of last year; Ming treasures and Munich atrocities; armour of which about a third was genuine; furniture indiscriminately Queen Anne, Sheraton, Jacobean, and Tottenham Court

Road; and pictures which ranged from a Sir Joshua (an indifferent specimen) to a recent Royal Academy portrait of Lord Claybody. A feature was the number of electric lamps to illumine the hours of darkness, the supports of which varied from Spanish altar-candlesticks to two stuffed polar bears and a turbaned Ethiopian in coloured porcelain.

Lady Claybody was a heavily handsome woman still in her early fifties. The purchase of Haripol had been her doing, for romance lurked in her ample breast, and she dreamed of a new life in which she should be an unquestioned great lady far from the compromising environment where the Claybody millions had been won. Her manner corresponded to her ambition, for it was stately and aloof, her speech was careful English seasoned with a few laboriously acquired Scots words, and in her household her wish was law. A merciful tyrant, she rarely resorted to ultimata, but when she issued a decree it was obeyed.

She was unaffectedly glad to see Janet, for the Radens were the sort of people she desired as friends. Two days before she had been at her most urbane to Agatha and the Colonel, and now she welcomed the younger daughter as an ambassador from that older world which she sought to make her own. A small terrier drowned her greetings with epileptic yelps.

"Silence, Roguie," she enjoined. "You must not bark at a fellow-countrywoman. Roguie, you know, is so high-strung that he reacts to any new face. You find me quite alone, my dear. Our daughters do not join us till next week, when we shall have a houseful for the stalking. Now I am having a very quiet, delicious time drinking in the peace of this enchanted glen."

She said no word of John Macnab, who was doubtless the primary cause of this solitude. Lord Claybody and Johnson, it appeared, were out on the hill. Janet chattered on the kind of topics which she felt suitable—hunting in the Midlands, the coming Muirtown Gathering, the political meeting of yesterday. "Claybody thought Sir Archie Roylance rather extravagant," said the lady, "but he was greatly impressed with Lord Lamancha's speech. Surely it is absurd that his part of the Highlands, which your sister says was so loyal to Prince Charlie, should be a hot-bed of radicalism. Claybody thinks that that can all be changed, but not with a candidate who truckles to socialist nonsense."

Janet was demure and acquiescent, sighing when her hostess sighed, condemning when she condemned. Presently the hot sun shining through the windows suggested the open air to Lady Claybody, who was dressed for walking.

"Shall we stroll a little before tea?" she asked. "Wee Roguie has been cooped indoors all morning, and he loves a run, for he comes of a very sporting breed."

They set forth accordingly, into gardens bathed in sunshine, and thence to the coolness of beech woods. The Reascuill, after leaving its precipitous glen, flows, like the Raden, for a mile or two in haughlands, which are split by the entry of a tributary, the Doran, which in its upper course is the boundary between Haripol and Crask. Between the two streams stands a wooded knoll which is a chief pleasaunce of the estate. It is a tangle of dwarf birches, bracken and blaeberry, with ancient Scots firs on the summit, and from its winding walks there is a prospect of the high peaks of the forest rising black and jagged above the purple ridges.

At its foot they crossed the road which followed the river into the forest, and Janet caught sight of a group of men lounging by the bridge.

"Have you workmen on the place just now?" she asked.

"Only wood-cutters, I think," said Lady Claybody.

Wee Roguie plunged madly into the undergrowth, and presently could be heard giving tongue, as if in pursuit of a rabbit. "Dear little fellow!" said his mistress. "Hear how he loves freedom!"

The ladies walked slowly to the crest of the knoll, where they halted to admire the view. Janet named the different summits, which looked ominously near, and then turned to gaze on the demesne of Haripol lying green and secure in its cincture of wood and water. "I think you have the most beautiful place in the Highlands," she told her hostess. "It beats Glenraden, for you have the sea."

"It is very lovely," was the answer. "I always think of it as a fortress, where we are defended against the troubles of the world. At Ronham one might as well be living in London, but here there are miles of battlements between us and dull everyday things. . . . Listen to Roguie! How happy he is! !"

Roguie's yelps sounded now close at hand, and now far off, as the scent led him. Presently, as the ladies moved back to the house, the sound grew fainter. "He will probably come out on the main avenue," his mistress said. "I like him to feel really free, but he always returns in good time for his little supper."

They had tea in the tapestried hall, and then Janet took her leave. "I want to escape the storm," she explained, "for it is certain to rain hard again before night." As it chanced she did not escape it, but after a wayside colloquy with a small boy, arrived at Glenraden as wet as if she had swum the Larrig. She had sent by Benjie a message to Crask, concerning her share in the plans of the morrow

That night after dinner, while the rain beat on the windows, John Macnab was hard at work. The map was spread out on the table, and Lamancha prepared the orders for the coming action. If we would understand his plan, it is necessary to consider the nature of the terrain. The hill behind Crask rises to a line of small cliffs not unlike a South African *kranz,* and through a gap in the line runs a moorland track which descends by the valley of the Doran till it joins the main road from Inverlarrig almost at Haripol gates. The Doran glen—the Crask march is the stream—is a wide hollow of which the north side is the glacis of the great Haripol peaks. These are, in order from west to east, Stob Ban, Stob Coire Easain, Sgurr Mor, and the superb tower of Sgurr Dearg. Seen from the Crask ridge the summits rise in cones of rock from a glacis which at the foot is heather and scrub and farther up steeps of scree and boulders. Between each peak there is a pass leading over to the deep-cut glen of the Reascuill, which glen is contained on the north by the hills of Machray forest.

It was certain that the navvy cordon would be an outer line

of defence, outside the wilder ground of the forest. Wattie expounded it with an insight which the facts were to justify. "The men will be posted along the north side o' the Doran, maybe half-way up the hill—syne round the west side o' Stob Ban and across the Reascuill at the new fir plantin'—syne up the Machray march along the taps o' Clonlet and Bheinn Fhada. They can leave out Sgurr Dearg, for ye'd hae to be a craw to get ower that side o't. By my way o' thinkin', they'll want maybe three hundred to mak a proper ring, and they'll want them thickest on the Machray side where the ground is roughest. North o' the Doran it's that bare that twa-three men could see the whole hill-side, and Macnicol's no the ane to waste his folk. The easy road intil the Sanctuary is fae Machray up the Reascuill, and the easy way to get a beast out wad be by the way o' the Red Burn. But the navvies will be as thick as starlin's there, so it's no place for you and me, my lord."

The Haripol Sanctuary lay at the headwater of the Reascuill, between what was called the Pinnacle Ridge of Sgurr Dearg and the cliffs of Sgurr Mor. As luck would have it, a fairly easy path, known generally as the Beallach, led from it to the glen of the Doran. It was clear that Lamancha must enter from the south, and, if he got a stag, remove it by the same road.

"I'll get ye into the Sanctuary, never fear," said Wattie grimly, "There's no a navvy ever whelpit wad keep you and me out. But when we're there, God help us, for we'll hae Macnicol to face. And if Providence is mercifu' and we get a beast, we've the navvies to get it through, and that's about the end o't. Ye canna mak yoursel' inconspicuous when ye're pu'in at a muckle stag."

"True," said Lamancha, "and that's just where Mr Palliser-Yeates comes in. . . . John, my lad, your job is to be waiting on the Doran side of the Beallach, and if you see Wattie and me with a beast, to draw off the navvies in that quarter. You had better move west towards Haripol, for there's better cover on that side. D'you think you can do it? You used to have a pretty gift of speed, and you've always had an uncommon eye for ground."

Palliser-Yeates said modestly that he thought he was up to the job, provided Lamancha did not attract the prior notice of the watchers. Once the pack got on his trail, he fancied he could occupy their attention for an hour or two. The difficulty lay in keeping Lamancha in view, and for that purpose it would be necessary to ensconce himself at the very top of the Beallach, where he could have sight of the upper Sanctuary.

To Leithen fell the onerous task of creating a diversion on the other side of the forest. He must start in the small hours and be somewhere on the Machray boundary when Lamancha was beginning operations. There lay the most obvious danger-point, and there the navvies would probably be thickest on the ground. At all costs their attention—and that of any Haripol gillies in the same quarter—must be diverted from what might be happening in the Sanctuary. This was admittedly a hard duty, but Leithen was willing to undertake it. He was not greatly afraid of the navvies, who are a stiff-jointed race, but the Haripol gillies were another matter. "You simply must not get caught," Lamancha told him. "If you're hunted, make a bee-line north to Machray and Glenaicill—the gillies won't be keen to be drawn too far away from Haripol. You won the school mile in your youth, and you're always in training. Hang it all, you ought to be able to keep Claybody's fellows on the run. I never yet knew a gillie quick on his feet."

"That's a pre-war notion," said Palliser-Yeates. "Some of the young fellows are uncommon spry. Ned may win all right, but it won't be by much of a margin."

The last point for decision was the transport of the stag. The moor-road from Crask was possible for a light car with a high clearance, and it was arranged that Archie should take the Ford by that route and wait in cover on the Crask side of the Doran. It was a long pull from the Beallach to the stream, but there were tributary ravines where the cover was good—always presuming that Palliser-Yeates had decoyed away the navvy guard.

"Here's the lay-out, then," said Lamancha at last. "Wattie and I get into the Sanctuary as best we can and try for a stag. If

172

we get him, we bring him through the Beallach; John views us and shows himself, and draws off the navvies, whom we assume to be few at that point. Then we drag the beast down to the Doran and sling it into Archie's car. Meanwhile Ned is on the other side of the forest, doing his damnedest to keep Macnicol busy. . . . That's about the best we can do, but I needn't point out to you that every minute we're taking the most almighty chances. We may never get a shot. Macnicol may be in full cry after us long before we reach the Beallach. The navvies may refuse to be diverted by John, or may come back before we get near Archie's car. . . . Ned may pipe to heedless ears, or, worse still, he may be nobbled and lugged off to the Haripol dungeons. . . . It's no good looking for trouble before it comes, but I can see that there's a big bank of it waiting for us. What really frightens me is Macnicol and the gillies at the Sanctuary itself. This weather is in our favour, but even then I don't see how they can miss hearing our shot, and that of course puts the lid on it."

A time-table was drawn up after much discussion. Leithen was to start for Machray at 3 a.m., and be in position about 8. Lamancha and Wattie, about the latter hour, would be attempting to enter the Sanctuary by the Beallach. Palliser-Yeates must be at his post not later than 9, and Archie with the car should reach the Doran by 10. The hour of subsequent happenings depended upon fate; the thing might be over for good or ill by noon, or it might drag on till midnight.

When the last arrangements had been settled Lamancha squared his back against the mantelpiece and looked round on the company.

"Of course we're all blazing idiots—the whole thing is insanity—but we've done the best we can in the way of preparation. The great thing is for each of us to keep his wits about him and use them, for everything may go the opposite way to what we think. There's no 'according to Cocker' in this game."

Archie was wrinkling his brows.

"It's all dashed ingenious, Charles, but do you think you have any real chance?"

173

"Frankly, I don't," was the answer. "The best we can hope for is to fail without being detected. I think there would be a far-away sporting chance if Macnicol could be tied up. That's what sticks in my gizzard. I don't see how it's possible to get a shot in the Sanctuary without Macnicol spotting it."

Wattie Lithgow had returned, and caught the last words. He was grinning broadly.

"I'm no positeeve but that Macnicol wull be tied up," he observed. "Benjie's here, and he's brocht something wi' him."

He paused for effect.

"It's a dog—a wee, yelpin' dog."

"Whose dog?"

"Leddy Claybody's. It seems that at Haripol her leddyship wears the breeks—that the grey mear is the better horse there—and it seems that she's fair besottit on that dog. Benjie was sayin' that if it were lost Macnicol and a'body about the place wad be set lookin' for't, and naething wad be thought of at Haripol till it was fund."

Archie rose in consternation.

"D'you mean to say—How on earth did the beast come here?"

"It cam here wi' Benjie. It's fine and comfortable in a box in the stable. . . . I'm no just clear about what happened afore that, but I think Miss Janet Raden and Benjie gae'd ower to Haripol this afternoon and fund the puir wee beast lost in the wuds."

Archie did not join in the laughter. His mind held no other emotion than a vast and delighted amazement. The lady who two days before had striven to lift his life to a higher plane, who had been the sole inspiration of his successful speech of yesterday, was now discovered conspiring with Fish Benjie to steal a pup.

11

HARIPOL—THE MAIN ATTACK

SOME men begin the day with loose sinews and a sluggish mind, and only acquire impetus as the hours proceed; others show a declining scale from the vigour of the dawn to the laxity of evening. It was fortunate for Lamancha that he belonged to the latter school. At daybreak he was obstinate, energetic, and frequently ill-tempered, as sundry colleagues in France and Palestine had learned to their cost; and it needed an obstinate man to leave Crask between the hours of five and six in the morning on an enterprise so wild and in weather so lamentable. For the rain came down in sheets, and a wind from the north-east put ice into it. He stopped for a moment on the summit of the Crask ridge, to contemplate a wall of driving mist where should have been a vista of the Haripol peaks. "This wund will draw beasts intil the Sanctuary without any help from Macnicol," said Wattie morosely. "It's ower fierce to last. I wager it will be clear long afore night."

"It's the weather we want," said Lamancha, cowering from the violence of the blast.

"For the Sanctuary—maybe. Up till then I'm no sae sure. It's that thick we micht maybe walk intil a navvy's airms."

The gods of the sky were in a capricious mood. All down the Crask hill-side to the edge of the Doran the wet table-cloth of the fog clung to every ridge and hollow. The stream was in roaring spate, and Lamancha and Wattie, already soaked to the skin, forded it knee-high. They had by this time crossed the moor-road from Crask to Haripol, and marked the nook where in the lee of rocks and birches Archie was to be waiting with the Ford car. Beyond lay the long lift of land to the Haripol peaks. It was rough with boulders and heather, and broken with small gullies, and on its tangled face a man might readily lose himself. Wattie disliked the mist solely because it prevented him from locating the watchers, since his experience of life made him disinclined to leave anything to chance; but he had no trouble in finding his way in it. The consequence was that he took Lamancha over the glacis at the pace of a Ghurka, and in half an hour from the Doran's edge had him panting among the screes just under the Beallach which led to the Sanctuary. Somewhere behind them were the vain navvy pickets, happily evaded in the fog.

Then suddenly the weather changed. The wind shifted a point to the east, the mist furled up, the rain ceased, and a world was revealed from which all colour had been washed, a world as bleak and raw as at its first creation. The grey screes sweated grey water, the sodden herbage was bleached like winter, the crags towering above them might have been of coal. A small fine rain still fell, but the visibility was now good enough to show them the ground behind them in the style of a muddy etching.

The consequence of this revelation was that Wattie shuffled into cover. He studied the hill-side behind him long and patiently with his glass. Then he grunted: "There's four navvies, as I mak out, but no verra well posted. We cam gey near ane o' them on the road up. Na, they canna see us here, and besides they're no lookin' this airt." Lamancha tried to find them with his telescope, but could see nothing human in the wide sopping wilderness.

Wattie grumbled as he led the way up a kind of *nullah,* usually as dry as Arabia but now spouting a thousand rivulets, right into the throat of the Beallach. "It's clearin' just when we wanted it thick. The ways o' Providence is mysteerious. . . . Na, na, there's nae road there. That's a fox's track, and it's the deer's road we maun gang. Stags will no climb rocks, sensible beasts. . . . The wind's gone, but I wish the mist wad come down again."

At the top of the pass was a pad of flat ground, covered thick with the leaves of cloudberries. On the right rose the Pinnacle

Ridge of Sgurr Dearg, in its beginning an easy scramble which gave no hint of the awesome towers which later awaited the traveller; on the left Sgurr Mor ran up in a steep face of screes. "Keep doun," Wattie enjoined, and crawled forward to where two boulders made a kind of window for a view to the north.

The two looked down into three little corries which, like the fingers of a hand, united in the palm of a larger corrie, which was the upper glen of the Reascuill. It was a sanctuary perfectly fashioned by nature, for the big corrie was cut off from the lower glen by a line of boiler-plates like the wall of a great dam, down which the stream plunged in cascades. The whole place was loud with water—the distant roar of the main river, the ceaseless dripping of the cliffs, the chatter and babble of a myriad hidden rivulets. But the noise seemed only to deepen the secrecy. It was a world in monochrome, every detail clear as a wet pebble, but nowhere brightness or colour. Even the coats of the deer had taken on the dead grey of the slaty crags.

Never in his life had Lamancha seen so many beasts together. Each corrie was full of them, feeding on the rough pastures or among the boulders, drifting aimlessly across the spouts of screes below the high cliffs, sheltering in the rushy gullies. There were groups of hinds and calves, and knots of stags, and lone beasts on knolls or in mud-baths, and, since all were restless, the numbers in each corrie were constantly changing.

"Ye gods, what a sight!" Lamancha murmured, his head at Wattie's elbow. "We won't fail for lack of beasts."

"The trouble is," said Wattie, "that there's ower mony." Then he added obscurely that "it might be the day o' Pentecost."

Lamancha was busy with his glass. Just below him, not three hundred yards off, where the ravine which ran from the Beallach opened out into the nearest corrie, there was a group of deer—three hinds, a little stag, and farther on a second stag of which only the head could be seen.

"Wattie," he whispered excitedly, "there's a beast down there—a shootable beast. It's just what we're looking for . . . close to the Beallach."

"Aye, I see it," was the answer. "And I see something mair. There's a man ayont the big corrie—d'ye see yon rock shapit like a puddock-stool? . . . Na, the south side o' the waterfall. . . . Well, follow on frae there towards Bheinn Fhada—have ye got him?"

"Is that a man?" asked the surprised Lamancha.

"Where's your een, my lord? It's a man wi' grey breeks and a brown jaicket—an' he's smokin' a pipe. Aye, it's Macqueen. I ken by the lang legs o' him."

"Is he a Haripol gillie?"

"He's the second stalker. He's under notice, for him and young Mr Claybody doesna agree. Macqueen comes frae the Lowlands, and has a verra shairp tongue. They was oot on the hill last week, and Mr Johnson was pechin' sair gaun up the braes, an' no wonder, puir man. He cries on Macqueen to gang slow, and says, apologetic-like,'Ye see, Macqueen, I've been workin' terrible hard the past year, and it's damaged my wund.' Macqueen, who canna bide the sight of him, says, 'I'm glad to hear it, sir. I was feared it was maybe the drink.' Gey impident!"

"Shocking."

"Weel, he's workin' off his notice. . . . I'm pleased to see him yonder, for it means that Macnicol will no be there. Macnicol"—Wattie chuckled like a dropsical corncrake—"is maist likely beatin' the roddydendrums for the wee dog. Macqueen is set there so as he can watch this Beallach and likewise the top of the Red Burn on the Machray side, which I was tellin' ye was the easiest road. If ye were to kill that stag doun below he could baith see ye and hear ye, and ye'd never be allowed to shift it a yaird. . . . Na, na. Seein' Macqueen's where he is, we maun try the wee corrie right under Sgurr Dearg. He canna see into that."

"But we'll never get there through all those deer."

"It will not be easy."

"And if we get a stag we'll never be able to get it over this Beallach."

"Indeed it will tak a great deal of time. Maybe a' nicht. But

178

I'll no say it's not possible. . . . Onyway, it is the best plan. We will have to tak a lang cast roond, and we maunna forget Macqueen. I'd give a five-pun-note for anither blatter o' rain."

The next hour was one of the severest bodily trials which Lamancha had ever known. Wattie led him up a chimney of Sgurr Mor, the depth of which made it safe from observation, and down another on the north face, also deep, and horribly loose and wet. This brought them to the floor of the first corrie at a point below where the deer had been observed. The next step was to cross the corrie eastwards towards Sgurr Dearg. This was a matter of high delicacy—first because of the number of deer, second because it was all within view of Macqueen's watch-tower.

Lamancha had followed in his time many stalkers, but he had never seen an artist who approached Wattie in skill. The place was littered with hinds and calves and stags, the cover was patchy at the best, and the beasts were restless. Wherever a route seemed plain the large ears and spindle shanks of a hind appeared to block it. Had he been alone Lamancha would either have sent every beast streaming before him in full sight of Macqueen, or he would have advanced at the rate of one yard an hour. But Wattie managed to move both circumspectly and swiftly. He seemed to know by instinct when a hind could be bluffed and when her suspicions must be laboriously quieted. The two went for the most part on their bellies like serpents, but their lowliness of movement would have been of no avail had not Wattie, by his sense of the subtle eddies of air, been able to shape a course which prevented their wind from shifting deer behind them. He well knew that any movement of beasts in any quarter would bring Macqueen's vigilant glasses into use.

Their task was not so hard so long as they were in hollows on the corrie floor. The danger came in crossing the low ridge to that farther corrie which was beyond Macqueen's ken, for, as they ascended, the wind was almost bound to carry their scent to the deer through which they had passed. Wattie lay long with his chin in the mire and his eyes scanning the ridge till he made up his mind on his route. Obviously it was the choice of the least among several evils, for he shook his head and frowned.

The ascent of the ridge was a slow business, and toilful. Wattie was clearly following an elaborate plan, for he zigzagged preposterously, and would wait long for no apparent reason in places where Lamancha was held precariously by half a foothold and the pressure of his nails. Anxious glances were cast over his shoulder at the post where Macqueen was presumably on duty. The stalker's ears seemed of an uncanny keenness, for he would listen hard, hear something, and then utterly change his course. To Lamancha it was all inexplicable, for there appeared to be no deer on the ridge, and the place was so much in the lee that not a breath of wind seemed to be abroad to carry their scent. Hard as his condition was, he grew furiously warm and thirsty, and perhaps a little careless, for once or twice he let earth and stones slip under his feet.

Wattie turned on him fiercely. "Gang as if ye was growin'," he whispered. "There's beasts on a' sides."

Sobered thereby, Lamancha mended his ways, and kept his thoughts rigidly on the job before him. He crept docilely in Wattie's prints, wondering why on a little ridge they should go through exertions that must be equivalent to the ascent of the Matterhorn. At last his guide stopped. "Put your head between thae rashes," he enjoined. "Ye'll see her."

"See what?" Lamancha gasped.

"That dour deevil o' a hind."

There she was, a grey elderly beldame, with her wicked puck-like ears, aware and suspicious, not five yards off.

"We canna wait," Wattie hissed. "It's ower dangerous. Bide you here like a stone."

He wriggled away to his right, while Lamancha, hanging on a heather root, watched the twitching ears and wrinkled nozzle. . . . Presently from farther up the hill came a sharp bark, which was almost a bleat. The hind flung up her head and gazed intently. . . . Five minutes later the sound was repeated, this time from a lower altitude. The beast sniffed, shook herself, and stamped with her foot. Then she laid back her ears, and trotted quietly over the crest.

Wattie was back again by Lamancha's side. "That puzzled the auld bitch," was his only comment. "We can gang faster now, and God kens we've nae time to loss."

As Lamancha lay panting at last on the top of the ridge he looked down into the highest of the lesser corries, tucked right under the black cliffs of Sgurr Dearg. It was a little corrie, very steep, and threaded by a burn which after the rain was white like a snow-drift. Vast tumbled masses of stone, ancient rockfalls from the mountain, lay thick as the cottages in a hamlet. At first sight the place seemed to be without deer. Lamancha, scanning it with his glass, could detect no living thing among the debris.

Wattie was calling fiercely on his Maker.

"God, it's the auld hero," he muttered, his eyes glued to his telescope.

At last Lamancha got his glasses adjusted, and saw what his companion saw. Far up the corrie, on a patch of herbage—the last before the desert of the rocks began—stood three stags. Two were ordinary beasts, shootable, for they must have weighed sixteen or seventeen stone, but with inconsiderable heads. The third was no heavier, but he had a head like a blasted pine—going back fast, for the beast was old, but still with thirteen clearly marked points and a most noble spread of horn.

"It's him," Wattie crooned. "It's the auld hero. Fine I ken him, for I seen him on Crask last back-end rivin' at the stacks. There's no a forest hereaways but they've had a try for him, but the deil's in him, for the grandest shots aye miss. What's your will, my lord? Dod, if John Macnab gets yon lad, he can cock his bonnet."

"I don't know, Wattie. Is it fair to kill the best beast in the forest?"

"Keep your mind easy about that. Yon's no a Haripol beast. He's oftener on Crask than on Haripol. He's a traiveller, and in one season will cover the feck o' the Hielands. I've heard that oreeginally he cam oot o' Kintail. He's terrible auld—some says a hundred year—and if ye dinna kill him he'll perish next winter, belike, in a snaw-wreath, and that's a puir death to dee."

"It's a terrible pull to the Beallach."

"It will be that, but there's the nicht afore us. If we don't take that beast—or one o' the three— I doubt we'll no get anither chance."

"Push on, then, Wattie. It looks like a clear coast."

"I'm no so sure. There's that deevil o' a hind somewhere afore us."

Down through the gaps of the Pinnacle Ridge blew fine streams of mist. They were the precursors of a new storm, for long before the two men had wormed their way into the corrie the mountain before them was blotted out with a curtain of rain, and the wind, which seemed for a time to have died away, was sounding a thousand notes in the Pan's-pipes of the crags.

"Good," said Lamancha. "This will blanket the shot."

"Ba-ad too," growled Wattie, "for we'll be duntin' against the auld bitch."

Lamancha believed he had located the stags well enough to go to them in black darkness. You had only to follow the stream to its head, and they were on the left bank a hundred yards or so from the rocks. But when he reached the burn he found that his memory was useless. There was not one stream but dozens, and it was hard to say which was the main channel. It was a loud world again, very different from the first corrie, but, when he would have hastened, Wattie insisted on circumspection. "There's the hind," he said, "and maybe since we're out o' Macqueen's sicht there's nae need to hurry."

His caution was justified. As they drew themselves up the side of a small cascade the tops of a pair of antlers were seen over the next rise. Lamancha thought they were those of one of the three stags, but Wattie disillusioned him. "We're no within six hundred yards o' yon beasts," he said.

A long circuit was necessary, happily in good cover, and the stream was not rejoined till at a point where its channel bore to the south, so that their wind would not be carried to the beasts below the knoll. After that it seemed advisable to Wattie to keep to the water, which was flowing in a deep-cut bed. It was a job for a merman rather than for breeched human beings, for Wattie would permit of no rising to a horizontal or even to a kneeling position. The burn entered at their collars and flowed steadily through their shirts to an exit at their knees. Never had men been so comprehensively and continuously wet. Lamancha's right arm ached with pulling the rifle along the bank—he always insisted on carrying his weapon himself—while his body was submerged in the icy outflow of Sgurr Dearg's springs.

The pressure of Wattie's foot in his face halted him. Blinking through the spray, he saw his leader's head raised stiffly to the alert in the direction of a little knoll. Even in the thick weather he could detect a pair of bat-like ears, and he realised that these ears were twitching. It did not need Wattie's whisper of "the auld bitch" to reveal the enemy.

The two lay in the current for what seemed to Lamancha at least half an hour. He had enough hill-craft to recognise that their one hope was to stick to the channel, for only thus was there a chance of their presence being unrevealed by the wind. But the channel led them very close to the hind. If the brute chose to turn her foolish head they would be within view.

With desperate slowness, an inch at a time, Wattie moved upwards. He signed to Lamancha to wait while he traversed a pool where only his cap and nose showed above the water. Then came a peat wallow, when his face seemed to be ground into the moss, and his limbs to be splayed like a frog's and to move with frog-like jerks. After that was a little cascade, and, beyond, the shelter of a big boulder which would get him out of the hind's orbit. Lamancha watched this strange progress with one eye; the other was on the twitching ears. Mercifully all went well, and Wattie's stern disappeared round a corner of rock.

He laboured to follow with the same precision. The pool was

easy enough except for the trailing of the rifle. The peat was straightforward going, though in his desire to follow his leader's example he dipped his face so deep in the black slime that his nostrils were plugged with it, and some got into his eyes which he dared not try to remove. But the waterfall was a snag. It was no light task to draw himself up against the weight of descending water, and at the top he lay panting for a second, damming up the flow with his body. . . . Then he moved on; but the mischief had been done.

For the sound of the release of the pent-up stream had struck a foreign note on the hind's ear. It was an unfamiliar noise among the many familiar ones which at the moment filled the corrie. She turned her head sharply, and saw something in the burn which she did not quite understand. Lamancha, aware of her scrutiny, lay choking, with the water running into his nose; but the alarm had been given. The hind turned her head, and trotted off up-wind.

The next he knew was Wattie at his elbow making wild signals to him to rise and follow. Cramped and staggering, he lumbered after him away from the stream into a moraine of great granite blocks. "We're no twa hundred yards from the stags," the guide whispered. "The auld bitch will move them, but please God we'll get a shot." As Lamancha ran he marvelled at Wattie's skill, for he himself had not a notion where in the wide world the beasts might be.

They raced to a knoll, and Wattie flung himself flat on the top.

"There," he cried. "Steady, man. Tak the nearest. A hundred yards. Nae mair."

Lamancha saw through the drizzle three stags moving at a gentle trot to the south—up-wind, for in the corrie the eddies were coming oddly. They were not really startled, but the hind had stirred them. The big stag was in the centre of the three, and the proper shot was the last—a reasonable broadside.

Wattie's advice had been due to his loyalty to John Macnab, and not to his own choice, and this Lamancha knew. The desire of the great stag was on him, as it was on the hunter in

Homer, and he refused to be content with the second-best. It was not an easy shot in that bad light, and it is probable that he would have missed; but suddenly Wattie gave an unearthly bark, and for a second the three beasts slowed down and turned their heads towards the sound.

In that second Lamancha fired. The great head seemed to bow itself, and then fling upwards, and all three disappeared at a gallop into the mist.

"A damned poor tailoring shot!" Lamancha groaned.

"He's deid for all that, but God kens how far he'll run afore he drops. He's hit in the neck, but a wee thing ower low. . . . We can bide here a while and eat our piece. If ye wasna John Macnab I could be wishin' we had brought a dog."

Lamancha, cold, wet, and disgusted, wolfed his sandwiches, had a stiff dram from his flask, and smoked a pipe before he started again. He cursed his marksmanship, and Wattie forbore to contradict him; doubtless Jim Tarras had accustomed him to a standard of skill from which this was a woeful declension. Nor would he hold out much hope. "He'll gang into the first corrie and when he finds the wund different there he'll turn back for the Reascuill. If this was our ain forest and the weather wasna that thick, we might get another chance at him there. . . . Oh, aye, he might gang for ten mile. The mist is a good thing, for Macqueen will no see what's happenin', but if it was to lift, and he saw a' the stags in the corrie movin', you and me wad hae to find a hidy-hole till the dark. . . . Are ye ready, my lord?"

They crossed the ridge which separated them from the first corrie, close to the point where it took off from the *massif* of Sgurr Dearg. It was a shorter road than the one they had come by, and they could take it safely, for they were now moving up-wind, owing to the curious eddy from the south. Over the ridge it would be a different matter, for there the wind would be easterly as before. But it was a stiff climb and a slow business, for they had to make sure that they were on the track of the stag.

Wattie trailed the blood-marks like an Indian, noticing

185

splashes on stones and rushes which Lamancha would have missed. "He's sair hit," he observed at one point. "See! He tried that steep bit and couldna manage it. There's the mark o' his feet turnin'. . . . He's stoppit here. . . . Aye, here's his trail, and it'll be the best for you and me. There's nothing like a wounded beast for pickin' the easiest road."

On the crest the air stirred freely, and, as it seemed to Lamancha, with a new chill. Wattie gave a grunt of satisfaction, and sniffed it like a pointer dog. He moistened his finger and held it up; then he plucked some light grasses and tossed them into the air.

"That's a mercifu' dispensation! Maybe that shot that ye think ye bauchled was the most providential shot ye ever fired. . . . The wund is shiftin'. I looked for it afore night, but no that early in the day. It's wearin' round to the south. D'yee see what that means?"

Lamancha shook his head. Disgust had made his wits dull.

"Yon beast, as I telled ye, was a traiveller. There's nothing to keep him in Haripol forest. But he'll no leave it unless the wund will let him. Now it looks as if Providence was kind to us. The wund's blawin' from the Beallach, and he's bound to gang up-wund."

The next half-hour was a period of swift drama. Sure enough, the blood-marks turned up the first corrie in the direction from which the two had come in the morning. As the ravine narrowed the stag had evidently taken to the burn, for there were splashes on the rocks and a tinge of red in the pools.

"He's no far off," Wattie croaked. "See, man, he's verra near done. He's slippin' sair."

And then, as they mounted, they came on a little pool where the water was dammed as if by a landslip. There, his body half under the cascade, lay the stag, stone dead, his great horns parting the fall like a pine swept down by a winter spate.

The two regarded him in silence, till Wattie was moved to pronounce his epitaph.

"It's yersel, ye auld hero, and ye've come by a grand end. Ye've had a braw life traivellin' the hills, and ye've been a braw beast, and the fame o' ye gaed through a' the country-side. Ye micht have dwined awa in the cauld winter an dee'd in the wame o' a snaw-drift. Or ye micht have been massacred by ane o' thae Haripol sumphs wi' ten bullets in the big bag. But ye've been killed clean and straucht by John Macnab, and that is a gentleman's death, whatever."

"That's all very well," said Lamancha, "but you know I tailored the shot."

"Ye're a fule," cried the rapt Wattie. "Ye did no siccan thing. It was a verra deeficult shot, and ye put it deid in the only place ye could see. I will not have seen many better shots at all, at all."

"What about the gralloch?" Lamancha asked.

"No here. If the mist lifted Macqueen micht see us. It's no fifty yards to the top o' the Beallach, and we'll find a place there for the job."

Wattie produced two ropes and bound the fore-feet and the hind-feet together. Then he rapidly climbed to the summit, and reported on his return that the mist was thick there, and that there were no tracks except their own of the morning. It was a weary business dragging the carcass up a nearly perpendicular slope. First with difficulty they raised it out of the burn channel, and then drew it along the steep hill-side. They had to go a long way up the hill-side to avoid the rock curtain on the edge of the Beallach, but eventually the top was reached, and the stag was deposited behind some boulders on the left of the flat ground. Here, even if the mist lifted, they would be hid from the sight of Macqueen, and from any sentries there might be on the Crask side.

Wattie flung off his coat and proceeded with gusto to his gory task. The ravens, which had been following them for the past hour, came nearer and croaked encouragement from the ledges of Sgurr Dearg and Sgurr Mor. Wattie was in high spirits, for he whistled softly at his work; but Lamancha, after his first moment of satisfaction, was restless with anxiety. He had still to get his trophy out of the forest, and there seemed many chances of a slip between his lips and that cup. He was impatient for Wattie to finish, for the air seemed to him lightening. An ominous brightness was flushing the mist towards the south, and the rain had declined to the thinnest of drizzles. He told Wattie his fears.

"Aye, it'll be a fine afternoon. I foresaw that, but that's maybe not a bad thing, now that we're out o' Macqueen's sight."

Wattie completed his job, and hid the horrid signs below a pile of sods and stones. "Nae *poch-a-bhuie* for me the day," he grinned. "I've other things to think o' besides my supper." He wiped his arms and hands in the wet heather and put on his coat. Then he produced a short pipe, and, as he turned away to light it, a figure suddenly stood beside Lamancha and made his heart jump.

"My hat!" said Palliser-Yeates, "what a head! That must be about a record for Wester Ross. I never got anything as good myself. You're a lucky devil, Charles."

"Call me lucky when the beast is safe at Crask. What about your side of the hill?"

"Pretty quiet. I've been here for hours and hours, wondering where on earth you two had got to. . . . There's four fellows stuck at intervals along the hill-side, and I shouldn't take them to be very active citizens. But there's a fifth who does sentry-go, and I don't fancy the look of him so much. Looks a keen chap, and spry on his legs. What's the orders for me? The place has been playing hide-and-seek, and half the time I've been sitting coughing in a wet blanket. If it stays thick I suppose my part is off."

Wattie, stirred again into fierce life, peered into the thinning fog.

"Damn! The mist's liftin'. I'll get the beast ower the first screes afore it's clear, and once I'm in the burn I'll wait for ye. I can manage the first bit fine mysel'—I could manage it a', if there was nae hurry. . . . Bide you here till I'm weel startit, for I don't like the news o' that wandering navvy. And you sir"—this to Palliser-Yeates—"be ready to show yourself down the hill-side as soon as it's clear enough for the folk to see

188

ye. Keep well to the west, and draw them off towards Haripol. There's a man posted near the burn, but he's the farthest east o' them, and for God's sake keep them to the west o' me and the stag. Ye're an auld hand at the job, and should hae nae deeficulty in ficklin' a wheen heavy-fitted navvies. Is Sir Erchibald there wi' the cawr?"

"I suppose so. The time he was due the fog was thick. I couldn't pick him up from here with the glass when the weather cleared, but that's as it should be, for the place he selected was absolutely hidden from this side."

"Well, good luck to us a'." Wattie tossed off a dram from the socket of Lamancha's flask, and, dragging the stag by the horns, disappeared in two seconds from sight.

"I'll be off, Charles," said Palliser-Yeates, "for I'd better get down-hill and down the glen before I start." He paused to stare at his friend. "By Gad, you do look a proper blackguard. Do you realise that you've a face like a nigger and a two-foot rent in your bags? It would be good for Johnson Claybody's soul to see you!"

12

HARIPOL—TRANSPORT

IT may be doubted whether in clear weather Sir Archie could ever have reached his station unobserved by the watchers on the hill. The place was cunningly chosen, for the road, as it approached the Doran, ran in the lee of a long covert of birch and hazel, so that for the better part of a mile no car on it could be seen from beyond the stream, even from the highest ground. But as the car descended from the Crask ridge it would have been apparent to the sentinels, and its non-appearance beyond the covert would have bred suspicion. As it was the clear spell had gone before it topped the hill, for Sir Archie was more than an hour behind the scheduled time.

This was Janet's doing. She had started off betimes on the yellow pony for Crask, intending to take the by-way from the Larrig side, but before she reached the Bridge of Larrig she had scented danger. One of the correspondents, halted by the roadside with a motor bicycle, accosted her with great politeness and begged a word. She was Miss Raden, wasn't she? and therefore she knew all about John Macnab. He had heard gossip in the glen of the coming raid on Haripol, and understood that this was the day. Would Miss Raden advise him from her knowledge of the country-side? Was it possible to find some coign of vantage from which he might see the fun?

Janet stuck to the simple truth. She had heard the same story, she admitted, but Haripol was a gigantic and precipitous forest, and it was preserved with a nicety unparalleled in her experience. To go to Haripol in the hope of finding John Macnab would be like a casual visit to England on the chance of meeting the King. She advised him to go to Haripol in the

190

evening. "If anything has happened there," she said, "you will hear about it from the gillies. They'll either be triumphant or savage, and in either case they'll talk."

"We've got to get a story, Miss Raden," the correspondent observed dismally, "and in this roomy place it's like looking for a needle in a hayfield. What sort of people are the Claybodys?"

"You won't get anything from them," Janet laughed. "Take my advice and wait till the evening."

When he was out of sight she turned her pony up the hill and arrived at Crask with an anxious face. "If these people are on the loose all day," she told Sir Archie, "they're bound to spoil sport. They may stumble on our car, or they may see more of Mr Palliser-Yeates's doings than we want. Can nothing be done? What about Mr Crossby?"

Crossby was called into consultation and admitted the gravity of the danger. When his help was demanded, he hesitated. "Of course I know most of them, and they know me, and they're a very decent lot of fellows. But they're professional men, and I don't see myself taking on the job of gulling them. *Esprit de corps,* you know. . . . No, they don't suspect me. They probably think I left the place after I got off the Strathlarrig fish scoop, and that I don't know anything about the Haripol business. I daresay they'd be glad enough to see me if I turned up. . . . I might link on to them and go with them to Haripol and keep them in a safe place."

"That's the plan," said Archie. "You march them off to Haripol—say you know the ground—which you do a long sight better than they. Some of the gillies will be hunting the home woods for Lady Claybody's pup. Get them mixed up in that show. It will all help to damage Macnicol's temper, and he's the chap we're most afraid of. . . . Besides, you might turn up handy in a crisis. Supposin' Ned Leithen—or old John—has a hard run at the finish you might confuse the pursuit. . . . That's the game, Crossby my lad, and you're the man to play it."

It was after eleven o'clock before the Ford car, having

slipped over the pass from Crask in driving sleet, came to a stand in the screen of birches with the mist wrapping the world so close that the foaming Doran six yards away was only to be recognised by its voice. All the way there Sir Archie had been full of forebodings.

"We're givin' too much weight away, Miss Janet," he croaked. "All we've got on our side is this putrid weather. That's a bit of luck, I admit. Also we've two of the most compromisin' objects on earth, Fish Benjie and that little brute Roguie. . . . Claybody has a hundred navvies, and a pack of gillies, and every beast will be in the Sanctuary, which is as good as inside a barb-wire fence. . . . The thing's too ridiculous. We've got to sit in this car and watch an eminent British statesman bein' hoofed off the hill, while old John tries to play the decoy-duck, and Ned Leithen, miles off, is hoppin' like a he-goat on the mountains. . . . It's pretty well bound to end in disaster. One of them will be nobbled—probably all three—and when young Claybody asks, 'Wherefore this outrage?' I don't see what the cowerin' culprit is goin' to answer and say unto him."

But when the car stopped in the drip of the birches, and Archie had leisure to look at the girl by his side, he began to think less of impending perils. The place was loud with wind and water, and yet curiously silent. The mist had drawn so close that the two seemed to be shut into a fantastic, secret world of their own. Janet was wearing breeches and a long riding-coat covered by a grey oilskin, the buttoned collar of which framed her small face. Her bright hair, dabbled with raindrops, was battened down under an ancient felt hat. She looked, thought Sir Archie, like an adorable boy. Also for the last half-hour she had been silent.

"You have never spoken to me about your speech," she said at last, looking away from him.

"Yours, you mean," he said. "I only repeated what you said that afternoon on Carnmore. But you didn't hear it. I looked for you everywhere in the hall, and I saw your father and your sister and Bandicott, but I couldn't see you."

"I was there. Did you think I could have missed it? But I was too nervous to sit with the others, so I found a corner at the back below the gallery. I was quite near Wattie Lithgow."

Archie's heart fluttered. "That was uncommon kind. I don't see why you should have worried about that—I mean I'm jolly grateful. I was just going to play the ass of all creation when I remembered what you had said—and— well, I made a speech instead of repeating the rigmarole I had written. I owe everything to you, for, you see, you started me out—I can never feel just that kind of funk again. . . . Charles thinks I might be some use in politics. . . . But I can tell you when I sat down and hunted through the hall and couldn't see you it took all the gilt off the gingerbread."

"I was gibbering with fright," said the girl, "when I thought you were going to stick. If Wattie hadn't shouted out, I think I would have done it myself."

After that silence fell. The rain poured from the trees on to the cover of the Ford, and from the cover sheets of water cascaded to the drenched heather. Wet blasts scourged the occupants and whipped a high colour into their faces. Janet arose and got out.

"We may as well be properly wet," she said. "If they get the stag as far as the Doran, they must find some way across. There's none at present. Hadn't we better build a bridge?"

The stream, in ordinary weather a wide channel of stones where a slender current falls in amber pools, was now a torrent four yards wide. But it was a deceptive torrent with more noise than strength, and save in the pools was only a foot or two deep. There were many places where a stag could have been easily lugged through by an able-bodied man. But the bridge-building proposal was welcomed, since it provided relief for both from an atmosphere which had suddenly become heavily charged. At a point where the channel narrowed between two blaeberry-thatched rocks it was possible to make an inclined bridge from one bank to the other. The materials were there in the shape of sundry larch-poles brought from the lower woods for the repair of a bridge on the Crask road. Archie dragged half a dozen to the edge and pushed them across. Then Janet marched through the water, which ran close to the top of her riding-boots, and prepared the abutment on the farther shore, weighting the poles down with sods broken from an adjacent bank.

"I'm coming over," she cried. "If it will bear a stag, it will bear me."

"No, you're not," Archie commanded. "I'll come to you."

"The last time I saw you cross a stream you fell in," she reminded him.

Archie tested the contrivance, but it showed an ugly inclination to behave like a see-saw, being insufficiently weighted on Janet's side.

"Wait a moment. We need more turf," and she disappeared from sight beyond a knoll. When she returned she was excessively muddy as to hands and garments.

"I slipped in that beastly peat-moss," she explained. "I never saw such hags, and there's no turf to be got except with a spade. . . . No, you don't! Keep off that bridge, please. It isn't nearly safe yet. I'm going to roll down stones."

Roll down stones she did till she had erected something very much like a cairn at her end, which would have opposed a considerable barrier to the passage of any stag. Then she announced that she must get clean, and went a few yards down-stream to one of the open shallows, where she proceeded to make a toilet. She stood with the current flowing almost to her knees, suffering it to wash the peat from her boots and the skirts of her oilskin and at the same time scrubbing her grimy hands. In the process her hat became loose, dropped into the stream, and was clutched with one hand, while with the other she restrained the efforts of the wind to uncoil her shining curls.

It was while watching the moving waters at their priest-like task that crisis came upon Sir Archie. In a blinding second he realised with the uttermost certainty that he had found his mate. He had known it before, but now came the flash of supreme conviction. . . . For swelling bosoms and pouting

194

lips and soft curves and languishing eyes Archie had only the most distant regard. He saluted them respectfully and passed by the other side of the road—they did not belong to his world. But that slender figure splashing in the tawny eddies made a different appeal. Most women in such a posture would have looked tousled and flimsy, creatures ill at ease, with their careful allure beaten out of them by weather. But this girl was an authentic creature of the hills and winds—her young slimness bent tensely against the current, her exquisite head and figure made more fine and delicate by the conflict. It is a sad commentary on the young man's education, but, while his soul was bubbling with poetry, the epithet which kept recurring to his mind was "clean-run." . . . More, far more. He saw in that moment of revelation a comrade who would never fail him, with whom he could keep on all the roads of life. It was that which all his days he had been confusedly seeking.

"Janet," he shouted against the wind, "will you marry me?"

She made a trumpet of one hand.

"What do you say?" she cried.

"Will you marry me?"

"Yes," she turned a laughing face, "of course I will."

"I'm coming across," he shouted.

"No. Stay where you are. I'll come to you."

She climbed the other bank and made for the bridge of larch-poles, and before he could prevent her she had embarked on that crazy structure. Then that happened which might have been foreseen, since the poles on Archie's side of the stream had no fixed foundation. They splayed out, and he was just in time to catch her in his arms as she sprang.

"You darling girl," he said, and she turned up to him a face smiling no more, but very grave.

Archie, his arms full of dripping maiden, stood in a happy trance.

"Please put me down," she said. "See, the mist is clearing. We must get into cover."

Sure enough the haze was lifting from the hill-side before them and long tongues of black moorland were revealed stretching up to the crags. They found a place among the birches which gave them a safe prospect and fetched luncheon from the car. Hot coffee from a thermos was the staple of the meal, which they consumed like two preoccupied children. Archie looked at his watch and found it after two-o'clock. "Something must begin to happen soon," he said, and they took up position side by side on a sloping rock, Janet with her Zeiss glasses and Archie with his telescope.

His head was a delicious merry-go-round of hopes and dreams. It was full of noble thoughts—about Janet, and himself, and life. And the thoughts were mirthful too—a great, mellow, philosophic mirthfulness. John Macnab was no longer an embarrassing hazard, but a glorious adventure. It did not matter what happened—nothing could happen wrong in this spacious and rosy world. If Lamancha succeeded, it was a tremendous joke, if he failed a more tremendous, and, as for Leithen and Palliser-Yeates, comedy had marked them for its own. . . . He wondered what he had done to be blessed with such happiness.

Already the mist had gone from the foreground, and the hills were clear to half-way up the rocks of Sgurr Mor and Sgurr Dearg. He had his glass on the Beallach, on the throat of which a stray sun-gleam made a sudden patch of amethyst.

"I see someone," Janet cried. "On the edge of the pass. Have you got it?—on the left-hand side of that spout of stones."

Archie found the place. "Got him. . . . By Jove, it's Wattie. . . . And—and—yes, by all the gods, I believe he's pullin' a stag down. . . . Wait a second. . . . Yes, he's haulin' it into the burn. . . . Well done, our side! But where on earth is Charles?"

The two lay with their eyes glued on the patch of hill, now lit everywhere by the emerging sun. They saw the little figure dip into a hollow, appear again and then go out of sight in the upper part of a long narrow scaur which held the headwaters of a stream—they could see the foam of the little falls farther down. Before it disappeared Archie had made out a stag's head against a background of green moss.

196

"That's that," he cried. "Charles must be somewhere behind protectin' the rear. I suppose Wattie knows what he's doin' and is certain he can't be seen by the navvies. Anyhow, he's well hidden at present in the burn, but he'll come into view lower down when the ravine opens out. He's a tough old bird to move a beast at that pace. . . . The question now is, where is old John? It's time he was gettin' busy."

Janet, whose glass made up in width of range what it lacked in power, suddenly cried out: "I see him. Look! up at the edge of the rocks—three hundred yards west of the Beallach. He's moving down-hill. I think it's Palliser-Yeates—he's the part of John Macnab I know best."

Archie found the spot. "It's old John right enough, and he's doin' his best to make himself conspicuous. Those yellow breeks of his are like a flag. We've got a seat in the stalls and the curtain is goin' up. Now for the fun."

Then followed for the better part of an hour a drama of almost indecent sensation. Wattie and his stag were forgotten in watching the efforts of an eminent banker to play hare to the hounds of four gentlemen accustomed to labour rather with their hands than with their feet. It was the navvy whose post was almost directly opposite Janet and Archie who first caught sight of the figure on the hill-side. He blew a whistle and began to move uphill, evidently with the intention of cutting off the intruder's retreat to the east and driving him towards Haripol. But the quarry showed no wish to go east, for it was towards Haripol that he seemed to be making, by a long slant down the slopes.

"I've got Number Two," Janet whispered. "There— above the patch of scrub—close to the three boulders. . . . Oh, and there's Number Three. Mr Palliser-Yeates is walking straight towards him. Do you think he sees him?"

"Trust old John. He's the wiliest of God's creatures, and he hasn't lost much pace since he played outside three-quarters for England. Wait till he starts to run."

But Mr Palliser-Yeates continued at a brisk walk apparently oblivious of his foes, who were whistling like curlews, till he was very near the embraces of Number Three. Then he went through a very creditable piece of acting. Suddenly he seemed to be stricken with terror, looked wildly around to all the points of the compass, noted his pursuer, and, as if in a panic, ran blindly for the gap between Numbers Two and Three. Number Four had appeared by this time, and Number Four was a strategist. He did not join in the pursuit, but moved rapidly down the glen towards Haripol to cut off the fugitive, should he outstrip the hunters.

Palliser-Yeates managed to get through the gap, and now appeared running strongly for the Doran, which at that point of its course—about half a mile down-stream from Janet and Archie—flowed in a deep-cut but not precipitous channel, much choked with birch and rowan. Numbers Two and Three followed, and also Number One, who had by now seen that there was no need of a rearguard. For a little all four disappeared from sight, and Janet and Archie looked anxiously at each other. Cries, excited cries, were coming up-stream, but there was no sign of human beings.

"John can't have been such a fool as to get caught," Archie grumbled. "He has easily the pace of those heavy-footed chaps. Wish he'd show himself."

Presently first one, then a second, then a third navvy appeared on the high bank of the Doran, moving aimlessly, like hounds at fault.

"They've lost him," Archie cried. "Where d'you suppose the leery old bird has got to? He can't have gone to earth."

That was not revealed for about twenty minutes. Then a cry from one of the navvies called the attention of the others to something moving high up on the hill-side.

"It's John," Archie muttered. "He must have crawled up one of the side-burns. Lord, that's pretty work."

The navvies began heavily to follow, though they had a thousand feet of lee-way to make up. But it was no part of Palliser-Yeates's plan to discourage them, since he had to draw them clean away from the danger zone. Already this was almost achieved, for Wattie and his stag, even if he had left the

198

ravine, were completely hidden from their view by a shoulder of hill. He pretended to be labouring hard, stumbling often, and now and then throwing himself on the heather in an attitude of utter fatigue, which was visible to the pursuit below.

"It's a dashed shame," murmured Archie. "Those poor fellows haven't a chance with John. I only hope Claybody is payin' them well for this job."

The hare let the hounds get within a hundred yards of him. Then he appeared to realise their presence and to struggle to increase his pace, but, instead of ascending, he moved horizontally along the slope, slipping and sprawling in what looked like a desperate final effort. Hope revived in the navvies' hearts. Their voices could be heard—"You bet they're usin' shockin' language," said Archie—and Number One, who seemed the freshest, put on a creditable spurt. Palliser-Yeates waited till the man was almost upon him, and then suddenly turned downhill. He ran straight for Number Two, dodged him with that famous swerve which long ago on the football field had set forty thousand people shouting, and went down the hill like a rolling stone. Once past the navvy line, he seemed to slide a dozen yards and roll over, and when he got up he limped.

"Oh, he has hurt himself," Janet cried.

"Not a bit of it," said Archie. "It's the old fox's cunning. He's simply playin' with the poor fellows. Oh, it's wicked!"

The navvies followed with difficulty, for they had no gift of speed on a steep hill-face. Palliser-Yeates waited again till they were very near him, and then, like a hen partridge dragging its wing, trotted down the more level ground by the stream side. The pursuit was badly cooked, but it lumbered gallantly along, Number Four now making the running. A quarter of a mile ahead was the beginning of the big Haripol woods which clothed the western skirts of Stob Ban, and stretched to the demesne itself.

Suddenly Palliser-Yeates increased his pace, with no sign of a limp, and, when he passed out of sight of the two on the rock, was going strongly.

199

Archie shut up his glass. "That's a workmanlike show, if you like. He'll tangle them up in the woods, and slip out at his leisure and come home. I knew old John was abso-lute-ly safe. If he doesn't run slap into Macnicol—"

He broke off and stared in front of him. A figure like some ancient earth-dweller had appeared on the opposite bank. Hair, face, and beard were grimed with peat, sweat made furrows in the grime, and two fierce eyes glowered under shaggy eyebrows. Bumping against its knees were the antlers of a noble stag.

"Wattie," the two exclaimed with one voice.

"You old sportsman," cried Archie. "Did you pull that great brute all the way yourself? Where is Lord Lamancha?"

The stalker strode into the water dragging the stag behind him, and did not halt till he had it high on the bank and close to the car. Then he turned his eyes on the two, and wrung the moisture from his beard.

"You needn't worry," Archie told him. "Mr Palliser-Yeates has all the navvies in the Haripol woods."

"So I was thinkin'. I got a glisk of him up the burn. Yon's the soople one. But we've no time to loss. Help me to sling the beast into the cawr. This is a fine hidy-hole."

"Gad, what a stag!"

"It's the auld beast we've seen for the last five years. Ye mind me tellin' ye that he was at our stacks last winter. Come on quick, for I'll no be easy till he's in the Crask larder."

"But Lord Lamancha?"

"Never heed him. He's somewhere up the hill. It maitters little if he waits till the darkenin' afore he comes hame. The thing is we've got the stag. Are ye ready?"

Archie started the car, which had already been turned in the right direction. Coats and wraps and heather were piled on the freight, and Wattie seated himself on it like an ancient raven.

"Now, tak a spy afore ye start. Is the place clear?"

Archie, from the rock, reported that the hill-side was empty.

"What about the Beallach?"

Archie spied long and carefully. "I see nothing there, but of course I only see the south end. There's a rock which hides the top."

"No sign o' his lordship?"

"Not a sign."

"Never heed. He can look after himsel' braw and weel. Push on wi' the cawr, sir, for it's time we were ower the hill."

Archie obeyed, and presently they were climbing the long zigzag to the Crask pass. Wattie on the back seat kept an anxious look-out, issuing frequent bulletins, and Janet swept the glen with her glasses. But no sign of life appeared in the wide sunlit place except a buzzard high in the heavens and a weasel slipping into a cairn. Once the watershed had been crossed Wattie's heart lightened.

"Weel done, John Macnab," he cried. "Dod, ye're the great lad. Ye've beaten a hundred navvies and Macnicol and a', and ye've gotten the best heid in the country-side. . . . Hae ye a match for my pipe, Sir Erchie? Mine's been in ower mony bog-holes to kindle."

It was a clear, rain-washed world on which they looked, and the sky to the south was all an unbroken blue. The air was not sticky and oppressive like yesterday, but pure and balmy and crystalline. When Crask was reached the stag was decanted with expedition, and Archie addressed Janet with a new authority.

"I'm goin' to take you straight home in the Hispana. You're drippin' wet and ought to change at once."

"Might I change here?" the girl asked. "I told them to send over dry things, for I was sure it would be a fine afternoon. You see, I think we ought to go to Haripol."

"Whatever for?"

"To be in at the finish—and also to give Lady Claybody her dog back. Wee Roguie is rather on my conscience."

"That's a good notion," Archie assented. So Janet was handed over to Mrs Lithgow, who admitted that a suitcase had indeed arrived from Glenraden. Archie repaired to the upper bathroom, which Lamancha had aforetime likened to a drain-pipe, and, having bathed rapidly, habited himself in a suit of a reasonable newness and took special pains with his toilet. And all the while he whistled and sang, and generally comforted himself like a madman. Janet was under his roof—Janet would soon always be there—the most miraculous of fates was his! Somebody must be told, so when he was ready he went out to seek the Bluidy Mackenzie and made that serious-minded beast the receptacle of his confidences.

He returned to find a neat and smiling young woman conversing with Fish Benjie, whose task had been that of comforter and friend to Roguie. It appeared that the small dog had been having the morning of his life with the Crask rats and rabbits. "He's no a bad wee dog," Benjie reported, "if they'd let him alane. They break his temper keepin' him indoors and feedin' him ower high."

"Benjie must come too," Janet announced. "It would be a shame to keep him back. You understand—Benjie found Roguie in the woods—which is true, and handed him over to me—which is also true. I don't like unnecessary fibbing."

"Right-o! Let's have the whole bag of tricks. But, I say, you've got to stage-manage this show. Benjie and I put ourselves in your hands, for I'm hanged if I know what to say to Lady Claybody."

"It's quite simple. We're just three nice clean people—well, two clean people—who go to Haripol on an errand of mercy. Get out the Hispana, Archie dear, for I feel that something tremendous may be happening there."

As they started—Benjie and Roguie on the back seat—Bluidy Mackenzie came into view, hungrily eyeing an expedition from which he seemed to be barred.

"D'you mind if we take Mackenzie," Archie begged. "We'll go very slow, and he can trollop behind. The poor old fellow has been havin' a lonely time of it, and there's likely to be such a mix-up at Haripol that an extra hound won't signify."

Janet approved, and they swung down the hill and on to the highway, as respectable an outfit as the heart could wish, except for the waterproof-caped urchin on the back seat. The casual wayfarer would have noted only a very pretty girl and a well-appointed young man driving an expensive car at a most blameless pace. He could not guess what a cargo of dog-thieves and deer-thieves was behind the shining metal and spruce enamel. . . . Benjie talked to Wee Roguie in his own tongue, and what Janet and Archie said in whispers to each other is no concern of this chronicle. The sea at Inverlarrig was molten silver running to the translucent blue of the horizon, the shore woods gleamed with a thousand jewels, the abundant waters splashing in every hollow were channels of living light. The world sang in streams and soft winds, the cries of plover and the pipe of shore-birds, and Archie's heart sang above them all.

Close to Haripol gates a tall figure rose from the milestone as the car slowed down.

"Well, John, my aged sportsman, you did your part like a man. We saw it all."

"How are things going?"

"Famously."

"The stag?"

"In the Crask larder."

"And Charles?"

"Lost. Believed to be still lurkin' in the hills. Look here, John, get in beside Benjie. We are goin' to Haripol and restore the pup. You'll be a tower of strength to us, and old Claybody will be tremendously bucked to meet a brother magnate. . . . Really, I mean it."

"I'm scarcely presentable," said Palliser-Yeates, taking off an old cap and looking at it meditatively.

"Rot! You're as tidy as you'll ever be. Rather dandified for you. In you get, and don't tread on the hound. . . . Bloody, you brute, don't you know a pal when you see him?"

13

HARIPOL—AUXILIARY TROOPS

HALF-WAY down the avenue, Archie drew up sharply.

"I forgot about Mackenzie. We can't have him here—he'll play the fool somehow. Benjie, out you go. You're one of the few that can manage him. Here's his lead—you tie him up somewhere and watch for us, and we'll pick you up outside the gates when we start home. . . . Don't get into trouble on your own account. I advise you to cut round to the bothies, and try to find out what is happenin'."

On the massive doorstep of Haripol stood Lady Claybody, parasol in one hand and the now useless dog-whip in the other. She made a motion as if to retreat, but thought better of it. Her face was flushed, and her air had abated something of its serenity. The sight of Janet—for she looked at Archie without recognition—seemed to awake her to the duties of hospitality, and she advanced with outstretched hand. Then a yelp from the side of Palliser-Yeates wrung from her an answering cry. In a trice Wee Roguie was in her arms.

"Yes," Janet explained sweetly, "it's Roguie quite safe and well. There's a boy who sells fish at Strathlarrig—Benjie they call him—he found him in the woods and brought him to me. I hope you haven't been worried."

But Lady Claybody was not listening. She had set the dog on his feet and was wagging her forefinger at him, a procedure which seemed to rouse all the latent epilepsy of his nature. "Oh, you naughty, naughty Roguie! Cruel, cruel doggie! He loved freedom better than his happy home. Master and mistress have been so anxious about Wee Roguie."

It was an invocation which lasted for two and a half minutes, till the invoker realised the presence of the men. She graciously shook hands with Sir Archie.

"I drove Miss Janet over," said the young man, explaining the obvious. "And I took the liberty of bringin' a friend who is stayin' with me—Mr Palliser-Yeates. I thought Lord Claybody might like to meet him, for I expect he knows all about him."

The lady beamed on both. "This is a very great pleasure, Mr Palliser-Yeates, and I'm sure Claybody will be delighted. He ought to be in for tea very soon." As it chanced. Lady Claybody had an excellent memory and a receptive ear for talk, and she was aware that in her husband's conversation the name of Paliser-Yeates occurred often, and always in dignified connections.

She led the way through the hall to a vast new drawing-room which commanded a wide stretch of lawns and flower-beds as far as the woods which muffled the mouth of the Reascuill glen. When the party were seated and butler and footman had brought the materials for tea, Lady Claybody—Roguie on a cushion by her side—became confidential.

"We've had such a wearing day, my dear," she turned to Janet. "First, the ruffian who calls himself John Macnab is probably trying to poach our forest. The rain yesterday kept him off, but we have good reason to believe that he will come to-day. Poor Johnson has been on the hill since breakfast. Then, there was the anxiety about Roguie. I've had our people searching the woods and shrubberies, for the little darling might have been caught in a trap. . . . Macnicol says there are no traps, but you never can tell. And then, on the top of it all, we've been besieged since quite early in the morning by insolent journalists. No. They hadn't the good manners to come to the house—I should have sent them packing—but they have been over the grounds and buttonholing our servants. They want to hear about John Macnab, but we can't tell them anything, for as yet we know nothing ourselves. I gave orders that they should be turned out of the place—no violence, of course, for it doesn't do to offend the Press—but quite firmly, for they were trespassing. Would you believe it, my dear? they wouldn't go. So our people had simply to drive them out, and it has taken nearly all day, and they may be coming back any moment. . . . Something should really be done, Mr Palliser-Yeates, to restrain the licence of the modern Press, with its horrid, vulgar sensationalism and its invasion of all the sanctities of private life."

Palliser-Yeates cordially agreed. The lady had not looked to Archie for assent, and her manner towards him was a trifle cold. Perhaps it was the memory of her visit a fortnight before when he was sickening for smallpox; perhaps it was her husband's emphatic condemnation of his Muirtown speech.

At this point Lord Claybody entered, magnificent in a kilt of fawn-coloured tweed and a ferocious sporran made of the mask of a dog-otter. The garments, which were aggressively new, did not become his short, square figure.

"I don't think you have met my husband, Miss Raden," said his wife. Then to Lord Claybody: "You know Sir Archibald Roylance. And this is Mr Palliser-Yeates, who has been so kind as to come over to see us."

Palliser-Yeates was greeted with enthusiasm. "Delighted to meet you, sir. I heard you were in the North. Funny that we've had so much to do with each other indirectly and have never met. . . . You've been having a long walk? Well, I know what you need. Cold tea for you. We'll leave the ladies to their gossip and have a whisky-and-soda in the library. I've just had a letter from Dickinson on which I'd like your views. Busy folk like you and me can never make a clean cut of their holiday. There's always something clawing us back to the mill."

The two men were led off to the library, and Janet was left to entertain her hostess. That lady was in an expansive mood, which may have been due to the restoration of Roguie, but also owed something to the visit of Palliser-Yeates. "My heart is buried here," she told the girl. "Every day I love Haripol more—its beauty and poetry and its—its wonderful traditions. My dream is to make it a centre for all the nicest people to come and rest. Everybody comes to the Highlands now, and we have so much to offer them here. . . . Claybody, I may as well admit, is apt to be restless when we are alone. He is not enough of a sportsman to be happy shooting and fishing all day and every day. He has a wonderful mind, my dear, and he wants a chance of exercising it. He needs to be stimulated. Look how his eye brightened when he saw Mr Palliser-Yeates. . . . And then, there are the girls. . . . I'm sure you see what I mean."

Janet saw, and set herself to cherish the innocent ambition of her hostess. In view of what might befall at any moment, it was most needful to have the Claybodys in a good humour. Then Lady Claybody, one of whose virtues was a love of fresh air, proposed that they should walk in the gardens. Janet would have preferred to remain in the house, had she been able to think of any kind of excuse, for the out-of-doors at the moment was filled with the most explosive material—Benjie, Mackenzie, an assortment of fugitive journalists, and Leithen and Lamancha somewhere in the hinterland. But she assented with a good grace, and, accompanied by Roguie, who after a morning of liberty had cast the part of lap-dog contemptuously behind him, they sauntered into the trim parterres.

The head-gardener at Haripol was a man of the old school. He loved fantastically shaped beds and geometrical patterns, and geraniums and lobelias and calceolarias were still dear to his antiquated soul. On the lawns he had been given his head, but Lady Claybody, who had accepted new fashions in horticulture as in other things, had constructed a pleasaunce of her own, which with crazy-paving and sundials and broad borders was a very fair imitation of an old English garden. She had a lily-pond and a rosery and many pergolas, and what promised in twenty years to be a fine yew-walk. The primitive walled garden, planted in the Scots fashion a long way from the house, was now relegated to fruit and vegetables.

Lady Claybody was an inaccurate enthusiast. She poured into Janet's ear a flow of botanical information and mispronounced Latin names. Each innovation was modelled on what she had seen or heard of in some famous country house. The girl approved, for in that glen the environment of hill and wood was so masterful that the artifices of man were instantly absorbed. The gardens exhausted, they wandered through the rhododendron thickets, which in early summer were towers of flame, crossed the turbid Reascuill by a rustic bridge, and found themselves in a walk which skirted the stream through a pleasant wilderness. Here an expert from Kew had been turned loose, and had made a wonderful wild garden, in which patches of red-hot pokers and godetia and *Hyacinthus candicans* shone against the darker carpet of the heather. Roguie led the way, and where Roguie's yelps beckoned his mistress followed. Soon the two were nearly a mile from the house, approaching the portals of the Reascuill glen.

Sir Edward Leithen left Crask just as the wet dawn was breaking. He had a very long walk before him, but at that he was not dismayed; what perplexed him was how it was going to end. To the first part, a struggle with wind and rain and many moorland miles, he looked forward with enthusiasm. Long, lonely expeditions had always been his habit, for he was the kind of man who could be happy with his own thoughts. Before it became the fashion he had been a pioneer in guideless climbing in the Alps, and the red-letter days in his memory were for the most part solitary days. He was always in hard condition, and his lean figure rarely knew fatigue; weather he minded little, and he had long ago taught himself how to find his road, even in mist, with map and compass.

So it was with sincere enjoyment that his legs covered the rough miles—along the Crask ridge till it curved round at the head of the Doran and led him to the eastern skirts of Sgurr Dearg. He knew from the map that the great eastern precipice of that mountain was towering above him, but he saw only the white wall of fog a dozen yards off. His aim was to make a circuit of the *massif* and bear round to the pass of the Red Burn, which made a road between Haripol and Machray. He would then be nearly due north of the Sanctuary and exactly opposite where Lamancha proposed to make his entrance. . . . A fortnight earlier, when he first came to Crask, he had gone for a walk in far pleasanter weather, and had been acutely bored. Now, with no prospect but a wet blanket of mist, and with no chance of observing bird or plant, he was enjoying every moment of it. More, his thoughts were beginning to turn pleasantly towards the other side of his life—his books and hobbies, the intricacies of politics, the legal practice of which he was a master. He reflected almost with exhilaration on a difficult appeal which would come on in the autumn, when he hoped to induce the House of Lords to upset a famous judgement. He had begun to relish his competence again, even to take a modest pride in his fame; what had been dust and ashes in his mouth a few weeks ago had now an agreeable flavour. Palliser-Yeates was of the same way of thinking. Had he not declared last night that he wanted to give orders again and be addressed as "sir," instead of being chivvied about the countryside? And Lamancha? Leithen seriously doubted if Lamancha had ever suffered from quite the same malady. The trouble with him was that he had always a large streak of bandit in his composition, and must now and then give it play. That was what made him the bigger man, perhaps. Charles might take an almighty toss some day, but if he did not he would be first at the post, for he rode more gallantly to win.

"I suppose I may regard myself as cured," Leithen reflected, as he munched a second breakfast of cheese-sandwiches and raisins somewhere under the north-eastern spur of Sgurr Dearg. But he reflected, too, that he had a horribly difficult day ahead of him, for which he felt a strong distaste. He realised the shrewdness of Acton Croke's diagnosis: he was longing once more for the flesh-pots of the conventional.

His orders had been to get somewhere on the Machray side by eight o'clock, and he saw by his watch that he was ahead of his time. Once he had turned the corner of Sgurr Dearg the wind was shut off and the mist wrapped him closer. He had acquired long ago a fast but regular pace on the hills, and, judging from the time and the known distance, he knew that he must now be very near the Machray march. Presently he had topped a ridge which was clearly a watershed, for the plentiful waters now ran west. Then he began to descend, and soon was brought up by a raging torrent which seemed to be flowing north-west. This must be the Red Burn, coming down from the gullies of Sgurr Dearg, and it was his business to cross it and work his way westward along the edge of the great trough of the Reascuill. But he must go warily, for he was very near the pass, by which, according to the map, a road could be found from Corrie Easain in the Machray forest to the Haripol Sanctuary—the road which, according to Wattie Lithgow, gave the easiest access and would most assuredly be well watched.

He crossed the stream, not without difficulty, and climbed another ridge, beyond which the ground fell steeply. These must be the screes on the Reascuill side, he concluded, so he bore to the right and found, as he expected, that here there was a re-entrant corrie, and that he was on the very edge of the great trough. It was for him to keep this edge, but to go circumspectly, for at any moment he might stumble upon some of Claybody's sentries. His business was to occupy their attention, but he did not see what good he could do. The mist was distraction enough, for in it no man could see twenty yards ahead of him. But it might clear, and in that case he would have his work cut out for him. Meanwhile he must avoid a premature collision.

He avoided it only by a hairsbreadth. Suddenly that happened which at the moment was perplexing Wattie Lithgow and Lamancha a mile off. Corridors opened in the air—dark corridors of dizzy space and black rock seamed with torrents. Leithen found himself looking into a cauldron of which only the bottom was still hid, and at the savage splinters of the Pinnacle Ridge. He was looking at something less welcome, for thirty yards off, on the edge of the scarp, was a group of five men.

They had been boiling tea in billies in the lee of a rock and had been stirred to attention by the sudden clearing of the air. They saw him as soon as he saw them, and in a moment were on their feet and spreading out in his direction. He heard a cry, and then a babble of tongues.

210

Leithen did the only thing possible. He strode towards them with a magisterial air. They were the real navvy, the hardiest race in the land, sleeping in drainpipes, always dirty and wet, forgetting their sodden labours now and then in sordid drink, but tough, formidable, and resourceful.

"What the devil are you fellows doing here?" he shouted angrily.

At first they took him for a gillie.

"What the hell's your business?" one of them replied, but the advance had halted. As he came nearer, they changed their minds, for Leithen had not the air of a gillie.

"My business is to know what you're doing here—on my land?"

Now Machray forest was not let that season, and this Leithen knew. If any arrangement had been come to with Haripol it could only have been made between the stalkers. It was for him to play the part of the owner.

The men looked nonplussed, for the navvy, working under heavy-handed foremen, is susceptible to the voice of authority.

"We were sent up here to keep a look out," one answered.

"Look out for what? Who sent you?"

"It was Lord Claybody—we took our orders from Mr Macnicol."

Leithen sat down on a stone and lit his pipe.

"Well, you're trespassing on Machray—my ground. I don't know what on earth Lord Claybody means. I have heard nothing of it."

"There's a man tryin' to poach, sir. We were told to wait here and keep a look-out for him."

Leithen smiled grimly. "A pretty look-out you can keep in this weather. But that doesn't touch the point that you're in a place where you've no right to be. . . . You poor devils must have been having a rotten time roosting up here."

He took out his flask.

"Here's something to warm you. There's just enough for a tot apiece."

The flask was passed round amid murmurs of satisfaction,

while Leithen smoked his pipe and surveyed the queer party. "I call it cruelty to animals," he said, "to plant you fellows in a place like this. I hope you're well paid for it."

"We're gettin' a pound a day, and the man that grips the poacher gets a five-pund note. The name o' the poacher is Macnab."

"Well, I hope one of you will earn the fiver. Now, look here. I can't have you moving a yard north of this. You're on Machray ground as it is, for my march is the edge of the hill. I don't mind you squatting here, and of course it's no business of mine what you do on Haripol, but you don't stir a foot into Machray. With this wind you'll put all the beasts out of the upper corries."

He rose and strolled away. "I must be off. See that you mind what I've said. If you move, it must be into Haripol. A poacher! I never heard such rubbish. Better my job than yours, anyway. Still, I hope you get that fiver!"

Leithen departed in an atmosphere of general good will, and as soon as possible put a ridge between himself and the navvies. It had been a narrow escape, but mercifully no harm was done. He must keep well below the skyline on the Machray side, for there would be watchers elsewhere on the Haripol ground and he was not ready as yet to play the decoy-duck. For it had occurred to him that he was still too far east for his purpose. Those navvies were watching the pass from the Red Burn, and had no concern with what might be happening in the Sanctuary. Indeed, they could not see into it because of the spur which Sgurr Dearg flung out toward the Reascuill. He must be farther down the stream before he tried to interest those who might interfere with Lamancha; so he mended his pace, and, keeping well on the Machray side, made for the hill called Bheinn Fhada, which faced Sgurr Mor across the Reascuill.

Then the mist came down again, and in driving sleet Leithen scrambled among the matted boulders and screes of Bheinn Fhada's slopes. Here he knew he was safe enough, for he was inside the Machray march and out of any possible prospect

212

from the Reascuill. But it was a useless labour, and the return of the thick weather began to try his temper. The good humour of the morning had gone, when it was a delight to be abroad in the wilds alone and to pit his strength against storm and distance. He was growing bored with the whole business and at the same time anxious to play the part which had been set him. As it was, wandering on the skirts of Bheinn Fhada, he was as little use to John Macnab as if he had been reading Sir Walter Scott in the Crask smoking-room.

It took him longer than he expected to pass that weariful mountain, and it was noon before he ate the remnants of the food he had brought in the hollow which lies at the head of the second main Machray corrie, Corrie na Sidhe. Here he observed that sight which at the same moment was perturbing Lamancha on the Beallach looking over to Crask. The mist was thinning—not breaking into gloomy corridors, but lightening everywhere with the sun behind it. The wind, too, had shifted; it was blowing in his face from the south. Suddenly the top of Stob Coire Easain in front of him stood clear and bright, and its upper crags, jewelled with falling waters, rose out of a rainbow haze. Far out on the right he saw a patch of silver which he knew for the sea. Nearer, and far below, was an olive-green splash which must be the Haripol woods. And then, as if under a wizard's wand, the glen below him, from a pit of vapour, became an enamelled cup, with the tawny Reascuill looped in its hollows.

It was time for Leithen to be up and doing. He crawled to a point which gave him cover and a view into the glen, and searched the place long and carefully with his glasses. There must be navvy posts close at hand, but from where he lay he could not command the sinuosities of the hill-side below him. He saw the nest of upper corries which composed the Sanctuary, but not the Beallach, which was hidden by the ridge of Sgurr Mor. . . . He lay there for half an hour, uncertain what he should do next. If he descended into the glen it meant certain capture, for he would be cut off by some lower post. The only plan seemed to be to show himself on the upper slopes

213

and then try to draw the pursuit off towards Machray, but he did not see how such a course was going to help Lamancha in the Sanctuary. The plan of campaign, he decided, had been a great deal too elaborate, and his part looked like a wash-out.

He made his way along the hill-side towards the Machray peak which bore the name of Clonlet and the wide skirts of which made one side of the glen above Haripol, the opposite sentinel to Stob Ban. He had got well on to the slopes of that mountain when he detected something in the glen below. Men seemed to be moving down the stream—three at least—and to be moving fast. His sense of duty revived, for here seemed a task to his hand. . . . He showed himself on an outjutting knoll and waited. The men below had their eyes about them, for he was almost instantly observed. He heard cries, he saw a hand waved, then he heard a whistle blown. . . . After that he began to run.

At this point the chronicler must retrace his steps and follow the doings of Mr Johnson Claybody. That young gentleman had taken the threat of John Macnab most seriously to heart: he felt his honour involved, his sense of property outraged, and he saw the pride of the Claybodys lowered if the scoundrel were victorious on Haripol as he had been at Strathlarrig. Above all he feared the Press, which was making a holiday feature of this monstrous insolence. He it was who had devised the plan of defence, a plan which did credit to his wits. Not only had he placed his sentries with care, but he had arranged for peripatetic gillies to patrol between the stations and form an intelligence service for head-quarters. His *poste de commandement* was at Macnicol's cottage just beyond the gorge of the Reascuill and some two miles from the house.

All morning his temper had been worsening. The news of the journalistic invasion of Haripol, brought to him about ten o'clock by a heated garden-boy, had been the first shock. He had sent a message to his father, handing over to him that problem, with the results which we have seen. Also he was lamentably short of the force he had hoped to muster, owing to his mother's insistence on keeping Macnicol and two of the gillies behind to look for her dog. It was not till close on midday that, after a furious journey to the house in a two-seater car, he was able to recover the services of the head-stalker. Macnicol, he felt, should have been on the edge of the Sanctuary at daybreak; instead he had had to send Macqueen, a surly ruffian whom he had dismissed for insolence, but whose hillcraft he knew to be of the first order. Johnson's plan was that towards midday he himself, with a posse, should patrol the upper forest, so that, if John Macnab should be lurking there, he might drive him north or south against the navvy garrison. East, Sgurr Dearg shut the way, and west lay the grounds of Haripol, where escape would be impossible, since every living thing there was on the watch. Johnson's blood was up. If John Macnab had made his venture, he wanted to share directly in the chase and to be in at the death.

It was after midday before the flying column started. It was composed of Macnicol, Cameron the third stalker, two selected gillies, and three of the navvies who were more mobile than their fellows. Macnicol had prophesied that the weather would clear in the afternoon, so, though the mist was thick at the start, they took the road with confidence. Sure enough, it began to lift before they were half a mile up the glen, and Macnicol grunted his satisfaction.

"Macnab cannot escape noways," he said. "But I do not think he has come at all, unless he's daft. He would not get in, but, if he is in, he will never get out."

Johnson's one fear now was that the assault might not have been made. It would be a poor ending to his strategy if the pool were dragged and no fish were found in it. But presently he was reassured, for at the foot of Bheinn Fhada he met one of the patrolling gillies with tremendous news. A man had been seen that morning by the navvies at the Red Burn. He had passed as the Laird of Machray, and had given them whisky. The gillie knew that the Laird of Machray was a child of three dwelling at Bournemouth, and he had demanded a description of the visitor. It was a tallish man, they said, lean and clean-shaven, rather pale, and with his skin very tight over his cheek-bones. He had looked like a gentleman and had behaved as such. Now the only picture of John Macnab known to the gillies was that which had been broadcast in talk by Angus and Jimsie of Strathlarrig, and that agreed most startlingly with the navvies account. "A long, lean dog," Angus had said, "and whitish in the face." Wherefore the gillie had hastened with his tidings to head-quarters.

The news increased Johnson's pace. John Macnab was veritably in the forest, and at the thought he grew both nervous and wroth. There was something supernatural, he felt, about the impudence of a man who could march quietly up to a post of navvies and bluff them. Were all his subtle plans to be foiled? Then, half a mile on, appeared Macqueen, just descended from his eyrie.

Macqueen had to report that half an hour before, when the mist cleared and he could get a view of the corries, he had seen the deer moving. The wind at the same time had shifted to the south, and the beasts in the corrie below Beallach were frightened. He had seen nothing with his telescope—the beasts had been moved some time before, he thought, for they were well down the hill. In his opinion, if John Macnab was in the forest, he was on or beyond the Beallach.

Johnson considered furiously. "The fellow was at the Red Burn just before nine o'clock. He must have gone through the Sanctuary to be at the Beallach half an hour ago. Is that possible, Macnicol?"

"I don't ken." Macnicol scratched his head. "Macqueen says that only the beasts in the corrie below the Beallach were moved, but if he had gone through the Sanctuary they would have been all rinnin' oot. I'm fair puzzled, sir, unless he cam' doun the water and worked up by Sgurr Mor. That Macnab's a fair deevil."

"We'll get after him," said Johnson, and then he stopped short. He had a sudden memory of what had happened at Glenraden. Why should not John Macnab have sent a confederate to gull them into the belief that he was busy in the

Sanctuary, while he himself killed a stag in the woods around the house? There were plenty of beasts there, and it would be like his infernal insolence to poach one under the very windows of Haripol. It was true that the woodland stags were not easy to stalk, but Macnab had shown himself a mighty artist.

Johnson had a gift of quick decision. He briefly explained to his followers his suspicions. "The man at the Beallach may not be the man whom the navvies saw at the Red Burn. The Red Burn fellow may have gone down the Machray side, and be now in the woods. . . . Cameron, you take Andrew and Peter, and get down the glen in double-quick time. If you see anybody on Clonlet or in the woods, hunt him like hell. I'll skin you if you let him escape. Drive him right down to the gardens, and send word to the men there to be on the look-out. You'll be a dozen against one. Macnicol, you come with me, and you, Macqueen, and you three fellows, and we'll make for the Beallach. We'll cut up through the Sanctuary, for it don't matter a damn about the deer if we only catch that swine. He's probably lying up there till he can slip out in the darkness. . . . And, Cameron, tell them to send a car up the Doran road. I may want a lift home."

It was Cameron and his posse who spied Leithen on the side of Clonlet. All three were young men; they had the priceless advantage of acquaintance with the ground, while Leithen knew no more than the generalities of the map. As soon as he saw that he was pursued he turned up-hill with the purpose of making for Machray. He had had a long walk, but he felt fresh enough for another dozen miles or so, and he remembered his instructions to go north, if necessary even into Glenaicill.

But in this he had badly miscalculated. For the whistle of Cameron had alarmed a post of navvies in a nook of hill behind Leithen and at a greater altitude, who had missed him earlier for the simple reason that they had been asleep. Roused now to a sudden attention, they fanned out on the slope and cut him off effectively from any retreat towards Corrie na Sidhe. There were only two courses open to him—to climb the steep face of

Clonlet or to go west towards the woods. The first would be hard, he did not even know whether the rock was climbable, and if he stuck there he would be an easy prey. He must go west, and trust to find some way to Machray round the far skirts of the mountain.

Cameron did not hurry, for he knew what would happen. So long as the navvies cut off retreat to the east the victim was safe. Leithen did not realise his danger till he found himself above the woods on a broad grassy ledge just under the sheer rocks of Clonlet. It was the place called Crapnagower, which ended not in a hill-side by which the butt of Clonlet could be turned, but in a bold promontory of rock which fell almost sheer to the meadows of Haripol. Long before he got to the edge he had an uncomfortable suspicion of what was coming, but when he peered over the brink and saw cattle at grass far below him, he had an ugly shock. It looked as if he were cornered, and cornered too in a place far from the main scene of action, where his misfortunes could not benefit Lamancha.

He turned and plunged downward through the woods direct for Haripol. There was still plenty of fight in him, and his pursuers would have a run for their money. These pursuers were not far off. Andrew had climbed the hill and had been moving fast parallel to Leithen, but farther down among the trees. Cameron was on the lower road, a grassy aisle among the thickets, and Peter, the swifter, had gone on ahead to watch the farther slopes. It was not long before Leithen was made aware of Andrew, and the sight forced him to his right in a long slant which would certainly have taken him into the arms of Peter.

But at this moment the Fates intervened in the person of Crossby.

That eminent correspondent, having inspired his fellow-journalists with the spirit of all mischief and thereby sadly broken the peace of Haripol, was now lying up from further pursuit in the woods, confident that he had done his best for the cause. Suddenly he became aware of the ex-Attorney-General descending the hill in leaps and bounds, and a gillie not fifty yards behind on his trail. . . . Crossby behaved like Sir Philip

218

Sidney and other cavaliers in similar crises. "Thy need is the greater," was his motto, and as Leithen passed he whispered hoarsely to him to get into cover. Leithen, whose head was clear enough though his legs were aching, both heard and saw. He clapped down like a woodcock in a patch of bracken, while Crossby, whose garb and height were much the same as his, became the quarry in his stead.

The chase was not of long duration. The correspondent did not know the ground, nor did he know of the waiting Peter. Left to himself he might have outdistanced Andrew, but he was watched from below by wily eyes. He reached the grassy path, turned to his right, and rounded a corner to be embraced firmly and affectionately by the long arms of the gillie. "That's five pund in our pockets, Andra, ma man," the latter observed when the second gillie arrived. "If this is no John Macnab, it's his brither, and anyway we've done what we were telled." So, strongly held by the two men, the self-sacrificing Crossby departed into captivity.

Of these doings Leithen knew nothing. He did not believe that Crossby could escape, but the hunt had gone out of his ken. Now it is the nature of man that, once he is in flight, he cannot be content till he finds an indisputable place of refuge. This wood was obviously unhealthy, and he made haste to get out out of it. But he must go circumspectly, and the first need was for thicker cover, for this upper part was too open for comfort. Below he saw denser scrub, and he started to make his way to it.

The trouble was that presently he came into Cameron's view. The stalker had heard the crash of Crossby's pursuit, and had not hurried himself, knowing the strategic value of Peter's position. He proposed to wait, in case the fugitive doubled back. Suddenly he caught sight of Leithen farther up the hill, and apparently unfollowed. Had the man given the two gillies the slip? . . . Cameron performed a very creditable piece of stalking. He wormed his way up-hill till he was above the bushes where Leithen was now sheltering. The next thing that much-enduring gentleman knew was that a large hand had been outstretched to grip his collar.

219

Like a stag from covert Leithen leaped forth, upsetting Cameron with his sudden bound. He broke through the tangle of hazel and wild raspberries, and stayed not on the order of his going. His pace downhill had always been remarkable, and Cameron's was no match for it. Soon he had gained twenty yards, then fifty, but he had no comfort in his speed, for somewhere ahead were more gillies and he was being forced straight on Haripol, which was thick with the enemy.

The only plan in his head was to make for the Reascuill, which as he was aware flowed at this part of its course in a deep-cut gorge. He had a faint hope that, once there, he might find a place to lie up in till the darkness, for he knew that the Highland gillie is rarely a rock-climber. But the place grew more horrible as he continued. He was among rhododendrons now, and well-tended grass walks. Yes, there was a rustic arbour and what looked like a summer-seat. The beastly place was a garden. In another minute he would be among flower-pots and vineries with twenty gardeners at his heels. But the river was below—he could hear its sound—so, like a stag hard pressed by hounds, he made for the running water. A long slither took him down a steep bank of what had once been foxgloves, and he found his feet on a path.

And there, to his horror, were two women.

By this time his admirable wind was considerably touched, and the sweat was blinding his eyes, so that he did not see clearly. But surely one of the two was known to him.

Janet rose to the occasion like a bird. As he stood blinking before her she laughed merrily:

"Sir Edward," she cried, "where in the world have you been? You've taken a very rough road." Then she turned to Lady Claybody. "This is Sir Edward Leithen. He is staying with us and went out for an enormous walk this morning. He is always doing it. It was lucky you came this way, Sir Edward, for we can give you a lift home."

Lady Claybody was delighted, she said, to meet one of whom she had heard so much. He must come back to the house at once and have tea and see her husband, "I call this a real romance," she cried. "First Mr Palliser-Yeates—and then Sir Edward Leithen dropping like a stone from the hill-side."

Leithen was beginning to recover himself, "I'm afraid I was trespassing," he murmured. "I tried a short cut and got into difficulties. I hope I didn't alarm you coming down that hill like an avalanche. I find it the easiest way."

The mystified Cameron stood speechless, watching his prey vanishing in the company of his mistress.

14

HARIPOL—WOUNDED AND MISSING

LAMANCHA watched Palliser-Yeates disappear along the hillside, and then returned to the hollow top of the Beallach, which was completely cut off from view on either side. All that was now left of the mist was a fleeting vapour twining in scarves on the highest peaks, and the cliffs of Sgurr Dearg and Sgurr Mor towered above him in gleaming stairways. The drenched cloudberries sparkled in the sunlight, and the thousand little rivulets, which in the gloom had been hoarse with menace, made now a pleasant music. Lamancha's spirits rose as the world brightened. He proposed to wait for a quarter of an hour till Wattie with the stag was well down the ravine and Palliser-Yeates had secured the earnest attention of the navvies. Then he would join Wattie and help him with the beast, and within a couple of hours he might be wallowing in a bath at Crask, having bidden John Macnab a long farewell.

Meantime he was thirsty, and laid himself on the ground for a long drink at an icy spring, leaving his rifle on a bank of heather.

When he rose with his eyes dim with water he had an unpleasing surprise. A man stood before him, having in his hands his rifle, which he pointed threateningly at the rifle's owner.

"'Ands up," the man shouted. He was a tall fellow in navvy's clothes, with a shock head of black hair, and a week's beard—an uncouth figure with a truculent eye.

"Put that down," said Lamancha. "You fool, it's not loaded. Hand it over. Quick!

For answer the man swung it like a cudgel.

222

"'Ands up," he repeated. "'Ands up, you ——, or I'll do you in."

By this time Lamancha had realised that his opponent was the peripatetic navvy, whom Palliser-Yeates had reported. An ugly customer he looked, and resolute to earn Claybody's promised reward.

"What do you want?" he asked. "You're behaving like a lunatic."

"I want you to 'ands up and come along o' me."

"Who on earth do you take me for?"

"You're the poacher—Macnab. I seen you, and I seen the old fellow and the stag. You're Macnab, I reckon, and you're the —— I'm after. Up with your 'ands and look sharp."

Mendacity was obviously out of the question, so Lamancha tried conciliation.

"Supposing I am Macnab—let's talk a little sense. You're being paid for this job, and the man who catches me is to have something substantial. Well, whatever Lord Claybody has promised you I'll double it if you let me go."

The man stared for a second without answering, and then his face crimsoned. But it was not with avarice but with wrath.

"No, you don't," he cried. "By ——, you don't come over me that way. I'm not the kind as sells his boss. I'm a white man, I am, and I'll —— well let you see it. 'Ands up, you ——, and march. I've a —— good mind to smash your 'ead for tryin' to buy me."

Lamancha looked at the fellow, his shambling figure contorted by hard toil out of its natural balance, his thin face, his hot, honest eyes, and suddenly felt ashamed. "I beg your pardon," he grunted. "I oughtn't to have said that. I had no right to insult you. But of course I refuse to surrender. You've got to catch me."

He followed his words by a dive to his right, hoping to get between the man and the Sgurr Mor cliffs. But the navvy was too quick for him, and he had to retreat baffled. Lamancha was beginning to realise that the situation was really awkward. This fellow was both active and resolved; even if he gave him the slip he would be pursued down to the Doran, and the destination of the stag would be revealed. . . . But he was by no means sure that he could give him the slip. He was already tired and cramped, and he had never been noted for his speed, like Leithen and Palliser-Yeates. . . . He thought of another way, for in his time he had been a fair amateur middle-weight.

"You're an Englishman. What about settling the business with our fists? Put the rifle down, and we'll stand up together."

The man spat sarcastically. "Ain't it likely?" he sneered. "Thank you kindly, but I'm takin' no risks this trip. You've got to 'ands up and let me tie 'em so as you're safe and then come along peaceable. If you don't I'll 'it you as 'ard as Gawd 'll let me."

There seemed to be nothing for it but a scrap, and Lamancha, with a wary eye on the clubbed rifle, waited for his chance. He must settle this fellow so that he should be incapable of pursuit—a nice task for a respectable Cabinet Minister getting on in life. There was a pool beside his left foot, which was the source of one of the burns that ran down into the Sanctuary. Getting this between him and his adversary, he darted towards one end, checked, turned, and made to go round the other. The navvy struck at him with the rifle, and narrowly missed his head. Then he dropped the weapon, made a wild clutch, gripped Lamancha by the coat, and with a sound of rending tweed dragged him to his arms. The next moment the two men were locked in a very desperate and unscientific wrestling bout.

It was a game Lamancha had never played in his life before. He was a useful boxer in his way, but of wrestling he was utterly ignorant, and so, happily, was the navvy. So it became a mere contest of brute strength, waged on difficult ground with boulders, wells, and bog-holes adjacent. Lamancha had an athletic, well-trained body, the navvy was powerful but ill-trained; Lamancha was tired with eight or nine hours' scrambling, his opponent had also had a wearing morning; but Lamancha had led a regular and comfortable life, while the navvy had often gone supperless and had drunk many gallons of bad whisky. Consequently the latter, though the heavier and more powerful man, was likely to fail first in a match of endurance.

At the start, indeed, he nearly won straight away by the vigour of his attack. Lamancha cried out with pain as he felt his arm bent almost to breaking-point and a savage knee in his groin. The first three minutes it was anyone's fight; the second three Lamancha began to feel a dawning assurance. The other's breath laboured, and his sudden spasms of furious effort grew shorter and easier to baffle. He strove to get his opponent on to the rougher ground, while that opponent manoeuvred to keep the fight on the patch of grass, for it was obvious to him that his right course was to wear the navvy down. There were no rules in this game, and it would be of little use to throw him; only by reducing him to the last physical fatigue could he have him at his mercy, and be able to make his own terms.

Presently the early fury of the man was exchanged for a sullen defence. Lamancha was getting very distressed himself, for the navvy's great boots had damaged his shins and torn away strips of stocking and skin, while his breath was growing deplorably short. The two staggered around the patch of grass, never changing grips, but locked in a dull clinch into which they seemed to have frozen. Lamancha would fain have broken free and tried other methods, but the navvy's great hands held him like a vice, and it seemed as if their power, in spite of the man's gasping, would never weaken.

In this preposterous stalemate they continued for the better part of ten minutes. Then the navvy, as soldiers say, resumed the initiative. He must have felt his strength ebbing, and in a moment of violent disquiet have decided to hazard everything. Suddenly Lamancha found himself forced away from the chosen ground and dragged into the neighbouring moraine. They shaved the pool, and in a second were stumbling among slabs and screes and concealed boulders. The man's object was plain: if he could make his lighter antagonist slip he might force him down in a place from which it would not be easy to rise.

225

But it was the navvy who slipped. He lurched backward, tripping over a stone, and the two rolled into a cavity formed by a boulder which had been split by its fall from Sgurr Mor in some bygone storm. It was three or four feet of a fall, and Lamancha fell with him. There was a cry from the navvy, and the grip of his arms slackened.

Lamancha scrambled out and looked back into the hole where the man lay bunched up as if in pain.

"Hurt?" he asked, and the answer came back, garnished with much profanity, that it was his —— leg.

"I'm dashed sorry. Look here, this fight is off. Let me get you out and see what I can do for you."

The man, sullen but quiescent, allowed himself to be pulled out and laid on a couch of heather. Lamancha had feared for the thigh or the pelvis and was relieved to find that it was a clean break below the knee, caused by the owner's descent, weighted by his antagonist, on an ugly, sharp-edged stone. But, as he looked at the limp figure, haggard with toil and poor living, and realised that he had damaged it in the pitiful capital which was all it possessed, its bodily strength, he suffered from a pang of sharp compunction. He loathed John Macnab and all his works for bringing disaster upon a poor devil who had to earn his bread.

"I'm most awfully sorry," he stammered. "I wouldn't have had this happen for a thousand pounds. . . ." Then he broke off, for in the face now solemnly staring at him he recognised something familiar. Where had he seen that long crooked nose before and that cock of the eyebrows?

"Stokes," he cried, "You're Stokes, aren't you?" He recalled now the man who had once been his orderly, and whom he had last known as a smart troop sergeant.

The navvy tried to rise and failed. "You've got my name right, guv'nor," he said, but it was obvious that in his eyes there was no recognition.

"You remember me—Lord Lamancha?" He had it all now—the fellow who had been a son of one of Tommy Deloraine's keepers—a decent fellow and a humorous, and a

226

good soldier. It was like the cussedness of things that he should go breaking the leg of a friend.

"Gawd!" gasped the navvy, peering at the shameful figure of Lamancha, whose nether garments were now well advanced in raggedness and whose peat-begrimed face had taken on an added dirtiness from the heat of the contest. "I can't 'ardly believe it's you, sir." Then, with many tropes of speech, he explained what, had he known, would have happened to Lord Claybody, before he interfered with the game of a gentleman as he had served under.

"What brought you to this?" Lamancha asked.

"I've 'ad a lot of bad luck, sir. Nothing seemed to go right with me after the war. I found the missus 'ad done a bunk, and I 'ad two kids on my 'ands, and there weren't no cushy jobs goin' for the likes of me. Gentlemen everywhere was puttin' down their 'osses, and I 'ad to take what I could get. So it come to the navvyin' with me, like lots of other chaps. The Gov'ment don't seem to care what 'appens to us poor Gawd-forgotten devils, sir."

The navvy stopped to cough, and Lamancha did not like the sound of it.

"How's your health?" he asked.

"Not so bad, barrin' a bit of 'oarseness."

"That explains a lot. You'll have consumption if you don't look out. If you had been the man you were five years ago you'd have had me on my back in two seconds. . . . I needn't tell you, Stokes, that I'm dashed sorry about this, and I'll do all I can to make it up to you. First, we must get that leg right."

Lamancha began by retrieving the rifle. It was a light, double-barrelled express which fortunately could be taken to pieces. He had some slight surgical knowledge, and was able to set the limb, and then with strips of his handkerchief and the rifle-barrel to put it roughly into a splint. Stokes appeared to have gone without breakfast, so he was given the few sandwiches which remained in Lamancha's pocket and a stiff dram from his flask. Soon the patient was reclining in comparative comfort on the heather, smoking Lamancha's tobacco in an ancient stump of a pipe, while the latter, with heavy brows, considered the situation.

"You ought to get to bed at once, for you've a devil of a bad cough, you know. And you ought to have a doctor to look after that leg properly, for this contraption of mine is a bit rough. The question is, how am I going to get you down? You can't walk, and you're too much of a heavy-weight for me to carry very far. Also I needn't tell you that this hill-side is not too healthy for me at present. I mean to go down it by crawling in the open and keeping to the gullies, but I can't very well do that with you. . . . It looks as if there is nothing for it but to wait till dark. Then I'll nip over to Crask and send some men here with a stretcher."

Mr Stokes declared that he was perfectly happy where he was, and deprecated the trouble he was giving.

"Trouble," cried Lamancha, "I caused the trouble, and I'm going to see you through it."

"But you'll get nabbed, sir, and there ain't no bloomin' good in my 'avin' my leg broke if Claybody's going to nab you along of it. You cut off, sir, and never 'eed me."

"I don't want to be nabbed, but I can't leave you. . . . Wait a minute! If I followed Wattie—that is my stalker—down to the Doran I could send a message to Crask about a stretcher and men to carry it. I might get some food too. And then I'll come back here, and we'll bukk about Palestine till it's time to go. . . . It might be the best way. . . ."

But, even as he spoke, further plans were put out of the question by the advent of six men who had come quietly through the Beallach from the Sanctuary, and had unostentatiously taken up positions in a circle around the two ex-antagonists. Lamancha had been so engaged in Stoke's affairs that he had ceased to remember that he was in enemy territory.

His military service had taught him the value of the offensive. The new-comers were, he observed, three navvies, two men who were clearly gillies, and a warm and breathless young man in a suit of a dapperness startling on a wild mountain. This young man was advancing towards him with a determined eye when Lamancha arose from his couch and confronted him.

"Hullo!" he cried cheerfully, "you come just in time. This poor chap here has had a smash—broken his leg—and I was wondering how I was to get him down the hill."

Johnson Claybody stopped short. He had rarely seen a more disreputable figure than that which had risen from the heather—dissolute in garments, wild of hair, muddy beyond belief in countenance. Yet these dilapidated clothes had once, very long ago, been made by a good tailor, and the fellow was apparently some kind of a gentleman. He was John Macnab beyond doubt, for in his hand was the butt-end of a rifle. Now Johnson was the type of man who is miserable if he feels himself ill-clad or dirty, and discovers in a sense of tidiness a moral superiority. He rejoiced to have found his enemy, and an enemy over whom he felt at a notable advantage. But, unfortunately for him, no Merkland had ever been conscious of the appearance he represented or cared a straw about it. Lamancha in rags would have cheerfully disputed with an emperor in scarlet, and suffered no loss of confidence because of his garb, since he would not have given it a thought. What he was considering at the moment was the future of the damaged Stokes.

"Who's that?" Johnson asked peremptorily, pointing to the navvy.

His colleagues hastened to inform him. "It's Jim Stokes," one of the three navvies volunteered. "What 'ave you been doing to yourself, Jim?" And Macnicol added: "That's the man that was to keep movin' along this side o' the hill, sir. I picked him, for he looked the sooplest."

Then the faithful Stokes uplifted his voice. "I done as I was told, sir, and kep' movin' all right, but I ain't seen nothing, and then I 'ad a nawsty fall among them blasted rocks and 'urt my leg. This gentleman comes along and finds me and 'as a try at patchin' me up. But for 'im, sir, I'd be lyin' jammed between two stones till the crows 'ad a pick at me."

"You're a good chap, Stokes," said Lamancha, "but you're a liar. This man," he addressed Johnson, "was carrying out your orders, and challenged me. I wanted to pass, and he wouldn't let me, so we had a rough-and tumble, and through no fault of his he took a toss into a hole, and, as you see, broke his leg. I've set it and bound it up, but the sooner we get the job properly done the better. Hang it, it's the poor devil's livelihood. So we'd better push along."

His tone irritated Johnson. This scoundrelly poacher, caught red-handed with a rifle, presumed to give orders to his own men. He turned fiercely on Stokes.

"You know this fellow? What's his name?"

"I can't say as I rightly knows 'im,"was the answer. "But 'im and me was in the war, and he once gave me a drink outside Jerusalem."

"Are you John Macnab?" Johnson demanded.

"I'm anything you please," said Lamancha, "if you'll only hurry and get this man to bed."

"Damn your impudence! What business is that of yours? You've been caught poaching and we'll march you down to Haripol and get the truth out of you. If you won't tell me who you are, I'll find means to make you. . . . Macnicol, you and Macqueen get on each side of him, and you three fellows follow behind. If he tries to bolt, club him. . . . You can leave this man here. He'll take no harm, and we can send back for him later."

"I'm sorry to interfere," said Lamancha quietly, "but Stokes is going down now. You needn't worry about me. I'll come with you, for I've got to see him comfortably settled."

"You'll come with us!" Johnson shouted. "Many thanks for your kindness. You'll damn well be made to come. Macnicol, take hold of him."

"Don't," said Lamancha. "Please don't. It will only mean trouble."

Macnicol was acutely unhappy. He recognised something in Lamancha's tone which was perhaps unfamiliar to his master—that accent which means authority, and which, if disregarded, leads to mischief. He had himself served in Lovat's Scouts, and the voice of this tatterdemalion was unpleasantly like that of certain high-handed officers of his acquaintance. So he hesitated and shuffled his feet.

"Look at the thing reasonably," Lamancha said. "You say I'm a poacher called John Something-or-other. I admit that you have found me walking with a rifle on your ground, and naturally you want an explanation. But all that can wait till we get this man down to a doctor. I won't run away, for I want to satisfy myself that he's going to be all right. Won't that content you?"

Johnson, to his disgust, felt that he was being manoeuvred into a false position. He was by no means unkind, and this infernal Macnab was making him appear a brute. Public opinion was clearly against him; Macnicol was obviously unwilling to act, Macqueen he knew detested him, and the three navvies might be supposed to take the side of their colleague. Johnson set a high value on public opinion, and scrupled to outrage it. So he curbed his wrath, and gave orders that Stokes should be taken up. Two men formed a cradle with their arms, and the cortege proceeded down the hill-side.

Lamancha took care to give his captors no uneasiness. He walked beside Macqueen, with whom he exchanged a few comments on the weather, and he thought his own by no means pleasant thoughts. This confounded encounter with Stokes had wrecked everything, and yet he could not be altogether sorry that it had happened. He had a chance now of doing something for an honest fellow—Stokes's gallant lie to Johnson had convinced Lamancha of his superlative honesty. But it looked as if he were in for an ugly time with this young bounder, and he was beginning to dislike Johnson extremely. There were one or two points in his favour. The stag seemed to have departed with Wattie into the *ewigkeit* and happily no eye at the Beallach had seen the signs of the gralloch. All that Johnson could do was to accuse him of poaching, *teste* the rifle; he could not prove the deed. Lamancha was rather vague about the law, but he was doubtful whether mere trespass was a grave

231

offence. Then the Claybodys would not want to make too much fuss about it, with the journalists booming the doings of John Macnab. . . . But wouldn't they? They were the kind of people that liked advertisement, and after all they had scored. What a tale for the cheap papers there would be in the capture of John Macnab! And if it got out who he was? . . . It was very clear that that at all costs must be prevented . . . Had Johnson Claybody any decent feelings to which he could appeal? A sportsman? Well, he didn't seem to be of much account in that line, for he had wanted to leave the poor devil on the hill.

It took some time for the party to reach the Doran, which they forded at a point considerably below Archie's former lair. Lamancha gave thanks for one mercy, that Archie and Wattie seemed to have got clean away. There was a car on the road which caused him a moment's uneasiness, till he saw that it was not the Ford but a large car with an all-weather body coming from Haripol. The driver seemed to have his instructions, for he turned round—no light task in that narrow road with its boggy fringes—and awaited their arrival.

Johnson gave rapid orders. "You march the fellow down the road, and bring the navvy—better take him to your cottage, Macqueen. I'll go home in the car and prepare a reception for Macnab."

It may be assumed that Johnson spoke in haste, for he had somehow to work off his irritation, and desired to assert his authority.

"Hadn't Stokes better go in the car?" Lamancha suggested in a voice which he strove to make urbane. "That journey down the hill can't have done his leg any good."

Johnson replied by telling him to mind his own business, and then was foolish enough to add that he was hanged if he would have any lousy navvy in his car. He was preparing to enter, when something in Lamancha's voice stopped him.

"You can't," said the latter. "In common decency you can't."

"Who'll prevent me? Now, look here, I'm fed up with your

232

insolence. You'll be well advised to hold your tongue till we make up our minds how to deal with you. You're in a devilish nasty position, Mr John Macnab, if you had the wits to see it. Macnicol, and you fellows, I'll fire the lot of you if he escapes on the road. You've my authority to hit him on the head if he gets nasty."

Johnson's foot was on the step, when a hand on his shoulder swung him round.

"No, you don't." Lamancha's voice had lost all trace of civility, for he was very angry. "Stokes goes in the car and one of the gillies with him. Here you, lift the man in."

Johnson had grown rather white, for he saw that the situation was working up to the ugliest kind of climax. He felt dimly that he was again defying public opinion, but his fury made him bold. He cursed Lamancha with vigour and freedom, but there was a slight catch in his voice, and a hint of anticlimax in his threats, for the truth was that he was a little afraid. Still it was a flat defiance, though it concluded with a sneering demand as to what and who would prevent him doing as he pleased, which sounded a little weak.

"First," said Lamancha, "I should have a try at wringing your neck. Then I should wreck any reputation you may have up and down this land. I promise you I should make you very sorry you didn't stay in bed this morning." Lamancha had succeeded in controlling himself—in especial he had checked the phrase "infernal little haberdasher" which had risen to his lips—and his voice was civil and quiet again.

Johnson gave a mirthless laugh. "I'm not afraid of a dirty poacher."

"If I'm a poacher that's no reason why you should behave like a cad."

It is a melancholy fact which exponents of democracy must face that, while all men may be on a level in the eyes of the State, they will continue in fact to be preposterously unequal. Lamancha had been captured in circumstances of deep suspicion which he did not attempt to explain; he had been caught on Johnson's land, by Johnson's servants; the wounded

233

man was in Johnson's pay, and might reasonably be held to be at Johnson's orders; the car was without question Johnson's own. Yet this outrageous trespasser was not only truculent and impenitent; he was taking it upon himself to give orders to gillies and navvies, and to dictate the use of an expensive automobile. The truth is, that if you belong to a family which for a good many centuries has been accustomed to command and to take risks, and if you yourself, in the forty-odd years of your life, have rather courted trouble than otherwise, and have put discipline into Arab caravans, Central African natives, and Australian mounted brigades—well, when you talk about wringing necks your words might carry weight. If, too, you have never had occasion to think of your position, because no one has ever questioned it, and you promise to break down somebody else's, your threat may convince others, because you yourself are so wholly convinced of your power in that direction. It was the complete lack of bluster in Lamancha, his sober matter-of-factness, that made Johnson suddenly discover in this potato-bogle of a man something formidable. He hesitated, the gillies hesitated, and Lamancha saw his chance. Angry as he was, he contrived to be conciliatory.

"Don't let us lose our tempers. I've no right to dictate to you, but you must see that we're bound to look after this poor chap first. After that I'm at your disposal to give you any satisfaction you want."

Johnson had not been practised in commercial negotiations for nothing. He saw that obstinacy would mean trouble, and would gain him little, and he cast about for a way to save his face. He went through a show of talking in whispers to Macnicol—a show which did not deceive his head-stalker. Then he addressed Macqueen. "We think we'd better get this fellow off our hands. You take him down in the car to your cottage, and put him in your spare bed. Then come round to the house and wait for me."

"This is my show, if you'll allow me, sir," said Lamancha politely. He took a couple of notes from a wad he carried in an inner pocket. "Get hold of the nearest doctor—you can use the post-office telephone—and tell him to come at once, and get everything you need for Stokes. I'll see you again. Don't spare expense, for I'm responsible."

The car departed, and the walking party continued its way down the Doran glen. Lamancha's anger was evaporating, philosophy had intervened, and he was prepared to make allowances for Johnson. But he recognised that the situation was delicate and the future cloudy, and, since he saw no way out, decided to wait patiently on events, always premising that on no account must he permit his identity to be discovered. That might yet involve violent action of a nature which he could not foresee. His consolation was the thought of the stag, now without doubt in the Crask larder. If only he could get clear of his captors, John Macnab would have won two out of the three events. Yes, and if Leithen and Palliser-Yeates had not blundered into captivity.

He was presently reassured as to the fate of the latter. When the party entered the wooded lower glen of the Doran it was joined by four weary navvies who had been refreshing themselves by holding their heads in the stream. Interrogated by Macnicol, they told a tale of hunting an elusive man for hours on the hillside, of repeatedly being on the point of laying hold of him, of a demoniac agility and a diabolical cunning, and of his final disappearance into the deeps of the wood. Questioned about Stokes, they knew nothing. He had last been seen by them in the early morning when the mist first cleared, but it was his business to keep moving high up the hill near the rocks and he had certainly not joined in the chase when it started.

Johnson's temper was not improved by this news. Twice he had been put to public shame in front of his servants by this arrogant tramp who was John Macnab. He had been insulted and defied, but he knew in his heart that the true bitterness lay in the fact that he had also been frightened. Anger, variegated by fear, is apt to cloud a man's common sense, and Johnson's usual caution was deserting him. He was beginning to see red, and the news that there had been an accomplice was the last straw. Somehow or other he must get even with this bandit and bring him to the last extremity of disgrace. He must get him inside the splendours of Haripol, where, his foot on his native heath, he would recover the confidence which had been so lamentably to seek on the hill. . . . He would, of course, hand him over to the police, but his soul longed for some more spectacular *dénouement*. . . .

Then he thought of the journalists, who had made such a nuisance of themselves in the morning. They were certain to be still about the place. If they could see his triumphant arrival at Haripol they would write such a story as would blaze his credit to the world and make the frustrated poacher a laughing-stock.

As it chanced, as they entered one of the woodland drives of Haripol, they met the gillie, Andrew, on his way home for a late tea. He was asked if he had seen any of the correspondents, and replied that he and Peter and Cameron had captured one after a hard chase, who at the moment was in Cameron's charge and using strong language about the liberty of the Press. Andrew was privately despatched to bid Cameron bring his captive, with all civility and many apologies, up to the house, with a message that Mr Claybody would be glad to have a talk with him. Then, with three navvies as a vanguard and four as a rear-guard, Lamancha was conducted down the glade between Johnson and Macnicol—the picture of a criminal in the grip of the law.

That picture was seen by a small boy who was lurking among the bracken. To the eyes of Benjie it spelt the uttermost disaster. The stag was safe at Crask, but the major part of John Macnab was in the hands of his enemies. Benjie thought hard for a minute, and then wriggled back into the covert and ran as hard as he could through the wood. To him at this awful crisis there seemed to be but a single hope. Force must be brought against force. The Bluidy Mackenzie, now tied up under a distant tree, must be launched against the foe. The boy was aware that the dog had accepted him as an ally, but that it had developed for Lamancha the passion of its morose and solitary life.

236

The prisoner's uneasiness grew with every step he took down the sweet-scented twilit glade. He was being taken to the house, and in that house there would be people—women, perhaps—journalists, maybe—and a most embarrassing situation for a Cabinet Minister. The whole enterprise, which had been so packed with comedy and adventure, was about to end in fiasco and disgrace, and it was he, the promoter, who had let the show down. For the first time since he arrived at Crask Lamancha whole-heartedly wished himself out of the thing with a clean sheet. There was something to be said, after all, for a man keeping to his groove. . . .

They emerged from the trees, and before them stretched the lawns, with a large and important mansion at the other end. This was worse than his wildest dreams. He stopped short.

"Look here," he said, "isn't it time to end this farce? I admit I was trespassing, and was fairly caught out. Isn't that enough?"

"By Gad, it isn't," said Johnson, into whose bosom a certainty of triumph and revenge had at last entered. "Into the house you go, and there we'll get the truth out of you."

"I'll pay any fine in reason, but I'm damned if I'm going near that house."

For answer, Johnson nodded to Macnicol, and the two closed in on the prisoner. Lamancha, now really desperate, shook off the stalker and was about to break to his left, when Johnson tackled high and held him.

At the same moment the Bluidy Mackenzie took a hand in the game.

That faithful hound, conducted by Benjie, had just arrived on the scene of action. He saw his adored Lamancha, the first man who had really understood him, being assaulted by another whose appearance he did not favour. Like a stone from a sling he leaped from the covert straight at Mr Johnson Claybody's throat.

It all happened in one crowded instant. Lamancha felt the impact of part of Mackenzie's body, saw Johnson stagger and fall, and next observed his captor running wildly for the house with Mackenzie hot on his trail. Then, with that preposterous instinct to help human against animal which is deeper than reason, he started after him.

Never had a rising young commercial magnate shown a better gift of speed, for a mad dog was his private and particular fear, and this beast was clearly raving mad. Macnicol and the navvies were some twenty yards behind, but Lamancha was a close second. Crying hoarsely, Johnson leaped the flower-beds and doubled like a hare in and out of a pergola. Ahead lay his mother's pet new lily-pond, and, remembering dimly that mad dogs did not love water, he plunged into it, and embraced a lead Cupid in the centre.

Mackenzie loved water like a spaniel, and his great body shot after him. But the immersion caused a second's delay and enabled Lamancha to take a flying leap which brought him almost atop of the dog. He clutched his collar and swung him back, making a commotion in the fountain like a tidal wave. Mackenzie recognised his friend and did not turn on him, but he still strained furiously after Johnson, who was now emerging like Proteus on the far side.

Suddenly the windows of the house, which was not thirty yards off, opened, and the stage filled up with figures. First the amazed eyes of Lamancha saw Crossby entering from the right, evidently a prisoner, in the charge of two gillies. Then at one set of windows appeared Sir Edward Leithen with a scared face, while from the other emerged the forms of Sir Archibald Roylance, Mr Palliser-Yeates, and a stout gentleman in a kilt who might be Lord Claybody. To his mind, keyed by wrath and confusion to expectation of tragedy, there could only be one solution. Others besides himself had failed, and the secret of John Macnab was horridly patent to the world.

"Archie," he panted, "for God's sake call off your tripe-hound. I can't hold on any longer. . . . He'll eat the little man."

Lord Claybody had unusual penetration. He observed his son and heir dripping and exhausted on the turf, and a figure, which looked like a caricature in the Oppositon Press of an eminent Tory statesman, surrendering a savage hound to a small and dirty boy. Also he saw in the background a group of gillies and navvies. There was mystery here which had better be unriddled away from the gaze of the profane crowd. His eye caught Crossby's and Lamancha's.

"I think you'd better all come indoors," he said.

15

HARIPOL—THE ARMISTICE

THE great drawing-room had lost all its garishness with the approach of evening. Facing eastward, it looked out on lawns now dreaming in a green dusk, though beyond them the setting sun, over-topping the house, washed the woods and hills with gold and purple. Lady Claybody sat on a brocaded couch with something of the dignity of the late Queen Victoria, mystified, perturbed, awaiting the explanation which was her due. Her husband stood before her, a man with such an air of being ready for any emergency that even his kilt looked workmanlike. The embarrassed party from Crask clustered in the background; the shameful figures of Lamancha and Johnson stood in front of the window, thereby deepening the shadow. So electric was the occasion that Lady Claybody, finically proud of her house, did not notice that these two were oozing water over the polished parquet and devastating more than one expensive rug.

Lamancha, now that the worst had happened, was resigned and almost cheerful. Since the Claybodys had bagged Leithen and Palliser-Yeates and detected the complicity of Sir Archie, there was no reason why he should be left out. He hoped, rather vaguely, that his captors might not be inclined to make the thing public in view of certain episodes, but he had got to the pitch of caring very little. John Macnab was dead, and only awaited sepulture and oblivion. He looked towards Johnson, expecting him to take up the tale.

But Johnson had no desire to speak. He had been very much shaken and scared by the Bluidy Mackenzie and had not yet recovered his breath. Also a name spoken by his father, as they entered the room, had temporarily unsettled his wits. It was Lord Claybody who broke the uncomfortable silence.

"Who owns that dog?" he asked, looking, not at Lamancha, but at his son.

"The brute's mine," said Archie penitently. "He followed the car, and I left him tied up. Can't think how he got loose and started this racket."

The master of the house turned to Lamancha. "How did you come here, my lord? You look as if you had been having a rough journey."

Lamancha laughed. Happily the waning light did not reveal the full extent of his dirt and raggedness. "I have," he said, "I'm your son's prisoner. Fairly caught out. I daresay you think me an idiot, unless Leithen or Palliser-Yeates has explained."

Lord Claybody looked more mystified than ever.

"I don't understand. A prisoner?"

"He's John Macnab," put in Johnson, whose breath was returning, and with it sulkiness. He was beginning to see that there was to be no triumph in this business, and a good deal of unpleasant explanation.

"Well, a third of him," said Lamancha. "And as you've already annexed the other two-thirds you have the whole of the fellow under your roof."

Lord Claybody's gasp suddenly revealed to Lamancha that he had been premature in his confession. How his two friends had got into the Haripol drawing-room he did not know, but apparently it was not as prisoners. The mischief was done, however, and there was no going back.

"You mean to say that you three gentlemen are John Macnab? You have been poaching at Glenraden and Strathlarrig? Does Colonel Raden—does Mr Bandicott know who you are?"

Lamancha nodded. "They found out after we had had our shot at their preserves. They didn't mind—took it very well indeed. We hope you're going to follow suit?"

"But I am amazed. You had only to send me a note and my

241

forest was at your disposal for as long as you wished. Why—why this—this incivility?"

"I assure you, on my honour, that the last thing we dreamed of was incivility. . . . Look here, Lord Claybody, I wonder if I can explain. We three—Leithen, Palliser-Yeates, and myself—found ourselves two months ago fairly fed up with life. We weren't sick, and we weren't tired—only bored. By accident we discovered each other's complaint, and we decided to have a try at curing ourselves by attempting something very difficult and rather dangerous. There was a fellow called Tarras used to play this game—he was before your time—and we resolved to take a leaf out of his book. So we quartered ourselves on Archie—he's not to blame, remember, for he's been protesting bitterly all along—and we sent out our challenge. Glenraden and Strathlarrig accepted it, so that was all right; you didn't in so many words, but you accepted it by your action, for you took elaborate precautions to safeguard your ground. . . . Well, that's all. Palliser-Yeates lost at Glenraden owing to Miss Janet. Leithen won at Strathlarrig, and now I've made a regular hat of things at Haripol. But we're cured, all of us. We're simply longing to get back to the life which in July we thought humbug."

Lord Claybody sat down in a chair and brooded.

"I still don't follow," he said. "You are people who matter a great deal to the world, and there's not a man in this country who wouldn't have been proud to give you the chance of the kind of holiday you needed. You're one of the leaders of my party. Personally, I have always considered you the best of them. I'm looking to Sir Edward Leithen to win a big case for me this autumn. Mr Palliser-Yeates has done a lot of business with my firm, and after the talk I've had with him this afternoon I look to doing a good deal more with him in the future. You had only to give me a hint of what you wished and I would have jumped at the chance of obliging you. You wanted the thrill of feeling like poachers. Well, I would have seen that you got it. I would have turned on every man in the place and used all my wits to make your escapade difficult. Wouldn't that have contented you?"

242

"No, no," Lamancha cried. "You are missing the point. Don't you see that your way would have taken all the gloss off the adventure and made it a game? We had to feel that we were taking real risks—that, being what we were, we should look utter fools if we were caught and exposed."

"Pardon me, but it is you who are missing the point." Lord Claybody was smiling. "You could never have been exposed—except perhaps by those confounded journalists," he added as he caught sight of Crossby.

"We had the best of them on our side," Lamancha put in. "Mr Crossby has backed us up nobly."

"Well, that only made your position more secure. Colonel Raden and Mr Bandicott accepted your challenge, and in any case they were sportsmen, and you knew it. If they had caught one or the other of you they would never have betrayed you. You must see that. And here at Haripol you were on the safest ground of all. I'm not what they call a sportsman—not yet—but I couldn't give you away. Do you think it conceivable that I would do anything to weaken the public prestige of a statesman I believe in, a great lawyer I brief, and a great banker whose assistance is of the utmost value to me. I'm a man who has made a fortune by my own hard work and I mean to keep it; therefore in these bad times I am out to support anything which buttresses the solid structure of society. You three are part of that structure. You might poach every stag on Haripol, and I should still hold my tongue."

Lamancha, regardless of the condition of his nether garments, sat down heavily on an embroidered stool which Lady Claybody erroneously believed to have belonged to Marie Antoinette, and dropped his head in his hands.

"Lord, I believe you're right," he groaned. "We've all been potting at sitting birds. John, do you hear? We've been making godless fools of ourselves. We thought we had got outside civilisation and were really taking chances. But we weren't. We were all the time as safe as your blessed bank. It can't be done—not in this country anyway. We're in the groove and have got to stay there. We've been a pretty lot of idiots not to think of that."

Then Johnson spoke. He had been immensely cheered by Lord Claybody's words, for they had seemed to raise Haripol again to that dignity from which it had been in imminent risk of falling.

"I don't complain personally, Lord Lamancha, though you've given me a hard day of it. But I agree with my father—you really were gambling on a certainty and it wasn't very fair to us. Besides, you three, who are the supporters of law and order, have offered a pretty good handle to the enemy, with those infernal journalists advertising John Macnab. There may be a large crop of Macnabs springing up, and you'll be responsible. It's a dangerous thing to weaken the sanctities of property."

He found, to his surprise, a vigorous opponent in his mother. Lady Claybody had passed from mystification to enlightenment, and from enlightenment to appreciation. It delighted her romantic soul that Haripol should have been chosen for the escapade of three eminent men; she saw tradition and legend already glorifying her new dwelling. Moreover, she scented in Johnson's words a theory of life which was not her own, a mercantile creed which conflicted with her notion of Haripol, and of the future of her family.

"You are talking nonsense, Johnson," she said, "You are making property a nightmare, for you are always thinking about it. You forget that wealth is made for man, and not man for wealth. It is the personality that matters. It is so vulgar not to keep money and land and that sort of thing in its proper place. Look at those splendid old Jacobites and what they gave up. The one advantage of property is that you can disregard it."

This astounding epigram passed unnoticed save by Janet, for the lady, smiling benignly on the poaching trinity, went on to a practical application. "I think the whole John Macnab adventure has been quite delightful. It has brightened us all up, and I'm sure we have nothing to forgive. I think we must have a dinner for everybody concerned to celebrate the end of it. What Claybody says is perfectly true—you must have known you could count on us, just as much as on Colonel Raden and Mr Bandicott. But since you seem not to have realised that, you have had the fun of thinking you were in real danger, and after all it is what one thinks that matters. I am so glad you are all cured of being bored. But I'm not quite happy about those journalists. How can we be certain that they won't make a horrid story of it?"

"My wife is right," said Lord Claybody emphatically. "That is the danger." He looked at Crossby. "They are certain to want some kind of account."

"They certainly will," said the latter. "And that account must leave out names and—other details. I don't suppose you want the navvy business made public?"

"Perhaps not. That was Johnson's idea, and I don't consider it a particularly happy inspiration."

"Well, there is nothing for it but that I should give them the story and expurgate it discreetly. John Macnab has been caught and dismissed with a warning—that's all there is to it. I suppose your gillies won't blab? They can't know very much, but they might give away some awkward details."

"I'll jolly well see that they don't," said Johnson. "But who will you make John Macnab out to be?"

"A lunatic—unnamed. I'll hint at some family skeleton into which good breeding forbids me to inquire The fact that he has failed at Haripol will take the edge off my colleagues' appetites. If he had got his stag they would have been ramping on the trail. The whole thing will go the way of other stunts, and be forgotten in two days. I know the British Press."

Within half an hour the atmosphere in that drawing-room had changed from suspicion to something not far from friendliness, but the change left two people unaffected. Johnson, doubtless with Lamancha's behaviour on the hill in his memory, was still sullen, and Janet was obviously ill at ease.

Lamancha, who was suffering a good deal from thirst and hunger and longed for a bath, arose from his stool.

"I think," he said, "that we three—especially myself—owe you the most abject apologies. I see now that we were taking no

245

risks worth mentioning, and that what we thought was an adventure was only a *faux pas*. It was abominably foolish, and we are all very sorry about it. I think you've taken it uncommonly well."

Lord Claybody raised a protesting hand. "Not another word. I vote we break up this conference and give you something to drink. Johnson's tongue is hanging out of his mouth."

The voice of Janet was suddenly raised, and in it might have been detected a new timidity. "I want to apologise also. Dear Lady Claybody, I stole your dog. . . . I hope you will forgive me. You see we wanted to do something to distract Macnicol, and that seemed the only way."

A sudden silence fell. Lady Claybody, had there been sufficient light, might have been observed to flush.

"You—stole—Roguie," she said slowly, while Janet moved closer to Sir Archie. "You—stole—Wee Roguie. I think you are the— "

"But we were very kind to him, and he was very happy."

"*I* wasn't happy. I scarcely slept a wink. What right had you to touch my precious little dog? I think it is the most monstrous thing I ever heard in my life."

"I'm so very sorry. Please, please forgive me. But you said yourself that the only advantage of property was that you could disregard it."

Lady Claybody, to her enormous credit, stared, gasped, and then laughed. Then something in the attitude of Janet and Archie stopped her, and she asked suddenly: "Are you two engaged?"

"Yes," said Janet, "since ten minutes past one this afternoon."

Lady Claybody rose from the couch and took her in her arms.

"You're the wickedest girl in the world and the most delightful. Oh, my dear, I am so pleased. Sir Archibald, you will let an old woman kiss you. You are brigands, both of you, so you should be very very happy. You must all come and dine here to-morrow night—your father and sister too, and we'll ask the Bandicotts. It will be a dinner to announce your engagement, and also to say good-bye to John Macnab. Poor John! I feel as if he were a real person who will always haunt this glen, and now he is disappearing into the mist."

"No," said Lamancha, "he is being shrivelled up by coals of fire. By the way"—and he turned to Lord Claybody—"I'll send over the stag in the morning. I forgot to tell you I got a stag—an old beast with a famous head, who used to visit Crask. It will look rather well in your hall. It has been in Archie's larder since the early afternoon."

Then Johnson Claybody was moved to a course which surprised his audience, and may have surprised himself. His sullenness vanished in hearty laughter.

"I think," he said, "I have made rather a fool of myself."

"I think we have all made fools of ourselves," said Lamancha.

Johnson turned to his late prisoner and held out his hand.

"Lord Lamancha, I have only one thing to say. I don't in the least agree with my mother, and I'm dead against John Macnab. But I'm *your* man from this day on—whatever line you take. You're my leader, for, by all that's holy, you've a most astonishing gift of getting the goods."

EPILOGUE

Crossby, from whom I had most of this narrative, was as good as his word, though it went sorely against the grain. He himself wrote a tale, and circulated his version to his brother journalists, which made a good enough yarn, but was a sad anticlimax to the Return of Harald Blacktooth. He told of a gallant but frustrated attempt on the Haripol Sanctuary, the taking of the culprit, and the magnanimous release by young Mr Claybody of a nameless monomaniac—a gentleman, it was hinted, who had not recovered from the effects of the war. The story did not occupy a prominent page in the papers, and presently, as he had prophesied, the world had forgotten John Macnab, and had turned its attention to the cinema star, just arrived in London, whom for several days, to the disgust of that lady's agents, it had strangely neglected.

The dinner at Haripol, Crossby told me, was a hilarious function, at which four men found reason to modify their opinion of the son of the house, and the host fell in love with Janet, and Archie with his hostess. There is talk, I understand, of making it an annual event to keep green the memory of the triune sportsman who once haunted the place. If you go to Haripol, as I did last week, you will see above the hall chimney a noble thirteen-pointer, and a legend beneath proclaiming that the stag was shot on the Sgurr Dearg beat of the forest by the Earl of Lamancha on a certain day of September in a certain year. Lady Claybody, who does not like stag's heads as ornaments, makes an exception of this; indeed, it is one of her household treasures to which she most often calls her guests' attention.

Janet and Archie were married in November in the little kirk of Inverlarrig, and three busy men cancelled urgent engagements to be there. Among the presents there was one not shown to the public or mentioned in the papers, and a duplicate of it went to Junius and Agatha at their wedding in the following spring. It was a noble loving-cup in the form of a quaich, inscribed as the gift of John Macnab. Below four signatures were engraved—Lamancha, Edward Leithen and John Palliser-Yeates, and last, in a hand of surprising boldness, the honoured name of Benjamin Bogle.